Shards of Sunlight

by

Anand Nair

Copyright Anand Nair

Published by YouWriteOn.com, 2014

The author, Anand Nair, has asserted her moral right under the Copyright, Designs and Patents Act, 1988, to be identified as the author of this work

All Rights reserved. No part of this publication may be reproduced, copied, stored in a retrieval system, or transmitted, in any form or by any means, without the prior written consent of the copyright holder, nor be otherwise circulated in any form of binding or cover other than that in which it is published and without a similar condition being imposed on the subsequent purchaser.

A CIP catalogue record for this title is available from the British Library.

This book is a work of fiction. People, places, events and circumstances are the product of the author's imagination. Any resemblance to actual persons, dead or living, is purely coincidental.

For

My father, who taught me to think, and know right from wrong.

1

The pounding on the front door woke Indu up as she slept beside her father. Moments later she heard the clatter as someone pulled the wooden bars away from their front door. Must be Aunt Devi. Indu listened. The voices wafted up in the silence of the night.

'I have to see Gopalan *Vakil*,' a man's voice insisted. 'It's urgent.'

Who was coming to see her father in the middle of the night, when the lamps were doused and the house shuttered down? Someone must have died in our village, Indu decided. That's when they came like this clamouring at the door.

'Let me turn up the lamp,' Indu heard Devi say.

'No. No lamp please. If you'll just wake up *Vakil*. Tell him it is Ahmed, the Circle-Inspector.'

Then the flap-flap sound of flat-footed Aunt Devi climbing the wooden steps to come upstairs. Indu lay rigid in bed, waiting with eyes like saucers.

Shards of Sunlight

'It is Circle-Inspector Ahmed. He is asking for you,' Devi whispered apologetically, touching her brother, Gopalan, lightly on the shoulder.

Indu was only seven years old but she knew her father hated to be disturbed when he slept.

Indu's eyes followed Gopalan as he opened his eyes and looked at his sister blearily, then sat up, pulling his sarong tighter and tucking it into his meagre waist. The moonlight shifted on the walls as the palm leaves outside stirred in the wind.

His hand come down on the bulky law-book he had been studying in bed earlier; he seemed unsteady, swaying a little, as he slipped his feet into the wooden clogs below his bed. Indu didn't like the way his shoulders slumped as he passed his fingers through his chest-hair. It was a sure sign that he was worried.

She sat up in bed holding her breath – something unusual was happening.

'Go back to sleep, *Moley,*' Gopalan said as he pulled out his bedside chair in readiness for Ahmed to sit and rubbed the sleep out of his eyes.

'Ask the man to come upstairs,' he said to Devi.

Ahmed arrived soon after. The Circle Inspector of Police in Thalassery was an impressive looking Muslim man. He was built like a *phaelwan*, tall and beefy, with a well-tended moustache. He came to their house occasionally to play card games like *Twenty-eight.* When he was troubled he had a habit of twirling his moustache.

He looked everywhere except at Gopalan's questioning face. He was tugging at his moustache furiously, shifting from one foot to the other.

Shards of Sunlight

'The list has come, Gopala,' he admitted almost shamefacedly, 'and your name's on top of it.'

The list: nobody would tell Indu what this list was. Since Ahmed's visit the women in the kitchen talked about nothing else. That and something called *Swaraj*. What was that?

'What is this list, Ammammey?' Indu asked in her deliberately winsome voice the next morning, when Devi was performing her dawn ritual of lighting the devotional lamp. Sometimes an answer slipped out by mistake. 'Is it like the list you make when the dhobi comes?'

Devi didn't answer; she rarely had time for Indu's many questions. She muttered prayers under her breath and pulled out the crumpled newspaper pushed into the neck of the coconut oil bottle in the puja corner. She sniffed at it. Then she tore up a piece of old *mundu* for wicks, and twisted three-inch strips to make points to light. She placed the wicks in the saucer of the lamp to soak and drew one end of each towards her.

The bit Indu loved came next. Devi pulled out the usually damp matchbox she kept behind the plaster Krishnan's shoulder and started her battle with the matchsticks. Three fizzled out before she got a flame on the fourth, and the room filled with the familiar dawn smell of sulphur and coconut oil. When Indu had got her fill of that comforting smell she went out to sit in her favourite place on the veranda edge, carrying the dawn benediction with her. The sunbeams splintered into rainbow colours on the cracked cement floor. She put her hand over them and imagined she had caught the colours of the morning.

Shards of Sunlight

Devi came out a few minutes later with her *pan* box; this would be a good time to ask questions, Indu knew. Devi was always amiable when she was chewing pan.

'What's *Swaraj*, Ammammey?' Indu asked. She smelled the green betel leaf smell and the sharp tang of *chunamb*, the white lime paste, which Devi put in minute quantities on the leaf, as she chewed.

'Oh. It's like – self-government.' Devi said.

Just like adults. You ask them for the meaning of a short word and they give you a longer one. Indu gave up.

Gopalan left his house early next Sunday to see Damu. Damu was also a lawyer, a *vakil*, as they were called locally, and lived a few houses down the road; he was Gopalan's closest confidante and his sane alter ego. Indu tagged along a few paces behind her father.

'You're still in your night slip,' he called out. 'Go back home.'

Indu looked down, kicked a stone around, and pretended she had not heard. Gopalan walked back to her and picked her up. 'You-' he said, but held her close.

She smelled his Lux shaving soap and Navy Cut cigarettes. She put her face near his and felt the pre-shave bristles on his cheek.

'A bit early for you, Gopala. Don't tell me you ran out of cigarettes,' Damu called out cheerily as he saw his friend at the front gate. Gopalan often went round to cadge cigarettes late at night or early in the morning, when the shops were closed, but also to talk.

Gopalan put Indu down on a chair, but she jumped off and went to the widow sill, where there was

Shards of Sunlight

a collection of conches and sea shells. She got a whiff of ancient dust and she sneezed. The room had a reek of something sour, like spoilt food.

Gopalan helped himself to a cigarette from the packet of *Scissors* on the table and went up to Damu to light it off the one already smoking in his friend's mouth. He took his time over getting a good head on the cigarette and blew out his first puff before he started talking.

'That list.' he said. 'We have known about it for some time. The Government is just waiting to see if the Congress will pass Gandhiji's *Quit India* resolution next week.'

Indu heard the word *list* and pricked up her ears.

'Ahmed says *my* name is top of the list. He came by yesterday, I may be -'

Damu exploded. 'You are mad. Reckless to get involved in all this Congress - bongress speechmaking and processions when you have a family to look after.'

Indu, startled, looked at Damu and then at her father. Why was Damu so angry?

'I'll be arrested within a week if they pass the resolution on the twelfth,' Gopalan said. 'We know it's going to be passed; all the provincial committees have voted for it.'

'What's 'rrested? Indu wondered. It sounded bad.

'*Ende Bhagawane...*' Damu always called on his Gods when he was nonplussed. 'How are the women and children going to manage? A house without a man.'

'They'll have to cope. Devi will manage; I know her. It's the children I am worried about. Especially Indu. Mother dead for years, and now, no

Shards of Sunlight

father either. And Mani too. She hasn't heard from her parents in three years and she is not going to, any time soon. Not until the war in Malaya is over - and who knows when *that* is going to be?'

Mani was the only child of Gopalan's brother, Kannan; she was four years older than Indu. Mani had been sent to Thalassery to go to school. Kannan, a doctor, lived on a rubber estate near Penang; there were no schools on the estate suitable for his daughter. Since the war broke out the letters from Penang had stopped and the money orders had ceased. No one knew whether Kannan and his wife were dead or alive.

In the evening, when Indu returned from school, she went to the kitchen to beg a piece of jaggery from Shinnu. Shinnu was Gopalan's niece, the youngest daughter of a sister who had died in childbirth. She was one of the many waifs and strays who landed on his side of the fence for sustenance. When Indu's mother had died five years back, Indu had been a two-year-old toddler. It was Shinnu, only fourteen years old at that time, who carried her around, fed her and comforted her.

Shinnu broke off a piece of jaggery from the store and gave it to Indu.

Devi walked in on this scene. 'That girl's teeth will rot the way she eats that stuff,' she said. 'You spoil her.'

Devi sounded more bad tempered than usual. She moved firewood around in the fireplace and peered into pots. Finally she burst out. 'These silly young men like Gopalan who organise processions and speak against the British Government. They think they are brave. Stupid is what they are. They'll all go to jail.

Shards of Sunlight

And you know the first person to be arrested? Our Gopalan.'

Devi pleaded with her God, her first port of call. 'Padachone –'

A lump of anxiety stirred in Indu's stomach and started to work its way to her throat. Devi can't be right. How can Achan go to Jail? He is not a burglar. Only bad people went to jail. She ran upstairs to find her father.

He was looking at the books on his writing table when Indu reached him. He patted her head absent-mindedly and carried on reading the titles. She clung to his arm and would not let go. Finally he pushed the books away and turned to Indu.

'Something bothering this little head,' he said. He smoothed the hair on her forehead and tucked it behind her ears.

'Is 'rrested going to jail, *Acha*?' Indu asked. 'You won't go to jail, will you?' She looked at her father's face, but found no reassurance there.

He picked her up and sat her down on the writing table. 'Ah. It's like this, *Moley*. Achan will have to go to jail for a few weeks. Because we have been telling the British Government to go away and they don't like us for that.'

'I don't want you to go. They'll beat you and tie you with ropes.' She started to sob and the tears rolled down her cheeks.

'Well, I don't want to go either.' Gopalan hugged her. 'But sometimes we have to do things we don't want to do.'

Gopalan wiped her tears away with his fingers. 'My little one mustn't cry. Achan *always* comes back. Don't I?'

Indu jumped off the table and went downstairs. Why did it have to be *her achan*? Why couldn't someone else's achan go instead?

2

They came for Gopalan, Indu's father, a few days later. The police jeep arrived early in the morning as the maids turned up to sweep the front yards and draw water for the kitchens of the middle-class houses on the road. On that morning the roads were quiet except for the bicycle bell of the milkman and the creaks of the wheels of the shit carts.

The two policemen in the jeep were in *mufti*, and looked left and right furtively as they closed the doors of the jeep. They walked towards the house, throwing away their half-smoked *beedies*.

Gopalan, sleepless and weary, and Indu, saw them from the upstairs window and was ready for them, but when they took the handcuffs out, he blanched.

'Is that necessary?' he asked. His straight, spiky hair was dishevelled and anxiety pooled in his eyes.

The policemen looked at each other, then at Gopalan's bony wrists and his sparse body.

'See, my bag is packed and I am going with you,' Gopalan said. His voice trembled a little on the last phrase.

'It's not you we are worried about,' they said, but they put the handcuffs away.

Gopalan picked up his suitcase and went down the stairs in front of the men.

At the foot of the stairs was his mother's room; he stooped under the low wooden lintel of the door. He

Shards of Sunlight

had not thought of the words for this moment, he who had words for all occasions.

'Ammey, I'm going,' he said.

She was curled up on her bed in her dark cave of a room and he could just see her white face and the rough grey blanket pulled up to her shoulders. The room smelled faintly of the ripe bananas and rice for the household stored under her bed, and her medicines.

Ammini struggled up and let her legs dangle over the side of the bed. As she did so she took in the two men standing grimly behind him.

'Who are they? And where are you going?'

Gopalan put his case down and bent to touch her feet for her blessing, but she turned away from him and lay down again on her bed, turning her face to the wall.

'Ammey,' he pleaded, but she did not move.

Devi and Shinnu came out of the kitchen with Mani and looked at the scene in front of Ammini's doorway. They clutched each other, and the two girls stared, terrified.

'Time to go,' Gopalan said looking at Devi's frantic face. 'Don't upset the children.' He picked up his suitcase again.

'No,' Indu screamed as she hurled herself on her father, sobbing. 'No-o-o. Tell them to go away, Acha, tell them.'

Mani ran to him then. '*Elayacha*. If you go -' She was sobbing too.

Gopalan bent down and gathered the girls in his arms.

'Listen, Mani. You've got to look after both of you. And help Devi Ammamma. You mustn't cry. They'll all start crying and what will I do then?'

Shards of Sunlight

The two men stared woodenly as Gopalan turned to leave. They followed him out of the house and through the front gate. When they reached the jeep they bundled him into the back and got clumsily into the front, hurrying to get away.

As the car started, it became apparent why they had come so early and silently: a small crowd of men and boys walked towards the car. They looked belligerent and some of them had stones or sticks in their hands.

As the first stone hit the windscreen, the policeman at the wheel revved up the engine and accelerated away.

Indu and Mani ran to the gate.

'Come inside,' Devi called out, but there was too much noise and excitement and the girls pretended they had not heard. After the car drove away and the crowd dispersed they stood at the gate, watching the few loiterers.

'When will Elayachan come back?' Mani asked. She seemed more disturbed than Indu, who had not quite understood that this was an arrest, and her father was going to jail.

'In the evening,' Indu answered, a little contemptuously. Achan always came back in the evening. Mani started crying. Indu watched perplexed as this was a truly unusual thing, Mani normally bit her lip and shut her eyes tight against the world when she was upset, but refused to be seen crying.

Mani picked up Indu's hand and started walking towards the house. She did this also rarely; she was not given to demonstrations of affection.

When Achan did not come back in the evening, Indu slept in Devi's bed.

Shards of Sunlight

'Ammammey, wake me up when Achan comes,' she said to Devi. Both girls called her 'Ammamma' – mother's mother, as though to compensate for the fact that she was childless.

'Yes, soon as he comes,' Devi murmured, and for once she put her arms round the child and drew her close.

3

After Gopalan went away there was a lot of talk about Indu's mother's house. Indu didn't like the sound of it; from where did this mother's house thing come up? What were the adults planning for her now? Two weeks after Gopalan left, Indu overheard *Achamma*, Ammini, say she should be sent to Madras, where her maternal grandmother, Ammu Velyamma, lived. That was a strange thing to say! *This* was her home and she didn't want to go anywhere else. Achan would be really annoyed if he knew.

Until then Indu's world had been a safe and uneventful one, made up of boring routines like brushing her teeth and saying her prayers twice a day. Now there were chinks in that safe cocoon, and an unfamiliar, heartless world threatened to creep in through the holes.

She scratched at the spot on her left arm. There was a nagging itch there, which came up now and then. It had recently started again; she was scared it might start bleeding or weeping if she irritated it. Devi said it was something called ringworm and it would spread if Indu did not leave it alone. Indu generally scratched at it when she was worried or afraid.

Once a year, Indu's mother's family came down from Madras to their village, Kodiyeri, the same village as her father's, for the summer holidays. Ammu Velyamma was young and had several children younger than Indu. Indu liked the two little girls best; they were

Shards of Sunlight

closest to her in age and it was with them she played when she went visiting. They came in the hot season when all the schools closed but Indu knew it wasn't school holidays yet, because her own school, The Sacred Heart Girls' High School, had not closed yet. It was not yet time to start talking about her mother's family.

As far as Indu was concerned the fact she did not have a mother didn't bother her. In fact it worked in her favour really. Mani didn't have parents with her either, so she was *motherless* too, but it was Indu who got all the extra care and sympathy. The two women in the house often referred to Indu as the *poor, motherless child*. This meant she got a little extra love mixed in with her food and when they combed her hair for school, she felt the love in the bristles of the comb.

Indu's mother's parents seemed harmless enough, but she really did not know them well. They seemed like kind strangers who made a fuss over her when they saw her once a year. One of her uncles would come into town to take her when they came to the village for a few days. She liked that because she always returned with new clothes and ribbons for her hair, ribbons and slides never seen in a little town like Thalassery.

However, she was invariably relieved to be back home to the sprawling, ramshackle house in town where she and her cousins and aunt lived. She knew all the neighbours there and wandered to some of their houses whenever she felt like it. Most of all she liked to go to the house on the north side; this was where Mathu, their outside maid, lived. Leela, her daughter, was Indu's best friend.

Shards of Sunlight

Indu hardly noticed Mathu from day to day as she swept and swabbed and washed endlessly in her house, engaging with no one. She appeared each morning in the front yard with a broom, a lean, not very clean spectre, and left at midday with a bowl full of leftovers.

It was Leela, Mathu's daughter, only a year older than Indu, whom Indu adored. Now that Achan was away she could play with the 'riffraff' next door, as he called them, any time she liked. Devi didn't mind who she played with or how dirty they all got together, so long as she and Mani came in for meals and said their evening prayers – '*Ramaramarama...*' fifty times and sang the two *slogams,* devotional songs in praise of Saraswathi, the Goddess of prosperity and knowledge, and Shivan, the destroyer.

Leela knew many games to be played with stones and arecanut seeds. She knew how to make cattle out of jack-tree leaves and arrange them for sale to play *Going To the Market*. Above all, she knew how to tie a rag round Indu's short hair and do pretend plaits so she could walk about swinging them like all her friends in school with their long hair.

Indu tried not to think too much about her father being a prisoner because it made her want to cry. She didn't mention him in school either.

On the front bench Hameed sat on Indu's left and Girija on her right. She sat as far from Hameed as she could manage without getting noticed by Sister Theckla's lynx eyes, because Hameed would take bogeys from his nose and put them on her arm, if she was within reach.

She quite liked Girija, but on that day Indu was caught tying Girija's long plaits to the slats of the bench

Shards of Sunlight

on which they sat. Well, Indu admitted to herself, she *was* jealous of Girija's plaits which came to her waist. Achan had never let Mani or her grow their hair; he had insisted on keeping it no more than three or four inches long.

Just now she needed a mother, Indu decided. She would have known how important it was for Mani and her to have lovely long plaits that swung from left to right when they walked . What did Achan know about these things? 'Until you are grown up,' he always said. Indu felt deprived when she saw all her friends with plaits adorned with jasmine and chrysanthemum; the usual rules for girls did not seem to apply to them.

The lesson that day was *Fractions*. Indu could see Sister was making a right hash of it. Indu now, numbers of any kind were her friends; she could make them do somersaults for her.

Sister, however, had gone on and on getting more and more apoplectic as she repeated herself, trying to get the class to understand what she called Top numbers and Bottom numbers. Indu's attention wandered.

Tying up Girija's plait was a small diversion while the rest of the class caught up with her. And Girija, who sat next to Indu, was so smug today; in addition to her waist-length plaits tied up with red ribbons, she was also wearing a homemade red bead-chain, which Indu coveted. All Indu was ever allowed to wear was a silly old gold chain, which had belonged to her mother. The gold chain had a heart shaped pendant, which was good for chewing. It was now dented and Indu hated it.

Shards of Sunlight

Sister, meanwhile, had lost control: clearly, she could not manage Indu's mischief and the fractions at the same time.

'Indu, you wicked girl, trying to follow in your wretched father's footsteps.'

Indu looked at Sister, not comprehending what she was saying. What did all this have to do with Achan in Vellore jail?

'Criminal behaviour, just like your father's; don't know the difference between right and wrong. Disgraceful! You'll end up in jail too.'

This was Sister Theckla's territory; she was the expert on rights and wrongs, what with taking the Moral Science class first thing in the morning and leading the hymns at Assembly daily.

Hameed, sitting on Indu's left, sniggered, so she stuck her left elbow into his side without moving her torso. Girija meanwhile took both her plaits and arranged them in front over her shoulders where she could see them; she was establishing ownership. The sight of those plaits and Sister Theckla's mocking face enraged Indu, driving out all sense of caution.

'My father is a *detenue*, he's not a criminal.' Indu remembered that was what Vijayettan next door called him. What was a detenue anyway? 'And he went to jail to get freedom for India. For all of us.' Then she burst into tears as a collective gasp came up from the class.

This bit about freedom was something Vijayettan from next door always said to Indu when he came visiting her man-less house to ask whether the women needed any help with the shopping. Indu didn't understand what this freedom was but it must be something good. Achan wouldn't do anything bad. A

Shards of Sunlight

whiff of fear, however, had invaded the invisible mantle of certainties she carried with her for protection. She hated Sister – and Hameed – and Girija too.

Indu knew what happened to girls in her class when Sister got annoyed with them. She locked them up in the dark and dank umbrella-room next to the classroom. This room was the punishment for really bad misdemeanours – like pulling somebody's hair in a fight or forgetting your catechism book. It had happened before and she would get through it. The last time was when she spilled paint on sister's habit by mistake; sister Theckla insisted she had done it on purpose.

There were no windows to this room and the floor was wet and cold from the puddles of wet umbrellas. Hameed said the cockroaches in there were as big as rats. The worst of it was you never knew when she would let you out, and inside there, time tended to stretch and become infinite.

But, strangely enough, Sister didn't punish her; she looked a bit shamefaced instead and let it go. She looked down at the Maths book in front of her on the desk and appeared to have lost her place in it. At break Girija offered to let her wear the bead necklace for a little while. So they exchanged necklaces: Indu's old chomped up gold chain for Girija's red beads.

4

After Gopalan went to jail, many visitors from Indu's father's extended family came to her house: *ettans* and *echis*, the girls were instructed to call them, elder brothers and sisters. The rule was, if they were older than you, you got off your seat for them and treated them with due respect.

They came at lunchtime from the neighbouring villages, which were within walking distance. When Achan was around, he treated most of them with scant respect and Indu took her cue from him. Now, the visitors seemed to have gained confidence and ordered the women of the house around as though the house belonged to them.

For Indu it was a relief from the ever-present *moong* dhal, which Shinnu cooked daily: moong with rice conjee in the morning, moong with raw plantain in the evening. Garnished with coconut and finished off with mustard and chilli beans popped in oil, it was a tasty substitute for the more expensive channa or thoor dhal. But Indu got tired of it quickly.

Indu and Mani dropped handfuls of curried moong into their brass water mugs to avoid eating it. Sometimes they mixed the moong into their conjee and quietly walked away from the food. If Devi knew what was happening she gave no sign of it. Often, the leftovers were dumped into a big bowl and given to Mathu, the walking dustbin of the family.

Shards of Sunlight

Unniettan came rarely; Indu wondered how he was related to her family. She asked Shinnu the next time he visited.

'Is he your brother? You like him, don't you?'

'No. He is not my brother - someone from our clan, that's all. But he makes us all laugh,' Shinnu said. 'Even Devi. Did you see his imitation of nuns the other day? Wicked. He folded his hands on his stomach and walked with mincing steps, looking down a little. He calls them *black-and-white crows* because of their costume.' Shinnu laughed.

'He plays with me and Mani,' Indu said. 'Next time he comes he's going to show us how to make a ball with coconut fronds.'

That April, when Unniettan came, Shinnu made a special effort for him. Krishnan, the servant boy was stationed at the gate early in the morning to catch the fisherman when he went past in his breathless trot, with his dripping head-load of fish. Indu waited with Krishnan, swinging on the gate. Shinnu helped the fisherman lower his basket carefully on to the veranda ledge when he arrived, but some fishy juices spilt, the scent bringing all the neighbouring, feral cats mewling for their share. Then the haggling began.

Devi had a four-anna coin knotted into the corner of her mundu, and she carried the *chatti*, the earthenware fish-wok in which fish curry was always made. That day she got fifty sardines.

Shinnu spent the whole morning grinding chillies, turmeric and coconut to go into the fish sauce. There was a general air of excitement in the kitchen; mustard seed popped noisily in coconut oil, and lovely smells of ginger, shredded coconut and garlic frying spread through the house.

Shards of Sunlight

With Gopalan away, Indu thought, the house had relaxed luxuriously like a fat woman who had shed her corset. Mani and she played with the neighbouring urchins whom Gopalan had considered too low-class for them to consort with. The women raised their voices in laughter and gossip at all hours of the day and hung clothes to dry in the front yard where it had been forbidden.

Some strange things happened to Indu during that visit of Unniettan's, exacerbating the feeling that her world was turning topsy-turvy. He played games with her during the day but Mani refused to join. Killjoy, Indu thought. Unniettan was especially friendly with Indu that day, teaching her card tricks and playing *thalama* with her, with a ball made out of plaited coconut fronds.

Indu felt specially chosen; nobody had ever singled her out in this manner. She was so pleased with all the attention, she insisted she wanted to sleep in his bed. So Devi rolled out her father's mattress on his bed upstairs for the two of them.

Things started off well with him showing her how to make shadow animals on the wall. She was quite flattered and sleep was far away when he suggested, 'Show you another game.'

For this game he lifted her slip up. Then he parted his *mundu* and pulled his choo-choo out. Well, she hoped he knew she didn't have one of *those*. Indu had never seen this game before; it didn't look right. What was he going to do with his choo-choo, which he was stroking like a pet squirrel? She knew people were not supposed to show their choo-choos to others, but

21

Shards of Sunlight

she didn't want to offend him, so she kept quiet. What next?

As he stroked the choo-choo it seemed to grow bigger than any she had ever seen. She had seen her cousins from the village do peeing competitions sometimes when they visited. But this was in another league of bigness.

'Nice and soft,' he said touching her crotch. His fingers trembled slightly and his voice had gone up an octave. She didn't mind him touching her but it seemed unnecessary. Why would he want to do that?

'Here, touch me,' he said picking up her hand and placing it on his penis. It felt like a live creature with an inner struggle of its own. He moved her fingers up and down his huge thing and something slimy came off on her fingers.

'*Chee*. Like *mookkitta*,' she said firmly, pushing his hand away. Snot! But he was past listening and there was a strange look in his eyes, like Devi had when she was praying in front of the shrine in the puja room.

Unniettan tried to take her hand back to that quivering thing, but she pulled away and tugged her slip down. 'Don't like this game.'

But he wouldn't let her go. He pushed her slip up again and brought his choo-choo towards her. She smelled rotten rubber and sour sweat.

'I'll tell Devi,' she said trying to wriggle away from him, but he stretched out his arm to hold her.

'I'm going to tell Achan when he comes. He won't like this game.' Indu slid out from under his arm and scurried off to Devi's bed downstairs. Achan's name always gave protection even though he was not near; she knew that. It was her magic mantram when all

Shards of Sunlight

else defeated her. However, Indu felt betrayed without quite knowing why.

'What happened last night?' Devi asked the next morning when she saw Indu curled up next to her.

'Bad dreams,' Indu said, not quite knowing whether she had dreamt last night's events or they had been real.

Indu told Mani. 'Unniettan is not nice. He did bad things. I won't play with him again when he comes.'

Mani looked at Indu. 'Did you tell Devi?'

'I wanted to tell Devi, but I was afraid. She'll blame me.'

'He tried to do dirty things with me too once. Next time he comes you stick with me. We won't leave each other alone in the room with him.'

In the days that followed Indu's mind went back frequently to the incident though she wanted to forget it; she wanted to like Unniettan. Instead she felt guilty; it was like the oily after-taste of castor oil in your mouth, which Devi made her drink sometimes, 'to make your stomach clean.'

Indu's world was changing fast with Achan away and she found it difficult to fathom what was going on.

5

Thursdays and Sundays were holidays at Indu's school, The Sacred Heart Convent. The state schools closed dutifully on Saturdays and Sundays like the rest of the working world, but the nuns *had* to do something different, if only to establish their superiority. Leela, Indu's best friend, went to a local Primary school, so Sunday was the one day Indu had to spend with Leela.

Some time in the evening on Saturdays, when her *jutka* clip-clopped home from school, Indu would start thinking about playing with Leela. Would Leela's disagreeable father, Chathu, be at home to scream at them? It would be a good Sunday if he was sleeping off a drinking bout from the previous day; he would not emerge from his dark hole of a bedroom till mid-day, and then he would be half-asleep.

Before she set off towards Leela's house in the morning, Indu checked whether Mathu had started sweeping the front yard, making wide semicircles in the dust with her broom. And was Chathu up and about?

Today Leela's veranda was empty, so Indu wriggled through the fence at the kitchen end of her house and crossed the narrow path to Leela's mud-brick hut. It still gave her a sense of wrongdoing. When her father was around, going to Leela's house was strictly forbidden. According to him they were "useless people" and her grandmother called them "the unwashed tribe next door."

Now, however, her father was in Vellore Jail, because he was something called a freedom fighter, and

Shards of Sunlight

Indu could go where she wished. She tiptoed gingerly up the rickety quarry stones, which did duty for steps to Leela's hut; They had a habit of tilting if you caught the edge; she had stubbed her little toe on those a few times. Chathu's dilapidated deck chair was the only furniture on the veranda and his blue-and-white, crumpled *lungi* hung on the back as though he had thrown it there in a hurry. Indu gave the chair a wide berth though Leela's grim father was not sitting in it just then.

When she reached the front door she stopped for a moment and peered into the tiny, cramped corridor getting her eyes accustomed to the forbidding darkness inside.

'Leela, where are you?' she called uneasily, as she stepped inside. She could smell the mouth-watering farinaceous smell of roasting cassava, not something made in her own house very often. It was only in the houses of the poor that cassava was used as a staple instead of rice.

'In the kitchen. Come,' Leela shouted out.

Indu heard the rustling of dry leaves and knew Leela was in front of the three-stone fireplace shovelling dry leaves into it with her hands. In the morning Leela was often to be found there, warming up yesterday's fish curry or straining old rice from the cold water soak that kept it fresh.

Indu forced herself to step into the dark passage; the floor felt gritty and uneven. There was a bedroom on either side and if you peered in, it was always night in there and smelled of unwashed clothes and damp. Once safe past the rooms, the kitchen was light-filled and airy with a door leading outside, though it hung loose on one hinge. Outside the door was the large half

Shards of Sunlight

sphere of the bamboo basket under which Mathu kept her chickens. The leaves that Mathu swept up from the compounds where she worked, and the coconut fronds she begged off Indu's aunt Devi for firewood, were heaped just outside the door. Some were spread on the mud floor in front of the hearth.

Indu found the older girl squatting in front of the fire, blowing at the embers through a bamboo pipe. A fine patina of ash had settled on her matted shoulder length hair, which was more brown than black. Indu loved Leela's hair, wavy and thick and long, unlike her own no-nonsense crop.

Leela nudged the roasting cassava out of the fire towards her and beat at it with the bamboo pipe, testing whether the skin had flaked, ready to split open. Satisfied it was done she left it on the floor to cool and turned to Indu who was now squatting beside her.

'Play *kottamkallu*?' she asked.

It was Leela who generally took the lead in such important matters as what game to play each day. She was left so much to herself by her mother that she had grown beyond her years.

Mathu did not have much choice except to leave Leela to her own devices. What Chathu gave her for rice and fish each month, after he had drunk most of his salary, did not stretch beyond the middle of the month. She supplemented this income with working in Indu's house, sweeping and swabbing, spreading cow dung on the floors once a week, and beating the life out of clothes on the concrete slab at the back. For this she was given five rupees a month and food for her and Leela. Because of this work she knew her daughter would never go hungry.

Shards of Sunlight

'Mmm...' Indu murmured, too eager for the cassava to say anything properly. The two girls started beating at the hot cassava with their palms, loosening the burnt skin from the tuber, then peeling it off to bite greedily into the fluffy white flesh. They opened their mouths and blew *ha-ha* as the hot cassava threatened to burn their tongues. For Leela this would be breakfast but Indu had already eaten her *conjee* of well-cooked rice in its starchy water, and *moong* dhal curry, before she ventured out.

The two girls were so engrossed in their cassava they did not hear the clumsy footsteps outside, the thump of an umbrella on the floor, followed by the shuffle of a weight collapsing on the deck chair. Then someone cleared his throat, hawked and spat noisily.

'Father,' Leela said, standing up quickly, in her haste dropping the remnants of the cassava she was eating. Indu scrambled up too, but before she could escape Chathu was in the kitchen glaring at her, and Leela was nowhere to be seen.

'Where is the other one? Leela...' he called. His speech was slurred. 'Where is that *nayinde mole, koothicheende mole*?' He stretched out his arm to grab hold of Indu, and then thought better of it. In the process he lost his balance and fell back against the kitchen wall. Indu smelled his sour toddy breath as he glowered at her, and with it the stench of stale sweat.

He heaved himself up and leaned towards Indu. 'Eating my cassava! Mmm...Go, Go...Now – and don't let me see you here again.' The thick blob of mucous, which had hung under his left nostril was now smeared across his cheek.

Indu heard the menace in his voice; no one had ever spoken to her like that. He must be the reason she

Shards of Sunlight

was not allowed to go to Leela's house. She ran out of the back door and across the path. Wriggling through the fence she scratched her arm on the wooden post, but didn't stop till she reached her veranda. She was breathless and shaking, glad to be on familiar turf but also certain there would not be any sympathy for her if Devi got to know she had sneaked off next door.

Leela wandered on to Indu's veranda later. '*Kothamkallu?*' she asked. In her right hand she loosely held a fistful of stones; they threatened to dribble through her fingers. She sat down carefully on the cement floor, at the edge of the veranda – she would never come further in, as though there were some invisible lines that stopped her. She scattered the stones in her hand in a small spread in front of her. Then she selected her master stone and threw it up to head height in front of her, testing its path. Not satisfied, she repeated the action, scooping up five small stones from off the floor, as the big stone started to descend. She caught her master stone neatly with the same hand and smiled at Indu. Leela was very good at this game.

To Indu, Leela seemed almost a grown-up. Self-sufficient, because she made her own rules, and did not care what the adults thought or did. When she was younger she used to follow Mathu around when she came to work, always a few paces behind, left thumb firmly stuck in mouth. These days the thumb was definitely not in the mouth and Mathu came to work alone.

Indu knew there was no point asking Leela where she had been and why her father was so angry. Leela never said much about what happened in her home, concentrating on the games they played together.

Shards of Sunlight

It was always Indu who asked questions. When the questions became oppressive Leela would merely get up and saunter away.

'I thought he was going to hit me,' Indu volunteered, taking care not to *ask* anything this time.

'He won't hit you. Only Amma and me. He's scared of your father.'

One angry shout from her father was enough to make Indu want to pee, but he had never hit her, even that time when she had accidentally pushed one of his law books off the veranda ledge and into the rain. He said he didn't believe in hitting anyone, there were better ways to make children behave.

'But he's not here now.' Indu voice trembled on the *now*; suddenly she wanted her father. Chathu, she was certain, would not have dared shout at her if her father was around.

'That's right. So don't wait for him to save you. We just have to run fast when my father comes back from work. He's always too drunk to chase us.'

For Leela all of this appeared to be totally normal. Indu knew her friend lived in a more precarious and uncertain world, but she had never imagined she needed to run away and hide from her own father. Now Indu had to learn to run as well. And hide?

'Hide where?' Indu asked, bemused. There was nowhere to hide in Leela's little house with two rooms and a kitchen.

'In the gully at the back. There is a drumstick tree there and I sit behind it.'

Indu had always known there was a narrow path there; it was the place where Chathu's household went to shit since their old stone-and-thatch latrine came down in the last monsoon. Indu wondered what happened when it rained and you had to go. Did you hold an umbrella up with one hand while you did your business? The narrow channel flooded during the rains, bringing all the sewage from up the hill. You could see turds and the odd dead, bloated goat floating in that water. Leela in there? Sometimes Leela's world seemed so distant from hers.

'It's filthy,' Indu said.

Leela tossed her head, throwing the comment to the winds. It seemed this was not a worry for her. Indu thought about the elaborate cleaning rituals in her own home: rooms swept daily by Mathu, new cow dung spread on the floors every Friday and women in pristine white clothes, with shining, newly washed hair down their backs, to dry in the mornings.

No, Indu did not want to hide anywhere near that filthy gully; she must find another place for herself.

6

Three months passed quickly and Achan's absence gradually became a fact of life. Devi got up much earlier than Achan every morning, so Indu also stumbled out of bed at dawn. Her first job was to help Devi roll up the sleeping mat they shared and put it away in the corner of their room.

Now Indu had plenty of time to day-dream between waking up and going to school. She was sitting on the edge of the veranda steps one day, watching the leaves of the jack-fruit tree drift to the ground in the cool November winds, when her grand mother grabbed her and pulled her up. Ammini clutched Indu's hand in a tight, prehensile grip, as she shuffled forward, dragging the girl with her.

'*Va. Vegam va*,' she said. Come. Come *quickly*. Ammini, gasped with the effort of pulling her along.

They went down the short path from the veranda leading to the front gate. Indu looked up at the woman's face. Ammini never ventured out of the house this early in the morning since as far back as she could remember; she wouldn't even come out of her bed. It was the time when the *parachi* women, the untouchables, sneaked into the backs of houses to collect the shit pots and carry them to the municipal hand-cart, which they pushed along from street to street. Ammini hated seeing the night-soil women with their foul cargo walking past; she always said they were like a bad omen: if you

Shards of Sunlight

started your day with seeing one, the remaining hours would be full of misfortunes.

What was Ammini *doing*? Indu tried to slide her fingers out for a quick getaway, but this merely made the old woman tighten her grip and pull harder.

Ammini was having trouble walking: she was bent over like a question mark, wincing as her arthritic stick-legs negotiated the uneven path. She wore a *mundu*, a soft, white ankle-length cloth, wrapped round and tucked tightly into the hollow of her concave waist, above which her shrivelled breasts dangled. This was all she would normally wear inside the house. However, today, a *thorthu*, a thin white towel made of coarse cotton, was thrown over her naked shoulders carelessly, a minor concession to the outside world of men. It hid nothing although she kept tugging it over her breasts as she walked.

Indu kept looking back at the veranda of the house, hoping someone would notice, but no one did. Ammini reached the end of the walkway and hesitated at the iron gates, in front of the steps leading down to the dusty road. In the house opposite a young woman was drying her waist length hair in the morning sun, slowly, sensuously, as though she had the whole day to do this.

Ammini pushed at the gate feebly, glancing back to the house as she did so, and squeezed through, pulling the girl along with her. As she looked at the wide, endless-seeming road in front of her, she gulped and her breath quickened.

On Indu's left, the owner of the *dabba* next to her house, was dismantling his shop front, one plank at a time, ready to put out his wares. He arranged the planks in a neat stack, leaning against the wall at one

Shards of Sunlight

end of the shop. While Indu watched, he went inside for a moment and came out with a big aluminium pot. He peered into it, then rinsed the dregs left over from the previous day by swirling them around and threw the remnants on to the road.

Indu glanced at the road uncertainly - she could step on it now if she wanted, something she was never allowed to do on her own. The most she ever managed was swing in a half-circle on the gate when no one was watching. Now Ammini had dumped her into this forbidden world where there was so much happening.

'*Poicko*,' she said, go, giving Indu a shove. 'No need to wait. There is nothing here for you.'

Indu tugged at her white night-slip in a sudden access of modesty now that she was standing on the road, and tested the dry, powdery soil with her bare feet. She put her right heel down and turned round on it, drawing a circle in the mud with her big toe. The soft, red dust rose, making Ammini sneeze as she darted quick, furtive glances left and right, then pushed the girl on to the tarmac, letting go of her hand.

Down the hill, where the road levelled out towards the Kuyyali River, a bus screeched to an unscheduled stop to pick up a passenger who had held out his arm for it.

'There,' the old woman said. 'They have tied your father behind that bus and they are dragging him. The police are killing him. Can't you hear him screaming?' She covered her ears with her hands as if to shut out that screaming, which Indu couldn't hear. 'He is not coming back,' she added grimly, almost to herself.

Shards of Sunlight

She pushed Indu again. '*Poicko, vegam poicko.*' Go quickly, *go*. To your mother's house. They will look after you.'

Ammini looked around distractedly before shuffling off towards the house with the air of a job well done. Indu stayed on the edge of the road looking around, as the morning came into focus like a slow-developing film. She looked towards the bus, which had started moving again, searching for her father, but didn't see anyone being dragged behind it.

On the crest of the hill, Thalassery's resident madman, Vasu, was doing his usual morning duties, picking up the litter from the sides of the road and depositing each find neatly in the middle. Occasionally, he kicked up the dust with his toes as he tried to dislodge plantain peels stuck into the dirt. He talked to himself all the time as he made his zigzag way up the hill, often going back some distance if he had missed an empty cigarette box or a torn banana leaf. Indu was engrossed watching his morning trail.

As he approached, Indu got back on the walkway to the house, poised for a hasty retreat if he pursued her. Today had started badly, she decided, it was an anything-could- happen kind of day. However, Vasu did not look at Indu; he shuffled past muttering to himself, 'Mahatma Gandhi, *Sindabad*, Congress Party, *Sindabad*,' holding up a dry banana frond like a flag.

'Mahatma Gandhi, *Sindabad*,' Indu tried out tentatively. Not satisfactory at all. She picked up a banana frond from her garden and held it up as she marched back to the house. 'Congress Party, *Sindabad*,' she shouted more enthusiastically; now she had a flag to wave, it felt much better.

Shards of Sunlight

When Indu got back to the veranda, she sat down on the cement steps and laid her flag down carefully at her feet; something was bothering her, a stray unease like a hovering mosquito. So she poked her right thumb into the seam of her white sleep-in slip, where the stitches had come out. When Indu felt threatened in any way, the hole in that seam got bigger.

She looked at the shards of sunlight dancing on the steps where she sat, as the leaves of the coconut palm overhanging the veranda moved in the wind. The cement floor under her near-naked behind was rough with grit and cold on her thighs. She cast a glance towards the south end of the veranda, which her father had made his domain. There he used to talk to his clients, bargain for fees and write up his files. The rickety wooden bench on which his clients sat had one front leg shorter than the others; it jumped up and came down with a thud when they sat on the end alerting Indu and Mani to be especially quiet as Gopalan worked with his clients..

The single chair with the adjustable back was Gopalan's, and no one else used it except he, even when he was not around. The backrest had a top layer of plywood with a yellow flower design on it; the plywood was peeling off in places and sometimes it had left red imprints on her father's pale skin. Looking at the chair Indu remembered his morning smell of *Chandrika* Sandalwood soap and Wills Navy Cut cigarettes.

Indu walked over to the chair and looked more closely; her legs had taken her there without any conscious decision on her part. She passed a finger over the yellow design and climbed in, sniffing for her

Shards of Sunlight

father's smell as she did so, but all she got was dry wood.

Lying back, she listened to the neighbour's children getting ready for school at the well in their compound– the plop of the scoop made out of arecanut fronds as it hit the surface of the water, the clatter of old Ovaltine tins and zinc buckets as the children bathed, the shouts and admonitions of mothers as they coaxed and cajoled the tribe to clean their teeth, bathe and change for school. She curled herself into a ball, put her head down on the arm of the chair and closed her eyes.

Indu started up as she heard Aunt Devi's voice in the corridor.

'That girl! She is forever daydreaming, forgetting the things she has to do. I wonder: has she done her homework? She didn't say her morning prayers either today.'

Morning prayers, Indu remembered. Had she said them or not? Indu often forgot to say her prayers, this was only one of the many sins of omission she chalked up in a regular week

Devi's harassed second call told Indu it was time for action.

'Indoo... Where has this child gone? Hasn't cleaned her teeth or washed. She'll be late for school.'

Devi often talked like this, to no one in particular – her woes addressed to the world at large.

Indu slipped off the chair and crept round the back of the house, before Devi could find her and berate her for not getting ready for school. Where was Shinnuedathy, the only person in the house, who always had time for her? Even if she was stoking the three-stone fire in the kitchen or chopping vegetables for

Shards of Sunlight

lunch, she would stop and talk to Indu and Mani. Indu *had* to tell her about Ammini.

Indu found Shinnu eventually in the kitchen cleaning out the hearth, sweeping the ash and gathering it into a flat piece of cardboard with a small broom. The room smelled of damp wood.

'Shinnuedathy,' she called.

'Entha Moley? Shinnuedathy can't come now, see. I'm cleaning out this fireplace. But you can come over and watch me,' she added, when she saw Indu's face - and the finger still working away at the seam.

'Achamma - I *don't* like her. I'll tell Achan when he comes back.'

'What are you going to tell him? That old woman! What has she been saying to you now?' Shinnu asked. 'She's getting madder by the day. Don't take any notice of her.'

By this time Indu was clinging, so Shinnu dumped the broom and cardboard and hugged her in spite of her dirty hands. She smoothed Indu's hair back behind the ears, leaving streaks of soot on the upturned face. Indu rubbed her face into Shinnu's blouse and took the opportunity to wipe some incipient snot off on it; she could not get close enough to Shinnu. She smelled Shinnu's familiar, comforting smells of shallots, wood ash and affection.

'You'll get late for school, Indu. Go and wash your face. See, I've made it really dirty.'

Indu wandered off reluctantly in the direction of the bathroom.

After her bath, Indu went in search of Mani. She found her bathed, cow-licked and dressed for school; she had her satchel ready and was busy rubbing her face

Shards of Sunlight

with a *thorthu,* trying to get any remnant of coconut oil off her face. Indu knew exactly how that felt; why did the women insist on putting coconut oil on their heads and faces every morning before their baths? The moong paste, green gram ground on stone, used for baths instead of soap, did not remove the oil properly. On bad days you could see the shine on the hair and forehead; Mani hated that. Indu did not usually waste much time on cleaning the oil off; she knew it was a lost cause.

Seeing Mani ready for school, Indu remembered that Devi was going to get into a temper if she did not get her school clothes on very soon.

'Mani, did Achamma ask you also to go away and live in your mother's house?' she asked tentatively as she pulled on a clean pair of knickers.

Mani always had the answers; everyone said she was so much wiser than Indu, so Mani lived up to this generally.

'What? In Penang? There is a war there; how can she ask me to go now?'

Indu thought for a moment. 'Do you think Achamma hates me now that Achan is not here? Shinnuedathy says Achamma is mad.'

Mani ignored that, Indu asked many questions and Mani often did not know the answers. 'Get that dress on soon or you will make me late. You are always making us late. The *jutka-man* will be here in a moment and all the children in the jutka will blame us for keeping them waiting.'

Indu had trouble getting her school dress over her head; she had forgotten to pull the press-studs apart.

Mani leaned over and unbuttoning the dress, tugged it down. Indu smoothed the rough cotton with her palm, trying unsuccessfully to iron out the creases,

Shards of Sunlight

make it look tidy and pretty like the dresses of her classmates. It smelled of rice-starch and damp; she flapped the skirt of the dress about, trying to dispel the odour.

'Get your school bag quickly,' Mani urged. And as an after thought, 'They say Achamma is going mad; I heard Devi say so to Vijayettan, next door.'

Devi bustled in then. 'Forget about Devi saying... Ramu is ringing the jutka-bell – out, the two of you.'

Devi sighed deeply. She did that a lot recently, so the girls did not even look her way.

Shards of Sunlight

7

Gopalan had been in jail for three months when the first letter arrived from Vellore. The postman delivered it with a sense of occasion.

'From Vellore,' he offered, as he handed the letter to Devi. 'Look at all the stamps on it.'

There were a great many purple seals and stamps on it, even on top of the address, making it difficult to read. He waited a moment, probably hoping Devi would open the letter in front of him and tell him what it was about.

Devi turned it this way and that; then she looked pointedly at the postman till he felt obliged to go away.

'What are these bits in purple ink?' she asked Mani, showing her the envelope. Devi did not know any English.

Mani read it out for her. 'Censored. By order of the Superintendent. Vellore Jail.'

Devi fumbled and tugged the envelope open. She read the three pages not allowing her mind to pause, like a starving man consuming food. It was full of instructions: the school fees were due soon when the Convent reopened in September; the clerk, Sukumaran, must be reminded to give some of the case records back to clients he could no longer represent, and collect some monies owing to him; his small library of law books must be protected from white ants and silverfish; Devi must get a tarpaulin to cover the shelves…

Shards of Sunlight

'He's not here, we haven't heard from him for a long while and what has he to say? Instructions! What about where he is? Is it comfortable, are they feeding him, do they treat him well? What have I got here to say to Amma?'

The two girls listened to Devi ranting.

'Devi Ammammey, is there anything for us? What does Achan say?' Indu called out. 'We must tell him about our quarterly exam results. He will be pleased, won't he?'

Actually, Indu had done only moderately well and stood eleventh in the class, whereas Mani had come first in the fifth standard.

'Here's a page for you two girls,' Devi said, handing over the last page.

It was written in English and started:
Dear Indu and Mani.

Then there was a one-inch block of Indian ink across the paper – two or three lines crossed off and made unreadable. The girls peered at it and held it up to the light, but they could not see through the dense black of the ink. They read the bits below it.

'What is this, Ammammey?' Mani asked. 'Why has Elayachan crossed off this bit with black ink?

'It's not Elayachan,' Devi said. 'See my letter. It is full of those blocks of black ink. Must have been done by the jail people. But, what could he write to you two that could possibly upset the government?'

'Maybe he told us about the jail,' Mani said cannily. 'They won't like people talking about how it is in the jail.'

The children continued fiddling with the page, trying to see through the ink. They passed it from one to the other reading the few sentences that were not inked.

Shards of Sunlight

"*Are you reading books and doing your homework, both of you? I am reading a book by someone called Trevelyan. It is a history of the British people and it is beautifully written.*"

The bit above that was blacked out. Then it said:

"*I am missing my girls; hope I can come back home soon.*"

'Can't see what Achan wanted to tell us,' Indu said, sounding forlorn. 'I want him home too.'

'Maybe we should write to him in Malayalam next time,' Mani said. 'They won't know Malayalam in Vellore, will they?'

They had got used to not knowing where he was and not getting letters; now it seemed the unread bit really made them dissatisfied.

Next morning Indu was on the veranda, sharpening her slate-pencil on the steps, when Devi came out with her brass box. She kept her housekeeping money in the bottom compartment and her betel leaves and accessories for chewing, arecanut, *chunamb* (lime) and tobacco, in the top.

Indu watched her take out coins and a few one rupee notes from the bottom and count them back into the tray. She did this twice as though something baffled her. When she noticed Indu looking at her, she closed the box and attempted a smile.

'Always less than I thought.'

'Can I have a quarter-anna for gooseberries?' Indu asked, seizing the moment. This was one of the many freedoms Indu had acquired after her father left for jail. He had disapproved of the girls buying any kind of food at the school gates, insisting the fruit was unwashed and would give them diarrhoea. She had

Shards of Sunlight

often begged a few gooseberries off her friend, Uma, whose parents were obviously more relaxed about such things. High time she returned the favour, or Uma was going to get peeved.

'Let's see. Later, maybe,' Devi said, closing the box quickly, and Indu knew the gooseberries were but a dream.

In the first period after lunch, sister Theckla called attendance register. The girls did not usually settle down to lessons until after the register was closed and prayers were said.

'*Our Father, who art in Heaven,*' sister intoned and the girls followed. '*Give us this day our daily bread.*' Nobody eats bread, Indu thought when she came to that bit. How about, '*Give us this day our daily rice?*' At the end of prayers, when all were seated, ready for the history lesson, sister took out a list and addressed the class.

'Fees,' she began. 'Several of you have still not paid this term's fees.'

Indu was not listening too carefully as she was busy delving in her school bag for her history textbook. Achan always paid for the term on the first day and she felt rather sorry for the girls whose names were read out in public by Sister. After the name reading a buff envelope would be given to the offending girls to take home. Indu often wondered what dire punishments were threatened inside that humiliating envelope. She was glad she never received one of those.

Sister seemed to enjoy seeing the defaulters squirm.

'You can't even get the half-fees you pay on time, Seetha,' she called out. Seetha had a fee-

Shards of Sunlight

concession from the school because her mother was a widow. 'If your mother cannot pay fees, there are many non-fee-paying schools, you should tell her that.' Sister threw a contemptuous glance in the general direction of the Mission High School next door.

'Yes, Sister,' Seetha muttered, looking straight in front of her, as she walked up to take her letter.

Parvathy was the next on the list; everyone knew Sister hated Parvathy anyway, though no one knew why.

'Not enough having an oil bath and dressing up with flowers in your hair every day. Fees have to be paid on time.'

Sister looked at Parvathy as though daring her to say something, but Parvathy merely stared back at her stonily, refusing to be drawn in. She was used to Sister's nastiness; she made a funny face at the class as she turned her back to Sister and walked back to her seat.

Sister Theckla picked up her list and started calling the names again as Indu continued fiddling within her bag.

'K.P.Indu,' sister called out, but Indu was oblivious to the summons, until the sudden hush in the classroom made her realise something was amiss. She looked up and around; what was the matter?

'Come and take your letter,' Sister said. 'And come back with a reply tomorrow.'

Indu dropped her bag on the floor and stood up, clumsily dislodging pencils and books from her lap. She walked up to take her letter, feeling all those pairs of eyes boring into her.

Shards of Sunlight

Sister stared hard when she handed the letter to her. 'Tell your guardian, whoever that is now, to come and see me,' she instructed.

Indu had no idea who her guardian was. She walked back, not meeting the eyes of any of her classmates, and wriggled past Hameed and into her seat.

'Who is my guardian?' Indu asked Mani as they sat in front of the altar in the puja room before supper. 'Is it like guardian angels?'

'No, you idiot,' Mani whispered. 'It's who looks after you at home. Devi, I think, for both of us because Elayachan is not here.'

'As if Devi is going to see Sister,' Indu said. 'Devi never goes anywhere.'

'What's it for, anyway?'

'Something to do with the fees.'

'Oh, oh,' Mani said. 'I'm going to get it too.'

8

A few weeks later, on a Sunday, Indu sat in her favourite seat on the front veranda steps, waiting for the day to unfold and spread its wares out. Devi sat behind her on a bench, chewing betel leaves; a trickle of thin, red juice came down one corner of her mouth, tracing the worry lines that reached towards her chin. Indu knew that look on her face. Like chicken-licken the world had fallen on her head the day Achan went away.

It was the quiet hour: breakfast was over and done with and lunch was some hours away. The road in front of the house was beginning to wake up and next door, Leela's father could be heard in his favourite morning activity – hawking and spitting last night's phlegm on the path in front of his veranda.

The fisherman would come soon, hopeful of a sale, but these days there was no money for anything. Most days it was spinach or cucumber for lunch; thankfully, Shinnu was getting more inventive at making new, unnamed curries with those two cheap vegetables.

Indu specially loved the red spinach, which came with lots of curry leaves and grated coconut. As lunch time approached, Shinnu allowed Indu to help peel the shallots; the tears had been plentiful, but Indu felt she was being allowed into the world of adult women, to do important things like cook for the family.

While Indu wiped the tears away, the mouth-watering smell of frying shallots and ginger, and the

Shards of Sunlight

sounds of popping mustard seed filled the kitchen. It happened so quickly, with sleight of hand, Shinnu throwing things into the pan with both hands, one after the other. The scraped, white coconut on the deep magenta of the spinach looked pretty.

When the vegetables were cooked, Indu came out again and watched the road, Doctor Shetty drove up in his little Morris Minor.

'I came to check the child with whooping cough next door,' he said. 'Might as well have a look at Ammini Amma.'

Indu knew about that tortuous cough, she could hear a the long-drawn agony early in the morning. She wondered whether you could get that cough by listening to it. Indu's mother had died of tuberculosis and Achan lost his head whenever Indu had a cough.

Devi accompanied the doctor to her mother's bedside and Indu followed behind. Ammini appeared to be sleeping, the frayed grey blanket pulled up to her chin. The doctor and Devi talked about her as though she was deaf and dumb.

'Some days she's very lucid; she surprises you. Others, she's like this. Out of this world.' Devi sounded resigned, long-suffering.

The doctor took Ammini's pulse and temperature and put his stethoscope to her chest, his actions slow and studied, as though he had nothing else to do for the rest of the day. Ammini opened her eyes as he was packing his bag.

'How are you today?' he asked, but she didn't answer. She turned over and pulled her blanket up.

As he was leaving Devi quickly found a five-rupee note in her money box and offered it to him.

'Not every time I come here. What have I done today? Let Gopalan come first.'

'We haven't paid for the medicines even,' Devi said.

'Never mind. The red liquid is to keep her pressure down, the pills to make sure her bowels work and the tonic to make her strong.'

'All that money and she hardly drinks the stuff.'

'We have to try,' he said gently. 'We have to try.'

Ammini usually baulked at the medicines and spat them out, far into the corner of her bedroom, as soon as Devi turned her back.

'Medicines!' she would mutter in anger. 'To keep this wretch alive. This sinner who has outlived her sons.' This was becoming a regular chant.

After the doctor left Devi settled back on the veranda again, thoughtfully, her mind clearly somewhere else. She started counting the notes and coins in her money box. As she counted she was murmuring to herself. Bad sign, Indu thought. Definitely no money for fees. Indu was glad when Shinnu joined Devi on the bench; she knew how to lighten Devi's moods.

Shinnu had bright pink patches on her cheeks from blowing into the wood fire and her hair had a dusting of ash. Indu got up from the steps and went up to her; Shinnu put her arms round Indu as she leaned into her. She smelled of ginger mixed with green plantains. She always smells of food, Indu thought. And Devi smells of betel leaves and the sacred ash smeared on her forehead.

Shards of Sunlight

'Ah, the bottomless box,' Shinnu remarked turning to Devi. 'What are you murmuring?' Shinnu asked after a moment when the silence stretched.

'School fees. What's the point?'

'Point for what?'

'Sending the girls to school when we hardly have enough to eat. You and I did not go to school a lot, did we?'

'And look at us!' Shinnu laughed. 'You and I haven't got a clue about anything but what happens in the kitchen. We are supposed to be married and looking after our men, but you are fifty-eight and I don't see a man around.'

'Nobody wanted to marry me,' Devi said wryly. 'I had just the one proposal: a cousin. He was a few annas short of a rupee, wanting a second wife because the first one could not bear him a son.'

Devi had a faraway look in her eyes as though she was thinking about that long-ago proposal and how she had turned it down.

Indu listened with interest; a parallel universe in which Devi Ammamma had a husband was impossible to imagine.

'How old were you then?' Shinnu asked.

'Long past the age. Thirty-two. I was considered an old maid by then.'

'School,' Shinnu started again. 'Don't the girls have to know to read and write?' she asked, with her usual dog-with-a-bone tenacity.

'Gopalan's madness. Girls have to be educated, he keeps saying. Last thing he said to me was, "Pay the school fees on time."'

Indu liked it when Shinnu and Devi found time to sit down and talk companionably like this, as though

Shards of Sunlight

they were the same age. It made her feel secure. When Shinnu was near her, Devi seemed to shed her worries; occasionally Shinnu could even coax a laugh out of her.

As the women talked a small, dark head appeared at the gate.

'Next door Vijayan is coming,' Shinnu pointed out as the bolt on the gate clanged.

Vijayan walked briskly towards them; he was carrying a small gunny bag folded under his arm. His stiffly starched dothi swished like wet washing in the wind. This was one of the new phenomena in their lives: Vijayan walking in confidently, stopping to offer tit-bits about the political situation. Vijayan, who always got short shrift from Gopalan, who had no time for local gossip.

'I'm off to the market,' Vijayan said. 'Can I get you anything from there?'

Shinnu got up and walked towards the kitchen; young girl that she was, she was not supposed to stay when a man came visiting.

'No. We are not buying anything.'

Vijayan hesitated. Devi looked at him, waiting for him to say whatever he had come to say.

Indu knew how irritable Devi could be, but she did not show her usual impatience. If somebody dies in this house, it is the likes of him who will carry the stretcher, she often remarked. Who is going to die in this house? Indu wondered, for Devi to be suddenly so tolerant of Vijayan.

Indu knew a bout of politics was coming, because this was Vijayettan's bread and butter.

Shards of Sunlight

'They say people like Gopalan vakil may be transferred from Vellore to Thanjavoor jail,' he said after an uneasy pause.

Indu always felt sorry for any one trying to make small talk with Devi on a bad day. And today had started badly.

'How do you know that?' Devi asked.

'People are saying -'

Devi had not asked him to sit down; in any case there was nothing to sit on apart from the bench on which she sat. Vijayan stood stiffly on the top step of the veranda.

'Right. Nobody is going to know until it is all done and finished. I'm tired of these rumours: The other day he was in Kunnoor, then he was in Madras. He was tied up and beaten; he was fasting in protest. What are we to believe?' Devi put her hands out, palms upwards, in obvious exasperation.

'You see.' Vijayan sounded reluctant to proceed. He turned away a little from Devi and looked at the clock on the wall. 'There is a talk that some lawyers were planning to bring the Union Jack down from the top of the Court buildings and put the tricolour up.'

The connection was clear in Indu's mind – she knew her father. *If* there was such a scheme, he would have been involved.

Devi got up as though to go inside.

'What he has started… There are some of us who believe we have to finish it,' Vijayan was talking to Devi's back as she started towards the door.

She spun round and walked back.

'Not enough that there is desolation in this house; now you want to bring it on others, including

51

Shards of Sunlight

your own house.' Devi pushed her strands of weak, grey hair behind her ears impatiently and glared at him. Then she slumped on the bench, exhausted by the strength of her reaction; she covered her mouth as if to stop the rest of the tirade from escaping.

'It's not that big a thing. It is only your blessing we need,' Vijayan said.

Devi looked hard at Vijayan again, 'What do you intend to do?' she asked, lowering her tone.

She darted a quick, uneasy look at Indu, who pretended to be engrossed in the mango fly she was balancing on a twig. Most of the time the adults ignored her while she stacked up information for future use. Indu was growing up fast and the world was coming into sharper focus.

'We need someone who has no fear of heights and can keep his mouth shut. There is that coconut-tree-climber; he is used to heights. He painted the Court buildings a year ago and knows the place well. He is one of us; his son was caught in a procession last year and is still in Kunnoor jail.

'And what if he gets caught?'

'The watchman is an old drunkard. Buy him enough toddy and he won't know if you carry him and dump him somewhere else.'

'The police will get nasty.'

'Yes. Aren't they nasty now? They'll search some of our houses. They may come here too. I think you should know what to expect.'

'No, surely not,' Devi said, eyes widening, but the *no* tailed off uncertainly when she saw Vijayan's face.

Vijayan was looking everywhere but at Devi. 'Give a license to these policemen and…'

Shards of Sunlight

'And?'

'Well. You know that teacher woman, Karthi, who has been organising the women around here, making speeches. That tall one who always wears *kadhar*. Last week two policemen came to her house and ransacked it. Even took the clothes from the line and threw them into the mud. Wonder what they thought was hidden under the skirts of women. Scavengers! They love showing their power, marching around everywhere. There is your mother to consider...' he tailed off.

Devi's lips clamped together. She thrust her chin up and out.

'We, you – can't leave things as they are, can we? No. Must do what needs to be done,' she said.

Next week, Indu woke up on Monday morning with a sense of momentous events, larger than herself, larger than any one person, looming. Instead of her slow, dopey shuffle around the house and compound, she skipped and ran around making Shinnu ask, 'Why are you acting like a kitten before a storm – lifting your fluffed up tail and darting about?'

As she walked through to the kitchen Indu could hear the excited chatter of the milk boy as Shinnu held out the *lotta* for the day's milk.

Kodathi, she heard, and *pathaka*. The Courts and the flag. She went to the back door to listen.

'*Enthada?*' What is it, boy? 'Noise and chatter when people are still sleeping,' Devi said to the boy.

'Devi ammey, *kettilley.*' Haven't you heard?

'Heard what?' Devi sounded offhand.

Shards of Sunlight

'The Court grounds are crawling with policemen. Even the beach in front is crowded with people watching. Can you believe it? The flag flying on top of the building is ours.' The 'ours' had a jubilant, almost uxorious ring to it.

The boy was pouring milk into the *lotta*, looking up at the women as he talked, and the milk overflowed from the top of the brass pot.

'Look at the milk,' Shinnu shouted.

The boy sobered up and tried to wipe the side of the lotta with a piece of multi-purpose rag that adorned his neck as a sweat band; normally he carried it on the seat of his bicycle to cushion his bony buttocks. Shinnu pulled the milk-pot away in disgust.

As the boy went to the gate, Vijayan scurried in. 'The police are on their way,' he said to Devi and sprinted off breathlessly. 'Don't want to be seen here. Keep the door to Ammini Amma's room closed.'

He reached the gate, stopped a moment and rushed back breathlessly. His sleek, pomaded hair was dishevelled for once. 'Don't let them go too quickly from here.'

'That's great,' Devi started sarcastically, but Vijayan had already disappeared.

Indu and Mani ran to the gate to have a look.

Marching down the Court Road, the police, they saw, had gathered a tail of urchins. The neighbours spilled out to the edge of their compounds, pretending to look at the coconut trees, hang out clothes on the line, beat the door mats on the veranda steps... Anything to join the *mela*. The Inspector leading the group of policemen opened Indu's front gate and the men filed through. The last policeman shooed away the boys. '*Poda*,' he said almost in a whisper, *go*. He raised

Shards of Sunlight

his *lathi,* his swagger stick, in threat and the boys hung back for a moment, feigning fear. As soon as he turned away they came closer, whispering to each other.

Devi saw them coming but went inside. Her thin joyless lips were set into an even thinner line and she pulled her top-cloth over her shoulders. She intoned a few quick *ramaramaramas* under her breath. Indu knew all about those *ramaramas*. Devi needed her God because the problems were beyond her.

'Shinnu,' Devi called out as she walked to the door, 'Don't come to the veranda.'

The two girls, Indu and Mani, had followed the policemen to the veranda but escaped Devi's x-ray eyes. When Devi came out, the policemen were gathering in an uneasy group on the steps of the veranda, with the Inspector on the top step. Devi watched impassively.

'*Entha*?' she asked as though policemen on the doorstep were a daily event. What is it?

The Inspector took his time answering. Indu could not decide whether it was embarrassment that made him hesitate, or pompousness. Maybe he is waiting for Devi to be afraid, she thought.

'We need to search the house,' he said.

'What for?'

The Inspector clearly did not know what he was looking for. 'Search means looking for anything, everything. Move aside from the doorway.'

Devi was blocking the doorway, but she didn't move. The man took a step forward. Indu got a little closer to Mani.

'Mani -,' she whispered.

Mani clutched Indu's hand tight in hers.

Shards of Sunlight

The policeman made as if to push Devi away to enter inside, but Devi stood her ground, staring at him, as though challenging him.

'Stop there,' a breathless voice commanded from behind the police. 'Have you got a search warrant?'

It was Damu, from down the lane. He was wearing only a dothi and a vest and must have sprinted down the road. The dothi was doubled up and tucked into his waist for running.

'I don't need a search warrant. These are special times.'

'Yes, yes. Special time indeed when policemen can come and threaten women in houses where there are no men. Shameless lot. Go find some men to frighten.'

The Inspector took a step back from the doorway.

The lawyer turned to Devi. 'Don't open the door to anyone without letting me know. Search indeed!'

The Inspector stood back for a moment and then signalled to his entourage. They filed out of the veranda in an untidy group as the urchins turned round and giggled at them.

Devi breathed a sigh of relief; Indu and Mani followed her inside. Her courage lasted only till she reached the kitchen; there she collapsed in an untidy heap and started trembling.

'Keep that scum here indeed. What did Vijayan think I was going to do?'

By the time Vijayan scurried back to check on Gopalan's household, Devi had regained her usual haughty self-sufficiency.

Shards of Sunlight

'Don't be scared,' she said to the distraught Shinnu. 'In any case Damu vakil will not let them bully us.'

'Mmm hmm,' Shinnu snorted, looking unconvinced.

Everybody knew what a coward Damu could be, always towing the safe line, keeping his nose pointed in harmless directions, continually chiding Gopalan for his political activities, and keeping his conscience at bay with the occasional contribution tossed ungraciously to the Congress Party. Gopalan used to make fun of Damu for keeping his head below the parapet.

'Really, he was here, telling the police to disappear. He made them go. What could *I* have done?' Devi asked.

'I ran there when I left here,' Vijayan said. 'He came immediately; I've never seen him move so fast.'

'What other houses did they go to?' Devi asked.

'They went straight to that Karthi teacher's from here. You know the one who holds meetings in her house?'

'Tell her Vijaya,' Devi said firmly. 'I am going to be there at the next meeting.'

'What are you talking about?' Shinnu demanded to know. 'Do you want to end up in jail too?'

'These policemen are Indians. And yet, see what they have become! Lackeys for the British. We have to teach them a lesson.'

'Devi Ammamma is going to make speeches like that teacher,' Mani said to Indu. Maybe she'll let us go and watch.'

'I am going to see how Karthi teacher is,' Devi declared. 'Must see whether she is all right after a visit from those hooligans.'

Shards of Sunlight

She went inside for a few minutes and came out dressed for the street. She had put on a clean blouse and retied her sparse hair to sit in a little knot at her nape.

'Who will come with me?' As a respectable woman she needed someone to escort her on the street.

'I'll come,' Indu volunteered, but Devi called Mathu, their maid.

'They've arrested one or two people,' Vijayan said. 'That young man from the Koduvally School who sings the anthem, *Janaganamana,* at meetings in teacher's house, and teacher's husband too. Poor man, he does not have anything to do with all this and is always warning his wife not to be a hothead.'

'Will they be hurt?'

'Who knows what happens in that police den? We'll know when – and if- they come out.'

Indu and Mani ran to the gate to see what happened next. They watched as the policemen tried to shed their ragtag following of boys, but every time they turned and shooed the boys away, they hung back for a moment, and returned in good humour, like flies after a fish vendor. In the face of this following the men in khaki held their heads high and talked to each other loudly about the incident that had brought them to Court Road, asserting their power and demonstrating their disregard of the local community.

Indu followed them staying close to the urchins, so as not to miss any fun. A little voice in her head said Achan would never let her go on the road like this, but this was one of the freedoms she had acquired with Achan going.

The police jeeps were parked at the crest of the hill, near the rear-gate of the Court buildings. As Indu and the urchins approached the vehicle they noticed a flat tyre at the back, and then very rapidly the fact that all four tyres had collapsed.

The policeman in front swore.

'*Nayinde makkal...*'

The Inspector hurried up and bent down to examine the tyres one by one. The valves had been removed and someone had stuck a small paper tricolour on the bonnet of the car. The street boys gathered round pointing and giggling; again the policemen tried to drive them back, but it was as futile as sweeping ants into a sieve: when they chased one boy away another moved in.

'Court Road, they call it!' the Inspector muttered in disgust. 'This road has more *goondas* than anywhere in town.' He frowned and spat noisily on to the side of the road. One of the urchins hawked loudly and imitated him, producing a respectable sized glob of spit near by. All the boys guffawed.

Men spilled out from the teashop near by, hitched up their *lungis* and lighted up *beedies;* they blew smoke out impassively as the Inspector looked at their faces. They talked to each other in whispers. Indu decided she needed a front seat for *this* cinema. She slipped behind the boys and stood next to the men.

'*Ara polum?*' one of them said. Are they saying who?

'Vijayan and his lot, I'm sure,' a man answered, holding his hand to his mouth.

'There he comes,' another said, pointing to a dilapidated old man being dragged forward by an irate policeman. He was in an alcoholic stupor and did not know what was going on around him.

'Let go,' he pleaded, trying to pull his arm away. At this the policeman pushed him forward, and taking a pair of handcuffs out of his pocket, put them on his wrists. It was the watchman at the Courts and probably the only one who did not know about the flag on the Court building.

'*Edo*, look what they have dragged in,' the leader of the urchin pack said, loud enough to be heard by the police. The watchman was red-eyed and could barely hold himself up. He made no effort to wipe the drool marks on his chin. When he noticed the urchins he grinned slowly, exposing his crooked, brown, front teeth.

The policeman picked up some stones from the side of the road and hurled it at the boys. The men watching in front of the teashop stirred.

'If you lose in the market place you take it out on your mother, eh?' one called out to another. 'What have the boys done?' He was careful not to address this to any one in particular.

The policeman put the prisoner between two of them and started walking towards town; as they turned the corner on the brow of the hill a huge amused roar went up from the men on the scene.

9

The week after Sister Theckla sent the buff envelope home, Indu refused to get dressed for school.

'Stomach ache,' she said tearfully, when Mani tried to hurry her.

'Suddenly, a stomach ache,' Devi muttered, disbelieving, but Shinnu intervened.

'So - does it matter if she misses a day?' Shinnu hugged Indu. 'Show me where your stomach hurts,' she said. ' Let's see if I can make it better.'

'Maybe worms,' Devi conceded grudgingly. 'About time both you girls got your laxative.'

'Now see what you have done,' Mani wailed to Indu.

Mani turned to Indu and whispered, 'What's up with you anyway? You *like* going to school. You are usually counting the days for the school to re-open after holidays.'

'Yes. Home is boring.' Indu frowned.

'So what's this act, then?'

'Sister Theckla will punish me for not paying fees. I don't want to go until the fees are paid. And my stomach is really hurting.'

'No, it's not. And you better tell Devi about the fees,' Mani said.

Indu knew all about that laxative – half a cup of distilled senna pods, which tasted like melted metal and stayed on your palate for hours. You had to drink it early in the morning, on an empty stomach, and a cup

Shards of Sunlight

of hot tea followed an hour later. At all meal times you were given only *conjee* and a *pappadam*, roasted rather than fried. This went on till you had made several trips to the outside latrine and Devi declared your stomach well and truly evacuated. This routine happened once every six months, and six months hadn't quite passed.

'Not yet six months, Ammammey,' Mani called out hopefully.

'A little early, but it looks like Indu needs it.'

Indu looked apologetically at Mani, but the older girl stormed out with her school bag to wait at the gate for the *jutka*.

Halfway through the morning when Shinnu got busy in the kitchen, Indu hung about, not knowing where to go or what to do. She watched as Shinnu cut a coconut open into two halves with a thick machete and poured the smoky water inside into a brass mug.

'Nectar for my tiny girl.' Shinnu said. Indu gulped it down greedily.

Then Shinnu cut a neat swirl of coconut from the top edge of one of the coconut-halves and gave it to Indu. 'Now go and play,' she said. 'I have cooking to do.' She put the coconut scraper down on the floor and started scraping into a tin plate. The white shreds made a growing hillock.

Indu squatted down next to the plate and started taking pinches of coconut out. Some fell on her hand; she licked those. As she chewed, coconut milk dribbled down at the side of her mouth.

'Why are you lurking like a ghost searching for salvation today? Go and read a book or something.'

Indu went out of the kitchen and sat on the narrow ledge of the kitchen-veranda, facing Leela's house, and dangled her feet over the edge. A host of white moths fluttered around the okra bushes, which were beginning to flower in Shinnu's small vegetable patch.

Leela would be in school, but there were noises coming from Leela's house as though someone was lumbering about inside. After a little while, Leela's obnoxious father came out and settled himself on the stone steps leading down to the path between the houses. Indu moved a little so that a banana tree hid her from his line of vision; she peeped at him through the leaves.

He put two small dented cigarette tins on either side of him and removed the towel round his waist. Underneath she could see his *konakam*, the traditional g-string that men wore. Instead of the usual red cloth, Chathu had a greasy strip of sacking hitched to the black thread round his waist. He stretched his limbs out for a moment and looked up at the sky, talking to himself. He did that a lot.

Chathu dipped his hand in one of the tins and started oiling his body, beginning with his skinny legs, stretched out on the steps below him. Why was he at home on a Monday? Indu wondered, but she had nothing to do, so she watched him as he oiled his arms, face and torso slowly before proceeding to his crotch. Indu knew she should stop looking and disappear but, if she stood up now, he would notice her. At least that was her excuse to herself to continue staring.

Finally he loosened the *konakam* in front and let it hang slack as he slid his hands between his legs and applied the oil to all the cracks and crevices. Indu saw two long brown cucumber-like objects sitting flaccidly on either side of his penis. What were *they*?

Shards of Sunlight

Did they dangle on his thighs when he walked? She wished she could get closer to have a proper look. They looked disgusting; she didn't know anyone who had those.

When he was satisfied, he stood up, ready to oil his behind. He turned and Indu decided it was a good time to run inside.

'Shinnuedathy,' she asked. 'Why is Chathu at home today?'

'Why are *you* at home today? anyone might ask. Perhaps he has a stomach ache like you. How is your stomach anyway?'

'It's gone – the ache,' she answered, a little sheepishly. 'Leela is not at home,' Indu said, poking her finger into the seam of her frock.

'Well. They say someone important is coming to Leela's house today. That's why Chathu is there.'

'Who's that?'

'Someone who wants to see Leela as well, so she'll be there in the afternoon. You can play with her then.'

Halfway through the afternoon, when the neighbourhood had slowed down for the siesta hour, Indu sat on the front veranda of her house restlessly, looking for something to do. Shinnu was reading the Malayalam newspaper and she couldn't be disturbed; the paper was borrowed for an hour from a house down the road. Devi was resting in the middle room of the house, mouth open, snoring as she slipped in and out of a light sleep.

Staying at home on a school day was not fun at all, Indu decided. So, when the especially opulent *jutka*, which was called a *governor's cart,* came by with its

Shards of Sunlight

red velvet curtains on the side-windows and the padded steps, it was a welcome diversion. She ran to the gate to watch.

A middle-aged man got out and adjusted his *veshti* – his off-white shawl with an elegantly thin gold border. It had been folded and ironed into a long strip which decorated his silk shirt. The man was tall and fair, and looked distinguished, more distinguished than any man she'd ever seen. He stretched his hand out for the woman inside. She came down gingerly, hitching up her sari to avoid tripping on it, displaying green and gold slippers on dainty white feet.

Indu's mouth fell open and she stared unashamedly. The lady was covered in green and gold: the sari was the green of paddy fields when the new shoots come out, with thin gold checks, which shimmered as they caught the afternoon sun. She wore a necklace made of green stones set in gold, and her glass bangles, which clinked as she moved her arms, were green and gold too. Indu wanted to get closer and look at her, to take that dazzle in, but Devi would explode if she did that.

The two visitors walked briskly down the narrow path between Indu's and Leela's houses and stopped in front of Leela's veranda; Indu ran round her house and peeped through the kitchen window, careful not be caught gawping.

Why would such rich people want to visit that shack? Indu wondered. Shinnu came by and stood close to her and peered over her shoulder.

'I told you someone was coming there today. That's why Chathu was preening himself. His one bath in a year probably.' Shinnu laughed and pointed to the

Shards of Sunlight

visitors. 'See that couple? It seems they have no children. They want to adopt Leela.'

'What's adopt? Anyway, that woman is the man's daughter, isn't she?'

'No, she's his wife. They want Leela to go and live in their house and be their daughter.'

'You can't be someone else's daughter just like that,' Indu said firmly. 'Anyway, Leela won't go.'

'Apparently, they are offering a lot of money. They think Leela is very pretty and they want her. Chathu has no money to look after her properly. All his money goes to the toddy shop; we all know that.'

They watched as Chathu came out and started talking to the couple. This was a new Chathu Indu was seeing – he wore a clean white *mundu* and a blue shirt. His hair was cow-licked into place and he was smiling and gesticulating while he talked. He pushed his deck chair towards the visitor, clearly asking the man to be seated, but the man shook his head and remained standing. The lady stood aside, looking around as though her role there was entirely peripheral.

Shinnu moved away from the window after a little while, but Indu stayed glued, watching the silent drama in front of her. The evening shadows were beginning to lengthen. The lively chatter of school children walking back home filled the roads and Leela returned from school.

She looked exhausted; strands of hair had escaped from her plait, making her look bedraggled. The sight of the visitors stopped her in her tracks for a moment, then she tried to walk past them to go indoors. The man broke off from talking to Chathu and turned to her; Chathu put his hand out and caught her.

Shards of Sunlight

The adults started talking again while Leela stood, head down, stock still, like a lassoed animal, clutching her slate and books. Finally, Chathu let her go and she ran inside past the staring woman, who did not for a moment take her eyes off the captured girl.

When Mani came home from school soon after, Indu was full of questions.

'Have you heard about adoption? Going away and living with strangers and they become your parents?'

'Ye-es. But what's it got to do with you or me?'

'Someone wants to adopt Leela; they came to her house today. In a *governor's cart*.

'Another one of your tall stories – as if Mathu is going to give Leela to any one. She'll die for that girl.

10

The next morning the houses around Leela's house woke up to loud thumping noises and screams. Indu jumped out of bed and ran to the north veranda. The kitchen door was already open and Shinnu was staring across at Leela's house.

'No, no, don't. Please don't,' she called out as Chathu screamed at Mathu and slammed her into the wall of the veranda.

'Good-for-nothing slag. You think you are going to stop me? I'll see you dead first.'

Chathu was in a frenzy and beyond hearing. Leela was tugging at his sarong, pulling him away from her mother. He turned and swiped her away with a back-hander..

'Get away from me, you miserable worm.'

As he hit out at Leela, Mathu wriggled away from underneath his arm and ran out of sight.

'Earthworms! Trying to lift their hoods like cobras. I'll show them.'

'Morning show over,' Shinnu announced. 'Wait for the next instalment.'

Indu found Devi cleaning out the puja corner in the middle room. Her aunt wiped the dust off the plaster Krishna with a wet rag and used rice paste to stick back the tinsel and coloured paper decorations that had worked themselves loose from the wall.

Shards of Sunlight

Indu pushed at Devi's shoulder, rocking her back and forth.

'Ammammey, can't you ask Chathu to stop hitting Leela and Mathu? He'll listen to you.'

'No, he won't. He's crazy and when he's drunk, he's like a rabid dog. He might have listened to your father, but …'

'He's going to give Leela to those people who came in the jutka.'

'That's all talk. Drunken talk.'

'Let's go to the big house,' Indu said to Mani later as they sat on the veranda, looking at the huge, half-finished house across the road; it had been empty for as long they could remember. Rumour had it that someone had hung himself on the veranda. The brick work and roof had been completed, but the walls were not plastered. In front there was a veranda and steps that went along the length of it. The impressive looking portico made you think of American cars with long fins, sweeping between the sturdy pillars and disgorging richly clad groups. For now though, the house was home to squatters who cooked over three-stone fires on the veranda and used the scummy pond on the left of the house for water. Mani, Indu and Leela occasionally wandered over, but recently a goat had drowned in the pool and it was forbidden territory.

Yesterday some women of the family came to Indu's house to beg for dry coconut fronds, and the water, which had been drained off cooked rice. They had with them a rag-tag bunch of small children who hung to their clothes and hid behind them. The women made the universal signs of begging for food, touching fingers to their mouths and stretching out their palms.

They didn't speak the local language, Malayalam, and no one wanted to go near them, but Devi pointed to some dry coconut palms at the end of the garden and made signs for them to take them.

'I saw the municipal hand cart come there earlier,' Indu said to Mani as they walked. 'They took a long bundle away.'

The day was slipping smoothly into dusk when the children crossed the road and walked up to the abandoned house. When they reached within hearing distance, Indu called out to the little girl sitting on the steps.

'*Itha?*' Here. The girl, who looked the same age as Indu, smiled shyly and hugged herself. Near the wall at the back of the veranda, the three-stone fire had been dead a long time. Sad-looking rags of nondescript shades of grey and brown hung on a rope slung between two pillars.

A woman came forward and stood behind the girl; as she saw the children approaching, she started calling out and gesticulating forcefully for them to go away.

'Bad sickness here. Don't come close.'

'What sickness?' Mani asked.

'Very bad,' the woman said, and began crying. 'Ettan died this morning.'

The girls panicked when they heard 'died' and ran back to their house.

'Devi Ammammey, a man died in that house. The woman is crying.'

Devi told Shinnu to go down there and check; perhaps the children misheard. 'Find out if this is true and what he died of. Maybe starvation. We didn't even know,' she said.

Shards of Sunlight

Shinnu was gone only a moment. 'Something serious there,' she said grimly. 'That young man definitely died last night. The woman can't speak much Malayalam; she's talking in Tamil. I asked her why so suddenly, but she just sobbed. Poor wretch. The eldest boy said the municipal cart came to take the body away. No money to bury him.'

Early the next week, a Health Officer turned up with a man carrying spraying equipment; he talked to Devi.

'The post mortem is over' he told Devi. 'The hospital says smallpox. We've had a few deaths in town also.'

'What should we do?' Devi asked.

'Keep everyone indoors as far as possible. And don't cook greasy food in the house. The vaccinator will come to give a booster dose to every one.'

He picked up Indu's left arm and looked at the large vaccination scar on her upper arm.

'This is a good scar; shows the vaccination has taken well. Still, better get another one. We're sending the vaccinators and sprayers out all this week.'

The sprayer, with the canister of disinfectant strapped to his back, went round the house spraying all the open drains and finishing off with the bathroom and the latrine. The pungent smell of phenol made Indu's eyes water.

Devi asked Mathu to fetch cow-dung from the small *maidanam*, the open land near the beach where the cows grazed. When it came, she mixed it with water and poured it into halves of coconut shells.

'What's that for?' Indu asked.

Shards of Sunlight

'You'll see,' Devi said enigmatically. 'Here, you can help me carry two of these.'

Devi arranged them on both sides of the path to the gate.

'Why are you putting cow-dung down, Ammammey?' Indu asked, baffled.

Devi explained as she walked back to the house: 'The goddess Mariamma is the evil goddess who distributes the pox. But she will not go near cow dung. This will stop her from coming to our house.'

Every three or four days Indu watched as the municipal cart came and carried another bundle away from the house across the road. Sometimes the bundles were tiny and Indu knew it was one of the children. When this happened she went to the back of the house and squatted on the parapet there for a long time, crying.

'Child, what's the point?' Shinnu said. 'We all feel bad.'

'Give them some cow-dung, Shinnuedathy. Then Mariamma will leave them alone. They are all dying.'

'Don't mention this in front of Achamma,' Shinnu told Indu. 'Promise me. You know Achan's eldest brother died of smallpox some years ago. She'll freak out if she hears there is small-pox in the house across.'

'But Mariamma can't come here because of the cow-dung,' Indu said with confidence.

'Mmm, alright.' Shinnu didn't sound so sure; Indu wondered why. 'Come on then. You've got to help me with the potatoes for the *bondas*,' Shinnu tempted her.

Shards of Sunlight

Bondas were Indu's favourite snack, so she ran to the kitchen, ready to help.

Shinnu had already boiled potatoes in their skin. They had cooled now and she asked Indu to wash her hands well and mash the potatoes.

Indu sat down on the low kitchen stool and started breaking up the potatoes. Meanwhile, Shinnu cut onions, ginger and green chillies very fine and made a thick batter of golden yellow gram flower. Already the kitchen smelt like bondas.

Shinnu mixed everything and made balls of the mixture. She dipped the balls in the batter and threw them into hot oil. The pungent smell of frying chilli filled their throats and nostrils and Shinnu and Indu coughed.

'Have to suffer a little to eat bondas,' Shinnu said between coughs.

Indu couldn't wait. As soon as the bondas were ready, she popped one into her mouth. It was scalding hot and she open-mouthed *ha-ha-ha* as she tried to cool it down.

'Greed!' Shinnu said indulgently. 'Leave some for the others.'

The smell of bondas brought Mani and Devi into the kitchen.

'The health man said not to fry things,' Devi said uncertainly. 'I wonder what it has to do with smallpox.'

'Exactly as much as the cow-dung to prevent it.' Shinnu laughed.

'You can laugh,' Devi countered. 'But don't forget to make the lemon juice with *jaggery*. That does work; it was in the newspaper.'

Shards of Sunlight

Lemon juice was a treat but Indu preferred it with real granulated sugar, which was becoming a thing of the past. The ration for a household such as Indu's was two pounds, once a month. Devi used it like gold dust.

She kept the sugar in her bedroom on top of the tiny shelf above the door, and doled it out reluctantly, a half-spoon at a time. When Ammini had to take sour medicines Devi brought the sugar out like a conjurer's assistant, making it a selling point for the medicine. She also kept some in an empty Quaker Oats tin for coffee, when guests, particularly respected in-laws and elderly uncles, arrived.

The children moaned they were tired of the gritty brown lumps they got in their tea, so Devi decided to give them their share early in the month. Mani and Indu got their sugar in empty Capstan's Navy Cut cigarette tins, which Gopalan had thrown away. W.D. and H.O. Wills, the tins proudly declared, showing the picture of a ship and its captain on the outside.

'I don't care whether you eat it all today or it lasts a month. But that is all there is till the next ration comes in,' Devi said.

Mani husbanded her share carefully, using a little now and then, but Indu put it into everything, even cold water, calling sugared water her special drink. Her share finished soon, and after that she was down to begging off Mani. Mani relented sometimes and gave her tiny pinches, but this merely whetted Indu's appetite and she pestered Devi until she took the oats tin down again.

Shards of Sunlight

So, when Vijayan's sister turned up with a whole two pounds of sugar wrapped in newspaper and gave it to Indu and Mani, it was carnival time.

'Sugar for lime juice, now. No more rubbish jaggery,' Indu said happily.

'From where is this?' Devi asked, 'The sugar that no one has enough of.'

'In our house, most people have diabetes, so this is no good to us,' the woman said, but her face belied her statement.

'For nothing, you are giving diabetes to everyone, 'Devi said smiling. 'We are grateful.'

Perhaps the sugar brought back memories for Mani.

'My Amma used to make vermicelli pudding,' she said to Indu. And she flavoured it with vanilla and cardamom pods.' She had a faraway look in her eyes.

'Was it nice?' Indu asked.

'Lovely,' Mani said. 'And some times she made mymoon.' There was longing in her voice.

'What is that?'

'Something she learned from the Chinese.' Mani's parents were still in Penang and Indu knew there were Malays and Chinese there.

'When your amma comes after the war, maybe she will make us mymoon.'

Indu sat thinking, 'I wouldn't mind having someone like your mother, who is my own, *own,* person,' she said after a while.

'There is your Achan,' Mani said.

'Mmm…' Indu did not feel very sure. Her Achan seemed to belong to many people. He was definitely not her *own* person, though she slept in his bed, and no one else did that.

Shards of Sunlight

'There is Devi,' Mani prompted.

'Won't let me sit in her lap,' Indu said as though that was the end of the discussion. Just before she went to sleep, Indu often wanted a vacant lap and a cuddle.

The last time Indu sat on Devi's lap, she had jerked her arm suddenly, starting up when she saw an orange-and-black frog hopping on to the front steps. She caught the side of Devi's mouth and drew blood; Indu had been horrified.

'Arande mackale
Arandu pottiyal
ayiram vali
sammanam.'

Devi had recited in her dead pan voice.

('Love another's child,
For a full six years,
What do you get?
A thousand farts.')

'You're a bit big to sit in any one's lap, don't you think?' Mani said.

Indu was nine years old now and she knew she was being silly, so she let it go. But the mother-shaped hole inside her ached sometimes. With Achan going the hole got bigger.

11

The next week, early on Sunday, Indu woke to excited noises downstairs; they sounded like happy noises. Was it her father's voice? It sounded very like him. She jumped out of bed and raced to the veranda.

'Mani, Mani, it is Achan, I think,' she called out as she ran.

'Dreaming again,' Mani said as she turned over and pulled her sheet up to cover her ears.

When Indu reached the veranda, Devi was paying the rickshaw man and Achan was standing there, tired and beaming. Indu ran and threw herself at him. She clung to her father, hiding her face in his *mundu*; he felt less bony than he used to be and looked paler.

'Grown up a lot,' Gopalan said, holding her back. 'Look at you.'

'Acha, Acha, why didn't you say you were coming? Ammamma never said - '

'I didn't want you to be disappointed in case he didn't get his parole,' Devi said.

Mani came out of the front door hearing the commotion. When she saw Gopalan, she ran to him and hugged him. 'Elayacha, I didn't believe Indu when she said you had come.'

'And how is my big girl?' Gopalan asked, hugging her. 'Have you been looking after the small one?'.

'She is not small any more, Elayacha. And she knows everything now.'

Indu noticed the exchange and a small bindweed of jealousy attached itself inside her and started coiling round and up.

"What is parole?' Indu asked.

'Permission to come home,' Gopalan said, not adding his parole was only for fifteen days, to see his sick mother.

How did word get around? Within an hour the house was deluged with visitors. Devi sent Mathu out for more milk and prepared endless cups of tea for the friends coming to greet her brother. The girls hovered around for a while on the edge of the crowd, but soon realized they had no place there, and disappeared indoors. From inside, they could still hear his confident baritone, describing his life in prison.

Indu wanted sole possession of her father; there were a hundred questions she needed to ask him. But they had to wait. So she restrained herself for the only real time she ever had with him: at night. But this too was spoilt because he insisted Devi put a mattress down in the same room for Mani.

'Must have both my girls near me,' he said.

In bed, all the questions came out.

'You are fat, Acha. How come you are fat and white?'

'The food was better than here,' he said smiling. 'And I didn't go out in the sun.'

Mani had a question from the other end of the room where her mattress was.

'They say people were beaten and starved. Didn't they treat you badly?'

He laughed. 'Do I look treated badly?'

'No,' Mani said. 'You look as though you have been having a holiday.'

'The lawyers and doctors – professionals like me. They treated us with caution. But the poorer classes were starved and beaten. In the Kunnoor jail, some bad things happened.'

'Where are you now?'

'I'm in Tanjavoor. They moved me from Vellore because I organized protests in the jail.'

Though Gopalan came to see his sick mother, he did not spend much time with her. The first morning of his parole, he went into her room to talk to her. Indu was behind him. Ammini didn't seem to recognise him.

'Ammey, it's Gopalan. Amma's son. Look at me.'

She stared at him and turned away. Indu felt sad for Achan.

'He's dead. Are you his ghost? Leave me alone,' Ammini said.

Later that morning the party men came in twos and threes and swallowed him up. Indu and Mani left for school while they talked, and when they came home at four in the evening, he was getting ready to go out with his friends.

Some days he attended meetings and planned strategies with the party leaders. But Indu was glad he was there in the nights and if she opened her eyes, she could see him in the moonlight, often awake, with his finger stretched around his nose, deep in thought.

'What are you thinking about?' she asked him once, in the early hours of the morning.

Shards of Sunlight

'You, of course,' he said, making a joke of it. Indu was not satisfied.

Indu started referring to Gopalan in the third person as *Endachan*, my father, trying to establish ownership as he slipped away more and more into the public domain. Devi made an attempt to explain matters to her.

'Your father, yes. But he's also their special person. They are always going to need him too; you better get used to that now.'

Indu responded by tossing her head and walking away.

'That child,' Devi exclaimed. 'The father is all she's got; I wish he'd just stay and look after her.'

Once, while she was hanging about on the outskirts of Gopalan's coterie, Leela's head appeared at the fence.

'Indoo, Indoo, come,' she called urgently. 'I'm going to -...'

'My father is here. Later,' Indu replied dismissively.

An hour later, Indu caught a glimpse of Leela going out with her father. She had her best dress on, and her hair was neatly plaited. She kept turning back to look at Indu's house while Chathu tugged at her hand, which he was clutching.

Indu thought about going to the fence to ask her where she was going, but she was too excited about Gopalan's presence to do anything but hover around him.

The last day of his parole came very quickly. Indu had been counting the days. The crowds came again to wish him good bye. She had to leave for school at nine in the morning, and his train, the Madras Mail,

Shards of Sunlight

would leave at twelve, long before she got home. She hovered on the edges of the crowd around him, peeping through any space she could find, trying to get his attention. Finally, she caught his eye.

'Going to school,' she mouthed, but the words would not come out.

He nodded, smiled slightly, and turned back to his crowd. Indu's shoulders slumped and her fingers probed at her waist. He has no time for me, she thought. When will he come again?

Shinnu saw her coming down the steps. A sob escaped from Indu.

Shinnu bent down and hugged her. 'Let me see,' she said. She straightened the bobby pin on Indu's hair. 'They won't leave him alone, will they? You mustn't mind. It's like that because he's here only for a fortnight. In all the world, there is no one he loves more than you.'

Indu did not remember Leela even after her father left; she had many things to think about. When would Achan come back again? One day, she'd wake up and hear his voice in the veranda, she decided. She started waking up before dawn to listen for him. She pestered Mani in those early morning hours saying, 'Achan will come today, now.'

'I'll have to sleep in Achamma's room if you go on like this,' Mani said. 'Won't let anyone sleep in peace.'

A week passed before Indu gave up on that dream. The refrain became, 'Achan didn't come.' She scratched furiously at the patch of ringworm on her elbow till she drew blood. She refused food and cried for nothing.

Shards of Sunlight

Finally Shinnu said, 'Why don't you go over and find Leela?'

'Leela won't talk to me, I think. She must be *so* angry with me.'

'Why? What did you do?' Shinnu asked.

'She called me the other day when I was with Achan and I didn't go. I didn't want to leave him.' Indu started crying again.

'That's bad,' Shinnu said, but she hugged her. 'You could have gone after he went. It's a long time since. Better you go and find her now.'

Indu walked across uncertainly.

'Leela,' she called out at the front door, but no one answered. Indu walked round the house noticing it looked dead. The sorry-looking washing of tattered sarongs and frayed shirts and blouses was spread on top of green coconut palm fronds on the ground. Chickens were rooting around in the dry soil nearby, sending up dust as they scratched for worms. Indu shooed them away from the clothes as she went past. The back door was open and Indu peeped in, but there was no one in the kitchen either. The hearth looked as though it had not been lit that day. Indu stuck her finger down the hole in her slip and went home.

'Where is Leela, Shinnuedathy? Leela is not there,' she said a little forlornly.

'Maybe she's gone somewhere to play. You've not been going there much lately, have you? Try Vijayettan's house behind ours. She often goes there.'

'But school has not closed,' Indu began and then remembered how little consideration was given to school in Leela's house. Unlike hers where everything was secondary to going to school and passing exams.

Shards of Sunlight

The next Sunday, Mathu disappeared and another faceless woman came to sweep and wash clothes. No point in asking *her* anything, Indu thought. She wandered around in the compound for a while before settling down on the veranda to make a ball with coconut palm leaves. Mani found her there a few minutes later, tying a knot to the thin end of the stripped leaves and plaiting the leaves round the stones. She was not very good at it.

'Leela is clever at making balls,' Indu said.

'Not going to play with Leela?'

'No one there,' Indu said. 'Maybe she's gone over to that big unoccupied house with her mother, to collect dry leaves.-

'Mm, Mm,' Mani said, shaking her head. 'No one goes there after they got small pox. She won't be there.'

If only I had asked where she was going that day, Indu thought. Maybe she is angry with me. But how could I leave Achan?

A week later, Indu was brushing her teeth on the north veranda when she saw Mathu. She was making a fire outside their kitchen with dried coconut fronds and coconut husk.

'Mathu,' she called. 'Are you coming to sweep?'

Mathu looked up but did not answer. Something in her face made Indu decide not to ask any more questions. She went across instead, and looked at the fire to see what Mathu was burning so furiously.

Mathu dropped what looked like a new red blouse on top of the fire, which was burning fiercely now. She then picked up a mundu and top cloth out of a paper-wrap near her and laid it carefully on top of the fire.

'They're new,' Indu exclaimed.

'New. Yes, very new. Blood money.' Mathu began sobbing as she threw more clothes into the blaze.

'Got those in exchange for my daughter, didn't I? My beautiful Leela, who loved everyone so much, even that dog of a father of hers. *Ende moley,* ' she called hoarsely for her lost daughter.

Indu could not make sense of any of this: Mathu burning new clothes, and why was Leela lost? And what was blood money? She ran to Vijayan's wife.

'Why is Mathu acting like she's mad, burning clothes. And she says Leela is gone.'

'He's done it finally, it seems.'

'Done what?'

'Sold her for money. Oh God!'

The woman walked over to the demented Mathu and took her to her own house.

'Go home,' she said to Indu. 'I'll tell you later.'

In the evening the full story reached Devi. Indu listened to the adults talking.

'Not to that couple who came the other day,' Devi said to Shinnu. 'Some white couple at the European Club took her apparently. Paid a thousand rupees for her. And they've left town. No one knows where they went, not even Chathu.'

Indu had heard of children being abducted by beggars, but never about one that had been sold by a father. If only I had gone to her when she called me, she thought, poking her fingers into her night slip.

In the morning she took her best dress out of the pile of washing and cut it into strips, using an old rusty blade from her father's room. As she scored the cloth,

Shards of Sunlight

she cut her forefinger too and the blood dripped on to the dress.

'Blood money, blood money,' she kept repeating under her breath.

She brought the dress to the kitchen and threw it in the fire on which a big pot of rice was cooking. Shinnu saw her just in time.

'What madness is this?' she cried, pulling the charred dress out of the fire. Indu started crying.

'Burn all the clothes,' she kept saying. 'Blood money.'

Shinnu hugged her close for a long time, till her sobs subsided. 'Wait and see. Leela is a clever girl; she'll be back. Don't cry, please don't cry.'

12

Indu did not like everything changing around her. It was like being on a merry-go-round from which you couldn't get off. First, Achan had left her and Mani and gone off to jail; this was bad enough. Why did he have to do things that other children's fathers did not do? And now Devi was acting strangely too – going to meetings in that mad Karthi teacher's house and threatening to walk in processions, holding the Congress flag. What if she was also arrested by the police? Indu's household was shrinking in front of her and she did not know how to stop it happening.

Ammini, for example. She could hardly be called a person these days. She never got up from bed as far as Indu could see, though she heard shuffling noises early in the morning from her room, when Shinnu went in to take her to the latrine and wash her.

Devi would not talk to anybody much, but at least Indu knew she could rely on her to buy things and make sure there was food to eat. Though it was always moong, moong and more moong with conjee, and horrible wheat conjee instead of rice at the end of the month when the ration-rice was finished. This looked and tasted like cattle feed – or what Indu imagined cattle feed must taste like.

Last week, Devi dressed up in her best mundu and asked the servant boy to fetch a rickshaw. It was a big event because she rarely got out of the house.

'Where are you going?' Indu asked.

Shards of Sunlight

'To the office of the Sub-Collector. He needs to give us some money.'

'Can I come with you?'

'No,' she said quickly and then changed her mind. 'Wear your school clothes and come quickly.

'Does he give everyone money?'

'No. But they took away your Achan, so they have to help us. How are we to pay fees otherwise?'

Devi waited a long time to see the officer, but when she did, she was firm. Indu was surprised at her determination.

'This child needs her fees paid and I am not going anywhere till you give me an advance. The nuns are bullying her.'

The officer hemmed and hawed, but finally an allowance was made, courtesy of the government: thirty rupees every month for her and Mani's fees. At least Indu knew she would not get another of those cringe-producing buff envelopes, which Sister Theckla produced with such glee.

Later in the month, the shaming ritual was repeated in school: Sister went through the alphabets calling out the name of the defaulters – Fatima, Gauri, Hyma... After Hyma, Indu tensed for her name, but Sister went on to Janaki. Phew! That evening Indu rushed home and found Devi.

'Ammammey, you paid my fees. Sister didn't call my name.'

'It should never have happened,' Devi said. 'Your father made a huge fuss when he was here. Must pay the fees, he said, even if we don't eat.'

Ramu, the jutka man, rarely got paid either and he seemed not to notice it. Very occasionally Devi gave him some coconuts from the trees or the odd two-rupee

Shards of Sunlight

note. His wages were four rupees a month for the two girls, but he never asked. Achan's sister sent rice from the village, hidden under old cloth and jack fruit to fool the grain inspectors; somehow Devi made sure three meals appeared for everyone in the house every day.

The nuns had relaxed the dress codes for school in view of the cloth rationing, so Indu and Mani kept on wearing their old clothes to tatters. Mani's skirt did not reach her knees even when Shinnu took the hems down and Indu's school dresses looked faded and shabby. The only cloth available in ration shops was white *mulmul* for *mundus*, unbleached, coarse *cora* for underwear, and blue voile with a black print on it for everything else. Devi could not afford to buy even that. Indu didn't much fancy the ubiquitous blue voile anyway, because all the girls had to wear it like another school uniform. There was nothing else in the shops to choose from. Sometimes she dreamt of the soft, printed silks, deep green, maroon and blue, which her father used to bring home for her and Mani's dresses when he had a more than usually lucrative brief.

Now Mathu and Leela were also gone and another faceless woman, squat and surly, pushed the dust around in the front yard in the mornings. Indu kept fear at bay, fear that Achan would never come back, fear that no one would be there to love her if Devi got arrested, but the fear followed her like the smell of damp cloth, noticeable only when she thought about it.

'Will Devi Ammamma go to jail?' Indu asked Mani one morning from behind her towel. She had just bathed and was bent low from her waist, drying her hair, which was thrown forward, the way women with long hair did, though Indu's hair hardly reached her jaw

Shards of Sunlight

line. Indu liked doing that – pretending she had waist length hair.

'No-o,' Mani answered, but it sounded uncertain to Indu. 'If she goes, who will look after us?' For once Mani sounded forlorn.

Shinnu walked in on that. 'I'm looking after everybody right now,' she said, cheerily. 'Who wants to be looked after first?' She winked at Mani, but Mani continued to look lost.

The girls gathered round Shinnu.

'Shinnuedathy, you won't go to make any speeches at Karthi teacher's house, will you?' Indu asked.

'Never will I give speeches to anyone but my two tiny ones. Promise.' Shinnu hugged the two girls. 'Not so tiny any more,' she added.

Devi had started a whole new parallel life and her comings and goings were making everyone in the house, including Indu, twitchy. She conspired with Vijayan in whispers each morning, and in the afternoons, set off wearing her one *kadhi* mundu and top cloth, when she should have been enjoying her siesta.

'This cloth is rough and heavy. It makes my waist itch,' she would mutter as she wound it round and tucked a bulky corner in. 'The things that mad old man makes us do.'

Everyone knew she was talking about Gandhiji, who, in her view had caused all the problems in the household: poverty, absence of Gopalan… Indu also knew she adored the *'mad old man'* and would do most things for his cause.

Shards of Sunlight

Around the same time, Indu noticed Devi's new habit of caressing her midriff, making circles on it with her palm whenever she was lying down.

'You got a stomach ache, Ammamma?' Indu asked one day when she was lying next to Devi in bed.

As was happening a lot recently, Devi had got up in the middle of the night and gone to the dark, cold kitchen to drink water out of the mud *kooja*.

'A little ache, yes, 'Devi answered. 'It will go.'

Devi lay there, chanting the *sahasranamam*, the thousand names of Shiva. Indu could sense the desperation in her voice.

"*Ooshendappa*," she moaned, calling to her dead father about the pain.

Indu put her arm round her, but she always pushed it away.

'Hurts when you put your arm on me.'

The pain got worse when she was about to go to Karthi teacher's house the next week on a Sunday..

'Don't go, Ammammey. You are not well,' Indu said when she got her coarse *khadar* mundu on the next time.

Devi went to the latrine several times and Shinnu made her cumin water to keep the stomach calm. When Devi drank the water, she belched long and noisily and looked temporarily relieved.

One day Devi came back from a meeting and announced to the household, 'Next week we are going in a procession to the small *maidanam*. With flags and everything.'

The small maidanam was the tiny piece of green that faced the sea on one side and the courts across the road on the other. In between, the over-crowded

Shards of Sunlight

Thalassery- Kunnoor buses made their ponderous way to and fro. For the locals this maidanam was an important piece of green – their one common meeting place.

In the early morning, before the sun came up from the Arabian Sea, it was the domain of the locals who lived on the seashore. They made their way down to the beach to defecate, the children perching obediently on the curved concrete seats. In the late morning the goats came to scuff the grass and drop their much smaller black pellets about. In the evenings the town's leisure class came to take the air, carefully avoiding the hot, steaming piles left by the earlier visitors. For the meetings, the flag waving and the speech making, all prohibited, the concrete seats became soap boxes.

Shinnu stared unbelievingly at Devi.

'You get aches when you go to Karthi's house. What will happen if you go to a meeting and have to make speeches? The things you get up to in your middle-aged madness.'

Meanwhile Ammini retreated from the world, gradually, without sound.

'She has lice in her hair,' Shinnu announced one morning.

'Oh,' Devi said, looking helpless.

She hurried off into Ammini's bedroom. Indu followed her in, sensing another drama.

Ammini did not stir as Devi parted her hair randomly and looked at the exposed pink scalp. Ammini's eyes stayed closed. When Indu got close she could see the lice – white and translucent, tumbling

Shards of Sunlight

around on the strands near the scalp. There were a great many of them.

Devi fetched the special louse-comb and sat down next to her mother's head. She combed gently and after each time, she picked out the lice from the teeth of the comb. Indu helped her, putting the lice between her thumbnails and killing them with a satisfying plop. After a while her nails were stained red, but the lice seemed endless.

Devi did the combing daily for a week and Indu got into the habit of following her to help with the cull, but the lice seemed to multiply overnight.

'Hundreds,' Devi said to Indu, who watched them scurrying on top of each other. 'What do they live on in this wasted body?'

Finally, one day, she collected the scissors from the children's craft box and hacked at her mother's hair, leaving only irregular tufts about an inch long, in front. She could not cut the bits at the back because she did not want to turn Ammini over.

'Like death-bed lice,' Devi mumbled uneasily and Indu again felt that small curl of disquiet, which started at the bottom of her tummy and crawled up to her throat to lodge there and make her choke.

Indu watched the tufts of hair collect on the floor. She picked up a handful and passed her thumb through them. 'Golden, like the *madammas*,' she said.

'She had lovely hair,' Devi said. 'Down below her waist when she was young. She was so proud of it. Even when it started greying it did not turn the ugly mud colour mine did.'

Devi tugged at the untidy fly-away strands near her face. Her voice broke and the tears welled and

Shards of Sunlight

escaped her eyes. She took the tufts from Indu's hand and clutched them tight.

'She looked after *our* hair as well. When your father got married – I remember that day your mother came to us.'

Indu held her breath. Nobody ever told her anything about her mother, her father least of all.

'She oiled your mother's hair daily,' Devi continued shakily. 'Till it grew long and heavy. By the time Janu died her hair was down to her knees – a thick plait, which made her look like a woman, rather than the child she was. And I - such a disappointment to my mother in so many ways.' Devi wiped the tears from her eyes impatiently.

'My thin hair, which would never grow whatever she did, no husband, and dark unlike the rest of the family.' She touched her cheeks as though she could feel the brownness that had so confounded her mother.

Indu wanted to hug her, but she also knew Devi's hurts could not be cuddled away; they seemed to get worse if you touched her. She put out her hand nevertheless and Devi, for once, clutched that hand and kept it close.

A few days later Ammini's hands became swollen, the skin tight and red on the back of them. Doctor Shetty was called in when her temperature rose and she began moaning softly. He took her temperature and pulse and asked questions; his normally impassive doctor's face looked concerned. At the end he shook his head slightly.

'Did she urinate at all today?'

Shinnu was called to answer that question.

Shards of Sunlight

'I put her on the commode, but she just sat there listlessly and she did nothing. Didn't say anything either.'

'If the fever gets any higher–' he began.

'I'll send word,' Devi said.

'Whatever the time – day or night,' he added.

In the evening Devi hovered in Ammini's room. Mani was busy with revising for exams and Indu followed Devi around; Devi seemed not to notice her and didn't chase her away. She kept testing Ammini's forehead for temperature; eventually she called Vijayan from next door.

'Must get the doctor,' she said. 'She is burning hot.'

A little later Devi called Shinnu to sit with her.

' 'I'm boiling tapioca,' Shinnu said, but one look at Devi's face must have convinced her of the crisis because she damped the fire under the pot of tapioca and shifted it to the side.

'Need to get *thulasi* water,' Devi said.

Shinnu went to the front yard and plucked some leaves from the sacred *thulasi* plant used in worship. She washed them and put them into a brass mug of clean drinking water, which she took into the sick room.

Devi turned up the wick on the hurricane lantern, the only light in the room. It cast deep shadows on the walls, shadows that shifted and reformed as the women moved around. They were like dancing demons, looming and retreating, and Indu was afraid.

Ammini appeared to be in a deep sleep; her breathing was so shallow there was no way of knowing whether she was breathing or not. Devi held a small mirror to Ammini's nostrils. The faint condensation

Shards of Sunlight

showed she was still there – just. Shinnu called the household together and they gave Ammini a few drops of the sacred thulasi water, each in turn. Indu realised that these were the last minutes of Ammini's life and she clutched Mani's hand for comfort. She had heard that the demon of death, Yaman, would wait nearby to take the soul away when a person died, and Indu was petrified of his presence in that room. She remembered all those images of him and the stories from mythology, the animal face with the horns, and didn't know where to hide.

    The doctor arrived, breathless, a few minutes later, but all he had to do was take her pulse and pronounce her dead. The foxes had started wailing in the hills behind the houses and the dogs bayed; Indu knew that wild dogs and foxes had to howl when a soul was carried away by Yaman, their master. She wanted it to be morning, but the night would not give way.

Indu must have slept at some time on that black night, because she woke up at dawn to find herself near Mani, on a mat upstairs.

13

Girija asked Indu's about her father one day in school during break. He had been in jail for almost three years.

'Why does your father go to jail? My father will never leave me and go to jail.'

Indu had trouble getting the words out. 'The government 'rrested the Congress leaders. My father is a leader. He wants us all to be free.' She thought for a moment. 'Someone has to do it. Because, otherwise, we'll be slaves under the British forever. That's what he said.'

When Gopalan was released Indu was ten years old and her world had crystallised into recognisable parts: there was school, there was home, and then there had been father somewhere in Thanjavoor. A warm and proud memory that made her feel special. She had looked at the Atlas and found Thanjavoor in Andhra State. She read about it – a hot place with not much water and many poisonous rodents. That worried her; she hoped her father would be careful of the scorpions and the snakes.

In December that year, when an unexpected rickshaw turned up the gate in the evening, Indu was sitting in her jutka, returning from school, only a few yards behind the rickshaw.

'Who's coming to our house?' Indu asked, turning to Mani.

'Let's see,' Mani said, squeezing past the others in the jutka without ceremony as soon as it stopped. She hopped out and went to the gate.

Shards of Sunlight

'Indu, look,' she shouted happily. 'Elayachan.'

Indu had seen him by then. 'Achan,' she said as she ran to him.

She wrapped herself round his legs and Mani hovered near. He gathered both of them in his hug and walked with them towards the veranda. The rickshaw man waited, bemused.

'I've just come back from jail; I have nothing,' Gopalan said to the man. Devi came out, hearing the commotion.

'Who?' she began. And then, 'You didn't write.'

Her face broke into a smile that started in her eyes and made her face glow. Indu had not seen that smile in years.

'I didn't know myself till day-before-yesterday. They don't tell you anything there. Pay the rickshaw man, please. Four annas.' A question on the four annas; clearly he did not know what the current fare was from the railway station.

But the rickshaw man had picked up the handles of his rickshaw and was already walking away. 'It's all right. Next time,' he called out.

As Indu watched, she could hear him tell the next man that came by on the road: 'Vakil Gopalan is back from jail.' There was joy in his voice as though Achan was a member of *his* family too.

'Now everybody will start coming,' Indu complained to Mani.

She knew how it was with her father; she had to fight for a piece of him, of his world. She lived with a nagging doubt that she was only equal with the rest.

Shards of Sunlight

That evening, Indu hopped around Gopalan while he got ready for bed. She was already washed and wearing her nightslip. Mani stayed in the room too, not in any hurry to go to sleep or read her books, it seemed.

Shinnu had prepared curried green plantain with sardines, all mashed together, for dinner. It was Gopalan's favourite food. He ate with the two girls.

'This kind of food – you can't get this anywhere else,' Gopalan said. 'Amma used to make this for me all the time when I came back from College for holidays, when I was young.' Indu could see he was sad about his mother's death, and this made her sad too.

'Acha, Mani and I can make it for you too. Can't we Ammammey?'

'Oh, absolutely,' Devi said, smiling 'Starting tomorrow.'

Indu knew there was a catch in it somewhere, but that could wait. She was too happy to care.

'I am going downstairs to sleep,' Mani said finally, when it was past ten. She darted towards Gopalan and hugged him.

Indu jumped into bed then in her usual place next to the wall, and waited for her father to get in.

Gopalan called Shinnu. 'Make a bed for Mani in here,' he said. 'I need both my girls near me. I have missed them for too long.'

Indu, for once, was not jealous; it seemed right that she should share her Achan with Mani, whose father had not come back yet.

'Are you back for good, Acha?' Indu asked.

'Hope so,' he said.

Today was good, but tomorrow the whole world will come to claim her father, Indu thought as she fell asleep.

Shards of Sunlight

As it happened, not many worshippers turned up. Vijayan from next door arrived in the late afternoon and stood on the veranda steps.

'How is everything?' Gopalan asked.

'The war in Europe has finished, but you must know that. Here, people have lost interest in politics; they are struggling to make ends meet, to get rice for the family. The black market in kerosene and sugar is flourishing.'

'We didn't get newspapers, but we had the guards' grapevine. It was excellent. I knew the war was over in Europe, but it is still going on in the East.'

'I suppose I have to kick-start my practice again. Beginning tomorrow.' Gopalan said to Devi the next morning.

He did not look enthusiastic. Indu could see the dark circles under her father's eyes, which came only when he was ill. He kept rubbing his chin with his fingers as though feeling for stubble, but this also, Indu knew, with her special antenna where he was concerned, was a sign of worry and dismay.

'You look tired,' Vijayan said, when he came by.

'Tired and restless, if that is possible.'

As soon as Vijayan left, Gopalan spoke to Devi. 'Any of that money remaining?' He asked.

She laughed ruefully. 'No. That finished some months ago, but we started getting thirty rupees a month from the Government. And some rice came from our sister's house in the village. Thank God she is a farmer's wife. She has been helping us with coconuts and fruit and vegetables too.'

Shards of Sunlight

'Looks like I have to start earning soon.'

Next day, Indu watched nervously as her father took out his moth-eaten lawyer's gown from the drawer in his room and shook it out. She sneezed, but she liked the smell of old taffeta and moth balls. Gopalan found a yellowing old white shirt and a stiff collar to attach with buttons. He looked at it with disgust; Indu grimaced with him. When he tried the shirt on Indu saw it was a little tight round his shoulders.

'Your father has grown fat in jail,' Gopalan said to Indu. 'But it will have to do.'

How did that happen? Her father who had been a vain clothes–horse, who wore trousers with knife-edge creases and shirts starched to perfection now seemed not to care. Indu wasn't quite sure whether she liked this new casualness. She wanted everything to go back to normal in the blink of an eye.

Gopalan gave Indu a pair of old black leather shoes and some polish. Indu set to work with great enthusiasm; she rubbed hard with rags, coaxing the oil into the dry creases caused by disuse, and buffed them with pieces of newspaper till the shoes gleamed.

'Where did you learn this?' he asked when he saw the sheen on the shoes.

It seemed her father had not realised she had grown up and changed while he had been away. Maybe he didn't know her well anymore.

Indu watched Gopalan dress for the Courts. Damu, his friend down the road, came by in his usual flurry and swish of lawyer's gown, with case records tucked under his arm. The clerk accompanying him waited on the veranda outside, clutching another set of files.

Shards of Sunlight

'Not ready? No time to waste,' Damu insisted, watching Gopalan squeeze his shoes on.

'Mmm... After three years. Surely another half-hour won't do any harm.'

'I thought you might need an escort on your first day back in school.' Damu laughed.

'Does feel like school,' Gopalan said. 'I am really out of touch.' He sounded a little breathless from the effort of getting his shoes on.

'But I sent you so many law books while you were there.'

'Knowing the law by heart is one thing; I have to get some briefs, find my old tout...'

'Old tout is gone, I'm afraid. He is working for another lawyer now. But the briefs will come.'

The two friends left together and Indu was glad her father's shaken world was slowly falling into place again. The two heads turning to each other, walking to the gate -Damu's hair curly and well-oiled, her father's springy and straight as bristles - was as normal as daybreak.

Gopalan came home early from the Courts. Indu was waiting for him, swinging on the front gate.

'Did not even make one rupee today,' he said to Devi. 'I just hung about doing nothing. Feeling out of place. All the lawyers were brisk, coming to the library and talking to their clients. And me sitting there. They were looking at me like I was a caged animal, searching for signs of jail on me.'

'It's just the first day,' Devi consoled. 'Wait and see.'

Gopalan showed no enthusiasm the next day for getting ready for work. He sat on the veranda reading

Shards of Sunlight

his Malayalam newspaper, drinking half-cups of coffee and watching the activity on the road. Indu could see he was enjoying the familiar scenes, which he had not seen for a long time: schoolchildren in threes and fours walking down the road, satchels and plaits swinging, the fishmonger trotting away down the hill and the buses careening past.

'What did you see in front of the jail?' Indu asked.

'Bars,' he said, 'to keep us in.'

When Indu was ready for school she looked to see whether her father had moved from his seat. He was still there. Normally, he would be bustling around on a working day, to and fro from the bath room, his wooden clogs clip-clopping on the stairs, calling for coffee, chasing Shinnu for his shoes, his cuff-links, his collar...

'I'm going, Acha,' she said, but he was far away and hardly responded.

She walked up to the gate and came back. 'Aren't you going to the courts today?' she asked.

'Later,' he said, sounding uninterested. 'Ramu and the jutka will go without you. Go.'

Indu dragged herself off reluctantly, feeling something was not quite right. Mani looked at her as she climbed the steps to the jutka.

'Mani…' she began.

'It's after a long time,' Mani said, in their practised shorthand. 'He'll be alright.'

Next morning, as Gopalan was folding his newspaper, a group of three men arrived at the veranda steps. Indu was finishing her homework half-heartedly while she watched the sunlight dancing on the veranda.

'Mmm?' Gopalan asked.

Shards of Sunlight

'We went to Mr Damu; he said we should come to you. Our son has been arrested on an assault charge. We have to get bail.'

'Right,' he said, as though this had been a daily happening.

He got up slowly and walked indoors, but when he got to the stairs Indu saw him bounding up.

Gopalan dressed quickly and went with the three men, without discussing fees.

In the evening when Indu returned from school, her father had not returned. She waited, swinging on the gates as usual, looking up the hill whenever the gate swung to. In between she stuck her finger into the seam of her dress.

When he came Indu noticed the new spring in his step. His black silk lawyers' gown was on his left arm as he walked up to the house and his stride had purpose. At the gate he gathered Indu up. She sat on his hip and put her arms round his neck because the gown was slippery and she was in danger of sliding down.

Devi came out to greet him. 'Is today better?'

'Much,' he said. 'Many of the lawyers have been sending me briefs. "We did your work when you were away. Now you must take it back," one of them said. All of them struggle to make a living, so I am really grateful.'

'The clouds have gone from your face, I can see.'

'I have enough work for two or three months. After that, it will come on its own. But I don't know how to thank all those lawyers.'

Shards of Sunlight

As Gopalan re-established his practice, the frown lines disappeared from Devi's face. Indu wished she could stop Devi's stomach aches as well.

'Ammamma is not well, Acha. I'm scared she will die like Achamma,' she said.

'Nonsense,' Gopalan reassured her. 'Everybody gets aches and pains some times. My teeth hurt all the time. Doesn't mean I am going to die.'

'She gets up in the night some times and moans. Shinnu has to boil water with roasted cumin in it for her. Then she says "ramaramarama" for a long time. She doesn't sleep.'

'Mm. Maybe get Dr Shetty to have a look at her.'

Doctor Shetty came a week later with Gopalan. He poked and prodded at Devi's stomach and said, 'It looks like an ulcer.'

He prescribed medicines and Indu waited for Devi to get better. She now slept beside her father, so she didn't know whether Devi still got up in the middle of the night.

As the months passed Devi began shrinking. Indu smelt a dry-ash smell on her when she was near and the skin around her wrists felt leathery.

Soon her middle could barely hold her mundu up; where had those comfortable hips gone?

'Devi is all skin and bones,' Indu said to Mani, one day, as they were eating their evening conjee. 'Looks like she is starving.'

'She's got problems. Shinnu says she is shitting blood.'

When Gopalan came back from his evening walk, Indu was at the gate, swinging in half circles.

'You'll break your neck. Get off,' he said.

Shards of Sunlight

He called Devi.

'She's lying down. Don't call her.'

Gopalan looked at Indu sharply.

'She's crying with pain and shitting blood and that doctor did not give her the right medicine. She'll die.'

'Rubbish, where do you hear all this nonsense?'

He called Shinnu. 'This child says Devi is very ill. Passing blood in her stools. Why wasn't I told?'

'Devi did not want to bother you. She made me promise not to tell you.'

'So it's better to tell this child, is it?'

He went straight out again and came back with another doctor, a young one called Madhavan.

'All that worry, these last few years. Plays havoc with the stomach,' the doctor said.

This time the doctor prescribed more coloured solutions and pills. Devi grimaced as she swallowed them one after the other. Indu watched out for the stomach pains disappearing.

Indu decided she *had* to know how Devi was.

'I'm sleeping downstairs with Ammamma tonight,' Indu announced one evening to her father.

'Right,' he said. 'Any special reason?'

'Just-'

Indu snuggled around the bony back of Devi and slept until after midnight, when Devi became restless and started turning and tossing. Indu moved to the far side of the bed and tried to sleep. After a while Devi started stroking her stomach – round and round the hand went, and Indu slept fitfully.

At four in the morning, when it was still dark, Devi got up and went to the kitchen to move the ashes on top of the embers in the fireplace and stir it into

Shards of Sunlight

reluctant life. Indu sat hunched on a wooden stool near her, afraid to ask questions. Soon Shinnu came as well.

'Go and lie down. I'll bring the cumin water to you. And Indu – what are you doing here in the middle of the night? You have to go to school soon.'

Indu followed Devi to bed after she drank the cumin water and waited, tense with anxiety, as Devi moaned and started her chant. '*Ramaramarama...*' Indu wondered whether the God, Rama, actually heard her entreaties when she was in pain. If he did not heed Devi, who *would* he heed? Her aunt spent so many hours each day praying to him and making the rest of the household remember him.

Next morning, Indu harassed her busy father again till he lost his temper.

'Won't let me work in peace,' he burst out finally, but Indu seemed determined to get his full attention.

'That Madhavan doctor - does he know anything?'

'What's it with her now?'

'She was in pain in the night.'

'I wish the doctor could give you a pill to stop you bothering me like this,' he said, but he got Doctor Madhavan back again. This time the doctor insisted on urine tests and stools tests.

The news when it came was not good.

'There is a hard mass in her lower intestines. I think it might be – anything.'

Next time Indu asked to sleep downstairs Gopalan sat her down and explained carefully.

Shards of Sunlight

'There is a bad thing inside Devi's stomach and it won't go away quickly. You must leave her to sleep in peace. On that small bed you will disturb her.'

'But I have to take care of her.'

Indu was not certain where she should be, but she did not sleep downstairs after that.

Devi stopped getting up in the morning to say her prayers. Indu noticed she did not bathe in the mornings any more. She lay on her bed in a haze of half-life. When Indu went near she would give her a hug and tell her to go and play.

The doctor's visits became more frequent and her father looked thoughtful and sad when he left. One day when Indu came home from school someone had chopped off Devi's hair. It had been cut roughly with jagged tufts sticking out from her scalp. Indu had been in this place before and remembered how it all ended with Ammini, this hair-cutting business.

When Indu went close, Devi said.

'Lice,' Devi said. 'They come when they know you are on your way out.'

Indu looked in her aunt's hair. There were lice doubled up on the short tufts and dancing around. Indu picked some, but there was no end to them. She had a sudden vivid image in her head of her grandmother's last days.

'I wouldn't let them shave it off,' Devi murmured and turned to the wall.

'It will grow again, Ammamma.' Indu tried to smooth down the unruly tufts and failed. She swallowed. 'No one's going to touch a strand of your hair again. And nothing is going to happen to you.'

Shards of Sunlight

To Indu, sometimes, it appeared as though Devi had gone some place where she was another person. Once a week Shinnu washed Devi's hair in a basin with an oil cloth on the bed. She would also sponge her off and put fresh clothes on her every other day, but the starched white clothes had gone forever. If Indu happened to be about when Devi was washed, Shinnu would shoo her away and close the door.

Once she got a glimpse of Devi's naked body and she never wanted to see it again. Her aunt was lying on her back while Shinnu cleaned her face and stomach. Her breasts dangled to either side of her chest like empty pouches and her stick-legs twitched when Shinnu rubbed her down. Indu redoubled her prayers for Devi and pestered her father more each day. She also harassed God.

'I'll never forget my prayers again if you make Ammamma well. Don't let her die. She's all we have,' she pleaded, sitting on the prayer mat in front of the images in the puja room.

She even put a big finger-streak of sacred ash on her forehead and kept her face down like the elders did when praying. She wanted to sneak a quick look at the picture on the wall in front to check how the deity was reacting, but she thought she'd better play it safe. Mustn't anger the Gods. She also said three Hail Marys to hedge her bets.

When Doctor Madhavan came next, Indu ran outside to the back of the house, stuck her thumb in the waist of her skirt and sobbed. Shinnu found her there.

'What's the point of crying?' she asked. 'That's one clever young man, that Madhavan. Just came back from America. He'll know how to treat her. Wait and see.'

Shards of Sunlight

Madhavan started Devi on a course of injections. 'This is a new medicine they are using in the States for stomach ulcers,' he said to Gopalan. 'Still at the experimental stage. Let's hope it is not too late.'

After drinking her conjee or orange juice, Devi would lie back and close her eyes, exhausted. Indu remembered how Ammini had withdrawn from the world. Indu would not let Devi slip away into that twilight space. She engaged Devi in conversation even when it was apparent she was not listening.

'Ammammey, today we sang *sarigama* in our music lessons. Teacher said I was tone deaf and threw me out. She told me not to make a sound while the others sang. It's not fair.'

Devi opened her eyes. 'And-?'

'And nothing.'

'Maybe you should practice at home.' Devi closed her eyes again.

Another day: 'Devi ammammey, Shinnu is making ghee-rice today because we have a visitor. Can you smell it? I'm going to check in the kitchen.'

The tempting smell of onions frying in ghee wafted through the house.

When she came back a minute later, Devi had closed her eyes again. Indu sat at the end of the bed, picked up Devi's right foot and put it on her lap. It felt cold and clammy. Cold is bad, she decided. Like dead. So she started massaging the foot; it was a long time before warmth returned to that foot. Indu then picked up the other foot and carried on with her treatment. There was no escape for Devi.

She opened her eyes. 'What is my baby doing here when she should be out playing?'

Shards of Sunlight

'I made your feet warm.' Indu brought a sheet from the next room and covered her aunt's now-warm foot.

As she was tucking the sheet in, Gopalan came down the stairs and past Devi's room. He ducked under the lintels and peered in as he had taken to doing daily. When he saw Indu, he came in and put his hand on her head. The hand was cold and firm and Indu could feel the love that came through that palm and worked straight into her heart.

'Looking after Devi. That's good,' he said. Devi opened her eyes and looked at the tableau. She smiled and closed her eyes again.

Indu was determined: she was not going to allow Devi to die. It was just a question of not letting it happen. It was a three-pronged strategy: talk to her whether she listened or not, stay with her and touch her to let the warmth of life go from herself to Devi, and make her eat and drink more each day. To Indu it was all fairly simple – a negation of all that dying meant.

Sometimes it looked as though it was working. On those days Indu walked with her invisible tail up like an antenna. She sang tuneless film songs and pestered Shinnu in the kitchen, begging for swirls of coconut, tasting things being cooked in the wok before they were done and generally being everywhere at the same time.

'Mani,' Shinnu would call out in exasperation. 'Get this child out of my hair.' Indu would dance away with another bit of coconut or fried potato in her hand – for a little while. Mani knew she was uncontainable in this mood and would barely acknowledge her

Shards of Sunlight

quicksilver presence. Mani, in any case, always had her head buried in a school book.

'Haven't you got any studying to do?' was the most Indu could get out of Mani.

There were days, however, when Devi seemed listless and unwilling to try. On those days Indu hardly left the room after coming home from school. She chanted *ramaramarama* as Devi used to do before she fell ill and made pacts with God, whichever God came to her mind just then – there were so many of them. Shivan, Vishnu, Brahman and all their *avataram*s: Raman, Krishnan and then there were the spouses: Parvathy, Saraswathy... Some of those Gods had so many wives, it was hard to keep track, so Indu chose one or two at random. And then there were Mama Mary and Jesus to placate.

Doctor Madhavan came less often and only when sent for. Gopalan generally sent a jutka for him on Saturdays. One Saturday Madhavan took Devi's pulse and temperature and talked to her.

'Pain?' he enquired.

'No,' Devi answered.

'Sit up,' he said and helped to prop her up on pillows. He shifted the stethoscope around and turned to Gopalan.

'She's getting better,' he pronounced, with a surprised look. 'She needs to build up her strength. Eat better. The injections can stop now.'

As soon as she was spared the medicines Devi's appetite improved. Indu loved running into the garden to fetch a jack leaf, which Shinnu would fashion into a small scoop with a stick from the spine of the palm leaf to keep it together. Devi would not use a metal spoon, which she had dubbed 'the-stick-sucked-by-many.'

Indu sat with her while she ate her salted mango and conjee painfully slowly, tiring from the activity of sitting up. Soon she started complaining about the conjee, the mango and the room. She flung bed-clothes left and right and fought the pillow. Indu knew she was gradually coming back to her cantankerous best.

'Devi ammamma is getting well,' she announced to Gopalan.

'She didn't have much choice, did she?' he replied, smiling happily.

Indu knew it had been a close call.

14

From the prison, Gopalan had brought back claustrophobia and a tendency to bronchitis. But he still kept his cigarettes and his lighter in his shirt pocket and went through twenty cigarettes a day. He got into the habit of spending long hours on the edge of the beach watching the waves; Indu ran around the beach with other children. Mani sat on the concrete seats and watched. As the months passed Mani preferred to hang around in the kitchen and Indu went with her father alone.

Sometimes Gopalan would leave her on the shore and swim in the ocean. Indu would watch his head bobbing on the water like a dry coconut, going further and further away, until the panic set in. Was he going too far, could he swim back without tiring? She would have to stop playing then and wait, her throat constricted, for him to turn around and head back.

'You mustn't go to that rock. Two men died there on that creek some months ago. There are strong undercurrents that can pull you down, they say.' Indu sounded frantic.

Two brothers had indeed died there, one trying to rescue the other who had been caught in a swirl.

'I don't go that far,' Gopalan said, but Indu thought he was tempting fate. Invariably the swimming led to sniffles, which became coughs and lasted for weeks. He would run a slight fever and hold his chest while coughing.

Shards of Sunlight

'You get coughs like a baby,' the doctor teased when he came one time.

'This is something I got from the prison. I thought it was an allergic cough and would go away, but it seems to have dug in.'

'It's bronchitis; your lungs are taking a beating from all that smoking,' the doctor said. 'I would stop smoking and swimming if I were you. You'll end up with pneumonia.'

Gopalan ignored the doctor as he ignored every one else and eventually the dreaded pneumonia arrived.

His breathing became laborious and he panted when he talked. Indu hovered as her father was taken over by his carers – adults from his activist past who came to look after a man who had no wife and no other adult man in his life, strong enough to hold him or lift his torso when those hacking coughs started. Vijayan from next door came and stayed the night when Gopalan became delirious.

Shinnu was getting orders by the minute: bring a basin for him to spit, bring hot water, fetch a bandage – no, a clean, soft towel. Boil rice till it is mashed and bring it straight up. They spread the hot rice-mash on the towel and folded it in. Then they tied it carefully round his chest.

'He will get burnt,' Indu cried, but they ignored her.

She saw her father wince when they pressed the bandage down on his hollow chest and he coughed again. When she tried to go near him, they waved her away.

The men put red crepe paper round the electric bulb in his room so that they could dim the light and continue to nurse him in the night. The eerie glow

Shards of Sunlight

frightened Indu – there was some thing death-like in that room and she was terrified; she willed it to go away. She prayed, desperately: Hail Marys first and then to Shivan, saying the same words under her breath.

Vijayan held the basin to Gopalan when he coughed and spat phlegm mixed with traces of blood. When the maid carried it away in the morning Indu saw the pink mess and knew her father's life hung on a thread..

'Aren't you going to school?' they asked when she hovered in the morning. 'May be he'll be better by the time you come back.' Indu felt she needed to be near him to keep him anchored to her, to life.

She didn't want to go anywhere; her hands trembled when she tried to get her school-clothes on. Shinnu helped her to button up, but Indu could see she had been crying too. This was more frightening than anything else.

'Achan is going to die,' Indu sobbed, clutching Shinnu and Shinnu sobbed with her.

'No, no, no,' she said, and hugged Indu to her.

Indu could not concentrate on her lessons; her mind dwelt on her father's wan face and hollow chest, the basin full of pink phlegm, and his noisy breathing. She wanted to go home. The Maths teacher did Algebra that day, Indu's favourite topic. Simultaneous Equations, which were a doddle normally, but that day Indu watched the teacher's lips move but heard nothing. Finally she burst into tears.

'What?' the teacher asked in alarm.

'Her father is ill,' the girl sitting next to her told the teacher.

'He'll be all right,' the teacher said without knowing what was wrong with him.

Shards of Sunlight

The next morning the doctor gave Gopalan an injection.

'This medicine is called Penicillin. I have not given it to anyone, ever.' He sounded uncertain.

'Will he get better?' Indu demanded to know as the doctor got into his car.

'He should,' he answered, but looked uneasy.

Miraculously Gopalan started improving from the next morning. Indu was allowed back in his room. She massaged his feet and sat nearby ignoring the visitors who came to se him. The doctor gave more injections with confidence.

'Heard you cried in school,' one visitor said? His daughter was in Indu's class. 'Got scared, eh?'

Indu was embarrassed, but Gopalan smiled.

'She looks after me. Somebody has to worry about me.'

In 1946, the war in the East had come to an end. One morning a telegram arrived from out of nowhere. It was a radio message picked up by a kind stranger in Calcutta and forwarded to Thalassery.

'Coming home soon. Both of us are well. Anxious mother's health.' It was from Mani's father. His mother, of course, had been long dead, but Mani was ecstatic. No one had ever seen Mani so happy for a long time.

'Hard, not knowing whether your parents are alright?' Indu hugged Mani and for once didn't get pushed away.

'They'll come soon,' Mani said, beaming.

Gopalan's practice, meanwhile, had gained momentum and Indu could see he was happy. He got

Shards of Sunlight

the house wired for electricity and bought a small car. Indu, at eleven, was busy with school work and all the team games in school, which she loved: throw-ball and ball-badminton and netball. Mani remained her placid self, always top of the class and Indu's quiet guardian angel.

It was another two years before Mani's parents actually came back to India.

'Lost all my savings in the war. Had to save up again to buy our tickets,' Mani's father said.

They came with practically nothing. Kannan had kept himself and his wife in food by repairing clocks. It had once been the hobby of a busy doctor, a way to relax, he used to say, after spending the whole day with his hand probing the nether regions of the pregnant estate women.

'My employers left when Singapore fell and I left the estate hospital then. But the Japanese soldiers were soon all over the place. Couldn't practise medicine.'

Kannan's stories were hair raising. 'They trampled all over the house whenever they felt like it – looking for anything they could take away. Eggs from the chicken coop, whole chickens, pens, cooked food.

'I put up a large framed picture of Nethaji Subhas Chandra Bose on the sitting room wall.' Nethaji was the Commander of the Indian National Army, which was said to have aligned itself with the Japanese. 'This placated them, but they were unpredictable and we could not communicate with them. The women ran into the latrines and hid until they left – there were so many stories of rape and murder.'

The brothers sat long into the night talking to each other; Indu could see how close they were.

Shards of Sunlight

Kannan teased his kid brother and Gopalan talked about his life in jail, how lock-ups were threatened and how they went on hunger strike.

'We had a good life in jail generally, but they got a little nervous when Madras was bombed. What did they think we were going to do, a handful of activists from the south of India? Anyway we went on hunger strike and they gave in, but not until three days. It was touch and go.'

So many stories from both brothers, all being aired for the first time. They talked far into the night and the house resounded with their laughter. Their words tumbled out as though they could not keep pace with their thoughts.

When Indu went to sleep beside her father, she could feel the benediction of the brother's presence.

Neighbours called in to greet the elder brother and his wife. He regaled them with stories of the occupation of Singapore and they listened, open-mouthed. Mani's mother would quietly withdraw after the first ceremonial greetings of her husband's friends and spend time with her daughter.

Kamala was a woman of great grace and self-possession; Indu was a little in awe of her. She was fair and tall and wore silk saris that swished as she walked. Her hair was always pinned up in a little kondai and she wore a tiny nose-ring in her left nostril. Unlike the women of Indu's household, she knew a smattering of English and did not shrink away from the men of the house. They treated her with respect and you could see she considered it merely what was due to her, as the wife of the senior brother.

Shards of Sunlight

The morning after their arrival, Kamala looked at Mani's indifferent looking dresses and asked, 'Nothing else?'

'No,' Mani said perfunctorily, and it was left to Indu to explain how there were no textiles to buy since the war started.

Indu had no experience of mothers and how they behaved with their daughters. So she watched as her Kamala Velyamma fussed about Mani. She made Mani sit in front of her and combed her hair for a long time. She then curled her hair using strips of rags. This was a magical exercise, which Indu had never seen before. Above all she noticed how Kamala touched Mani all the time and kept her close. Sometimes she sat for long moments with her hand lightly caressing Mani's shoulder.

Kamala saw Indu watching at the door and called out to her. 'Come. Let me see whether I can curl *your* hair.' Perhaps she saw the little green glint of envy in Indu's eyes. Indu's hair, however, resisted all Kamala's efforts to subdue it: whatever she did it refused to curl and fell back straight as a horse's tail. At that moment Indu hated her hair. But she wished she had a mother like Kamala.

Next day Kamala took out a whole bagful of crisp Japanese money and the children played going-to-market with it. Mani, at fourteen was really too old for Indu's childish games, but she did not demur. Indu wished Leela could join them; Leela would have been so good at this.

No one told Indu about what was going to happen next, when Mani's parents eventually packed their bags and got ready to leave for their own home in

Shards of Sunlight

Ottappalam. Indu knew it was somewhere south of Thalassery and it took many hours by train to get there. But why did they want to take Mani away? And what about school? And was she going in the ship to Malaya with them? That was even further, lots further. Apparently it took two whole weeks in the steamer.

Indu accosted her father one day between his bath and going to Court.

'Why are they taking Mani away? What about school?'

Gopalan looked at his daughter's agitated face and picked her up like a baby. He deposited her on the edge of his writing table and said,

'They haven't seen her for six years. Like you have to be with me always, she has to be with them now they are here.'

Indu was not satisfied; there was a catch here somewhere, but she knew the adults did what they liked with children. So Mani would go. Did grown-ups ever think of how children felt, how she and Mani were being torn apart, when they had been each other's support system all these years?

Two weeks went by on wheels and the jutka came at 11.30 in the morning on a Saturday to take Mani and her parents to the railway station. She went next door to say her goodbyes to the family who lived behind their house: Vijayan's sisters and old mother. Vijayan plucked a red rose off his precious rose bush, which flowered rarely and only with lots of coaxing with goat droppings and wood ash. He presented it to Mani with some ceremony, and suddenly there were tears in her eyes. Mani appeared overwhelmed with her celebrity status, but she kept darting glances at Indu,

Shards of Sunlight

who followed her mutely. Finally, she picked up Indu's hand and that is how she walked to the jutka.

Mani's parents were already in the jutka, waiting for her, and the horse tossed its mane, rearing to go. The suitcases had been stowed under one of the seats. When Mani got in and looked back at Indu, she was swinging on the gate. Back and forth she went. Mani called out but Indu ignored her, jumped off the gate and ran into the house.

15

Maybe Gopalan saw Indu's desolate face when Mani left, but he started taking her everywhere he went: to the club, on walks by the Kuyyali river, to the beach and all his usual haunts. His friends soon got used to the fact that Gopalan came with this appendage – for the most part they ignored her. Some odd hanger-on would occasionally engage her in conversation, which she did not quite understand.

Some people that she met made her uneasy. Stating the obvious: 'With your father all the time, eh?' or, 'Don't you have homework to do?' When the questions got intrusive, Indu would glance at her father and he would say, 'Right, time to go.' He would walk away, leaving the man gawping, or the man would leave, a little bewildered and shamefaced. Other people had acid tongues, but my father has acid looks, Indu thought.

The women muttered that she was not learning any of the skills a young woman would need. No cooking, no sewing, and worst of all, she was not learning to look submissive and respectful when men were around. They did not understand the deliberate sabotage of traditional ways that Gopalan was attempting.

Indu was his Pygmalion and sometimes she rebelled. Most often than not she lost.

Shards of Sunlight

Most days, he got the servant boy to line up two cups of black coffee at four in the morning and threw her out of bed.

One morning Devi accosted him as he was drinking his coffee.

'The girl's is *grown up*. She should be learning the skills that a woman will need to manage her household when she marries. Not reading books and gadding about with you the whole time.'

Indu didn't want that particular *grown-up* discussed. Those cotton rags and bandages and bleeding were enough nuisance every month without bringing her father into it.

Achan ignored Devi's remarks and smiled at Indu. 'Grown up, my foot,' he said.

'Morning hours are precious. Things to do, Moley.'

Things? What things?

He lighted up a cigarette, picked up his carved walking stick and strode out of the house, his mundu hitched up to his knees to make walking freer; Indu ran to catch up.

'Walk always on the inside, to the right of me,' he said. 'So you are nowhere near those hurtling buses.' He made no concession to her size and she hurried to keep up.

'Acha,' she said accusingly, when she fell back; he grinned at her and stopped, putting his walking stick out to her, which he swung with each stride.

'Why are you carrying a stick when you are not old?' she asked.

'We get rabid dogs around here – and rabid men too. I can shoo them away with this. Then again, I can

Shards of Sunlight

point to things with it. Like that fox slinking away in among those bushes. Have to be careful.'

'Can't we go walking a little later?' Indu asked. The cold December mists hung low over the horizon and she shivered in her summer dress.

'The rest of the world will be up by then and we'll have to greet and talk and I won't want to do that. It stops me from thinking.'

Gopalan showed her the rivers and the creeks and took her balancing over precarious log-bridges to show her the birds in the sanctuary, in the middle of the lake near the railway lines. The riverside was lined with lean-tos, which were the latrines of houses, which edged the water.

'People perched in those ramshackle latrines – I wonder whether they ever fall into that muck,' Indu asked one day.

'These are poor people, they are survivors. Isn't it sad that people have to live this way?'

Once sleep had been shaken off, these dawns were magical, times when she owned her father totally, no politicians, neighbours or family staking claims.

Another day they went to Dharmadam beach and hunted for baby crabs. When Indu was with her father she felt that anything was possible and no harm would ever come to her. A notch above the rest of the world.

Not satisfied with what Indu learned at school, Gopalan took her education in hand, Tennyson's *Morte d'Arthur* was followed by Browning and then an assault on the Malayalam poets, Ashan and Vallathol.

Tennyson was never-ending and boring, she complained. So she got Shelley and Keats instead. '*Icicles on windows,*' – what on earth were they?

Shards of Sunlight

'You know what?' Indu challenged her father one day at the end of a demanding poetry session. 'You never bother me with Maths.'

'Don't know any Maths,' he admitted.

'That's my favourite,' Indu said.

'Don't know where you get that from. Must be your mother.'

Indu held her breath. Gopalan rarely mentioned his dead wife and Indu yearned to know about this shadowy figure in her past, that young woman who must have loved her.

'Was she good at numbers?' Indu probed gently, sensing regret or grief or something there in her father's face.

'Maybe,' Gopalan said and turned away, making it clear there was no more to be said.

In the summer, there was tenni-quoit in the front yard with a rope hitched to the window sill at one end and the coconut tree at the other, for a net. He ran her around the 'court' mercilessly till she collapsed laughing. Mani was forgotten and Indu ceased to feel alone.

At fourteen, Indu was a tall and healthy girl, good at sports and interested in many extra-curricular activities. Her teachers realised she was different, without quite knowing in what way.

However they protested when she started finishing her sums too quickly in the Mathematics lessons.

'Who's teaching you at home?' they asked, sounding disgruntled. 'These methods are different.'

'Nobody,' she insisted but they looked disbelieving.

Shards of Sunlight

'You won't leave me in peace,' she said to her father one day, when he insisted it was time she learned Hindi. 'We learn Hindi in school, isn't that enough? Teach me Maths instead.' She was trying a fast one.

'Don't know enough,' he said. 'Now History? Maybe.'

He sounded like a man with a winning idea. Next day he brought home an abridged version of Nehru's *Discovery of India*.

Gopalan kept going back to Hindi like a dog with a bone. He dug it up frequently.

'That pretence of teaching Hindi. The teachers never speak it; it comes out of books. No, you are getting a personal tutor.' Gopalan wouldn't budge

'Only if you let me grow my hair,' Indu negotiated. She had got him on the hop.

Gopalan looked at Indu as though seeing her after a long time. 'I guess you are old enough to manage long hair,' he said, 'but if I see lice in it, the hair gets cut.'

Indu's hair reached shoulder length in no time at all. So she gradually joined all the other girls in her class, who had two plaits at the back, swinging from side to side. It stayed obstinately straight as it grew, but it was thick and luxurious and Indu was soon very proud of it.

16

Gopalan's work kept him busy and happy. The money flooded in – thick wads of low-denomination old rupee notes smelling of tobacco and dry fish and everything in between. He bought a plot of land at the edge of the paddy fields, down the road. The household knew it was prosperous and adjusted their behaviour. New clothes arrived for everybody and Indu blossomed in the peacock hues of India's reviving textile industry.

Gopalan's house got built steadily and it was soon time to be moving into their new home down the road. Indu was proud of the fact that her father was the first lawyer on the road to build his own house, but she did not like the huge change this implied: leaving the old home, which had been the one unchangeable thing in all the years of upheaval, sickness, death.

Indu remembered all the people who had died in that house. Her grandfather and grandmother. And her mother, whom no one mentioned. Would all those shadow figures be wiped out if they lived in another house?

Above all, what about Leela? In this house she felt connected to Leela. Shinnu said she must be in the village with her mother because Mathu had disappeared a few days after Leela. Chathu also had left the next year. Some new people lived next door, but they had no children and Indu did not consider that place a part of her domain anymore. Still, it would be nice to see Leela

Shards of Sunlight

again. Where *was* she? How can people vanish into thin air and why was it no one cared?

Indu remembered Leela's prettiness and how she could disperse her worries with a toss of her brown-black hair.

Gopalan waited for a sunny break in the July monsoon of 1950 and the servants and helpers carried their few bundles down the road. He owned little furniture and the few chairs, tables and beds were carried on the heads of the men and women who came to help and participate in the house-warming. Indu walked from room to room of the old house, switching on lights and getting in the way of the movers.

She made a separate bundle of her books and stationary and carried it herself – her clothes could take care of themselves.

The new house had paddy fields on three sides and the main road on the fourth. The constant rumble of the buses hurtling down that side, and the blare of the impatient horns, became a familiar accompaniment. Soon Indu stopped noticing it; she developed a useful capacity to shut the rest of the world out when she read.

On the other sides of the house new rice seedlings were being planted and Indu spent hours listening to the women singing as they waded knee deep in muddy water. The songs celebrated stories of old chiefs and forgotten battles, of beautiful women, who had lit up the lives of the warriors, and the joys of a good harvest.

Next year Indu would be in College and studies would become more demanding; meanwhile she had nothing to do that summer except sit on the parapet of

Shards of Sunlight

their balcony, reading and listening to the soporific verses of the women.

Indu, at fourteen, was a big girl. In her joint household many boys and men came and went. They came for a day in town, to see the new house, for going to the cinema or asking Gopalan for help with school fees. Indu did not notice them; most looked green and clumsy and did not talk to her.

Until the day Sreedharan turned up. He was tall and fair. He looked straight at her when he talked to her and she could see his dark brown eyes asking questions to which she had no answer. He had come to stay for a week and he filled her with a strange disquiet, which no one else noticed.

He was a village-boy too, but he was educated. He had attended a local school, and had to come to town to sit his exams as there was no examination centre where he lived. He came with a huge bundle of books.

Devi gave him a mat and a quilt to sleep on the veranda and he made a little habitat there. Steel pens and pencil and ink in a straight line on the old table near him. The note books and text books in tidy heaps below them. A gunny bag contained his change of clothes. This slumped on the floor against the corner of the wall.

He was out at lunch but Devi served him breakfast and dinner, in the hall where Indu had her study desk. He always greeted Indu before sitting down on his wooden stool to eat. Devi talked to him as he ate and asked about his family in the village.

Indu did not gather much at these times from the book she was pretending to read. Sometimes she raised the flap of her desk and hid behind it when her face

Shards of Sunlight

grew hot at his passing engagement with her, which was never more than a glance and a smile.

Thus Indu found out about things she could never discuss with anyone. When the young man left after a week, she felt an emptiness within her for a while.

For the first time in Indu's life there was something about which she could not talk to her father.

Mani came that year after she finished her degree exams. 'Had to see Elayachan's new house,' she said.

Indu was a gawky, happy fifteen-year-old, with the world, she thought, at her feet.

'My, my, my,' was the first thing Mani said when she saw Indu. She had given Indu a huge hug, smelling of jasmine and could it be? cigarettes.

Never used to hug people, Indu thought, but was glad nevertheless. What other transformations would be revealed?

Some of them were apparent. Mani had grown lean and tall. Her hair was cut in a neat bob and she had an out-of-town elegance that no one in Thalassery could possibly aspire to. Gone was the grave little girl-woman who wore ankle length skirts in cheap cotton voile and tied her hair up with strips of cotton begged off the local tailor.

'You look like a *Madamma*, Shinnu exclaimed.

Mani just smiled and let all the comments pass by.

There was good reason for Shinnu to think she looked like a madamma. Mani had become quite fair and what with the short hair and the knee-length skirt, she could have been from anywhere. Her hair had been

Shards of Sunlight

dyed a brown-red colour in places, which added to her otherness.

She watched Indu and Shinnu gawping with something like amusement. 'You two...' she said, smiling. 'Time for mouths to close,' she added. 'You are still my two most favourite people in the whole world.' She thought for a moment and added, 'Bar none.'

'Don't let your parents hear that,' Shinnu muttered, but Mani only grinned.

Mani's visit made Indu realise the things missing in her life – the things that mothers normally managed.

In the mornings, after Indu had bathed, Mani combed her cousin's thick black mane out and plaited it with a fair amount of affection woven into the plaits. She fetched sprigs of dainty Yeshoda blooms and pinned it into Indu's hair.

'There,' she said when she had finished. 'Now the face. Almost perfect but a little colour would help.'

Mani fetched a sleek black leather make-up case and touched up Indu's face with pink powder. The older girl hummed a fragment of a Hindi song as she worked on Indu. She stood back and admired her handiwork.

'You're old enough now to do your own face really.'

'Do? Do what?'

Indu was aware that all the girls in her school wore black *mye* in their eyes and *pottus* on their forehead. Somehow they looked more *finished* compared to herself. Their clothes were ironed for one thing. But what was Mani going to do next?

Indu started picking her skirts and blouses out of the washed heap every week and putting them neatly

Shards of Sunlight

folded under her sleeping mat at night. They looked better but crinkles remained.

She looked hard at herself in the shaving mirror Gopalan generally propped up on one of the veranda pillars. The only other mirror in the house was spotted and not much larger than the pages of a note book. Indu could barely see her face in it and the rest of herself was totally out of sight.

One day Gopalan caught Indu examining herself in the mirror. The next day he brought home a small phial of red pottu and Indu started on the road to self-transformation. The family who live behind her house made mye out of a rag soaked in lime juice. They burned it against a clean mud-pot and caught the soot in it. The soot was then mixed with a drop of gingelly oil to make eye liner.

Soon after, Gopalan turned up with a tin of Cuticura powder. Upstairs, next to Indu's study desk, a large mirror appeared on the wall. Indu experimented. She loved the jasminy smell of the powder and pasted large quantities on her face. Indu's friends laughed at her and she learned to be more subtle.

Even the recalcitrant eye make-up, which generally smudged under her eyes learned to behave. Indu became expert at pulling the skin down from under her eye and drawing a neat line on the rim. The pottu, which refused to centre now found its place. All this added a good twenty minutes to Indu's morning schedule, but she was now stepping out as a confident teenager. Even her gait became relaxed and graceful, as though in some way, she had come to terms with her growing self.

Shards of Sunlight

To Indu it seemed the milestones in her life were coming at her too fast. College loomed and she had no intention of wearing long skirts and blouses to go there. She asked her father for saris.

Gopalan seemed lost for words. He looked at her confused. 'For you?'

'Yes. For College.'

Gopalan took her to the textile shop and let her loose. 'Girl wants saris,' he told the owner. 'Please show her some.'

'What kind of price range?' the man asked. Gopalan had never bought a sari in his life. He looked at Indu beseechingly.

'For college,' she said, firmly. 'Not very expensive.' Gopalan picked up the newspaper sitting on the shop-owner's table and sat as far as he could from the whole event.

Indu emerged an hour later with heavy bundles. 'Saris, six,' she said. 'And blouses, and material for under-skirts.' Gopalan paid up and they left.

Next week, Indu tried her first sari on, a thin green Khatau voile with a mango print. When she had coralled it and tucked it in, she went upstairs to find her father. He was delving in his bureau.

'Acha, look,' Indu said. Gopalan turned and looked and his breath caught.

'You look so grown up,' he pleaded.

'That's because I am,' she said mercilessly, but she went downstairs quickly and changed back to her child-self.

Indu loved her new home. This was theirs and she didn't mind that it was cold at night, surrounded as it was with water. Both Indu and her father caught colds frequently. She got over them quickly while he struggled with wracking coughs and fever and ended up having to see a doctor. Bottles of 'mixtures', with graduated labels showing doses on the outside, became the norm in the house.

Gopalan also suffered from toothaches; this was another problem that had started in jail and did not get treated. He had two molars pulled out that year and unlike others, he would bleed for a long time and end up having to take antibiotics.

'Stop pulling out teeth,' the doctor instructed.

The next time Gopalan had tooth ache even the dentist balked at pulling out another molar. Gopalan refused drilling and filling and opted for the quick solution. Indu was annoyed when he came home that evening with his jaw swollen and spitting blood.

'You'll soon run out of teeth to pull. What are you going to eat with if you keep on taking out your back teeth?'

'You'll have to cook *conjee* for me all the time, then, won't you?'

Indu was not amused.

17

Gopalan loved sitting at the far corner of what he called his kingdom in the evenings, looking at his domain.

'When no one's working in the fields that stretch of green is mine,' he would say. It rolled on endlessly to the Kuyyali river on the other side. Sometimes Indu joined him there with her current reading. Gopalan had started plying her with the plays of Bernard Shaw. The plays were set out in fine print as in a newspaper, with two columns down each page. She did not understand too much anyway. This was true of much of her reading because her father had no concept of children's books; the only books she saw were *his* books.

'Don't miss out the introductions,' he would say of Shaw. See how much detail he puts into those.'

If Gopalan's friends came to chat with him, Indu had to go indoors but, as she read her book on the upstairs balcony, she could hear their chatter and laughter like the singing at a faraway wedding.

'Hope you will send her to College,' the nuns at the Sacred Heart School said to Gopalan when he went in to pay her fees.

'She'll go. She can't wait. Wants to become a lawyer like me, but I keep telling her she should do something different. Like medicine.'

Shards of Sunlight

That summer three girls in Indu's class got married and Indu attended two of the weddings. The girls were dressed in white and gold saris and jasmines covered their hair; they looked like miniature women. They were all less than seventeen years old. The girls kept their heads down during the ceremony and Indu wondered what they thought of the whole pantomime. Were they scared? One was a good student; did she not want to go to College?

'Rema should have gone to College; she is really clever,' Indu said to her father as they travelled back to their house. 'Why did she want to get married?'

'Don't think she had much choice,' Gopalan answered shortly. 'Now *you* – you are going to study as much as you want. No hanging about in the kitchen gossiping either.'

Indu was pleased and proud her father thought differently from the families of many of her friends. 'I'm going to do Maths at College and become a lawyer like you,' Indu said. 'Make lots of money.'

'Don't know about the lots of money.'

When did Gopalan start handing over the household to Indu? She hardly noticed it. Initially it was, 'Take eight annas from my drawer for the fisherman.' Then it became, 'Make sure you have enough money for the fish and vegetables today,' before he left the house.

Even later, it became, 'How much did we spend this week?' When he came back from work he started giving the fees for that day to her. He'd pull it out of both of his jacket pockets, folded into wads or crumpled up.

'Count it and put it away.'

Shards of Sunlight

The wads got bigger and the money accumulated; Indu wondered what he was going to do next. She did not have to wonder for too long: a little grey-blue car, a Standard-8, arrived with a weather-flap on the roof and a driver to take the family around.

Sometimes Gopalan and his friends stayed up late into the night and continued out there perched on the edge of his empire until they tired of the sound of their own voices. Indu and Devi were not surprised when he went into another bout of coughs and fever. His friends came to his bedroom to visit, but he did not have the energy to talk to them. He complained about chest pain when he coughed. Indu send for the doctor.

The doctor took his temperature and felt his pulse.

'Why have you not called me before this?' he said sternly to Indu.

'He won't let me. Says it's only 'flu.'

'I have a case to go to in Thalipparambu in two days time,' Gopalan said. 'Can't lie about in bed all week.'

'You won't go anywhere this week,' the doctor instructed.

On Thursday, Gopalan dragged himself out of bed and put his lawyer's clothes on. He had to sit down halfway through because he was short of breath. Indu put his shoes down near his feet. His palm was hot to her touch.

'Don't go today. I'll tell your tout to get it postponed,' she insisted.

'I have debts from building this house. Can't afford to leave it for later.'

Shards of Sunlight

When Gopalan returned in the evening, he went straight to bed. In the next room, Indu could hear him moaning softly in the night. When she touched his forehead in the morning it was burning hot.

She sent for the doctor again. When he came, Gopalan was in a troubled sleep and slightly delirious.

'Call my brother – I have things to say to him,' he said.

No one took any notice as he seemed to be rambling. He called Indu by her mother's name, Janu, and told her to make tea for his father, who was long dead.

The next day the doctor came without being called.

'Send a telegram to my brother,' Gopalan kept saying. 'Things to say.'

Indu sent a telegram to her uncle to come over urgently, but she was certain the doctor's injections would cure her father as they had in the past.

Gopalan's brother, Kannan, turned up the next morning from Ottappalam, where he had a private practice as a GP. When Gopalan saw him he held on to his hand.

'If something happens to me…'

'Nothing's happening.' Kannan laughed it off.

'Listen,' Gopalan said desperately. He was finding it difficult to talk. 'You have to take care of Indu and Shinnu and Devi. Indu must study.'

'All right,' Kannan answered, as though to indulge him. 'Now try to sleep. All this talking seems to tire you.'

'She must study,' Gopalan repeated, as though this was the one message he needed his brother to remember.

Shards of Sunlight

Gopalan closed his eyes and slipped off into a febrile sleep, moaning while he exhaled.

The doctor came early the next morning. Gopalan opened his eyes as the doctor ministered to him. His breathing became laborious and he panted when he talked. Indu hovered as her father was taken over by his carers –Vijayan from next door stayed the night to help Kannan Indu kept going to his room to check on him, hoping for a miraculous recovery, but all she saw was the twilight room, with lights dimmed and Vijayan sitting, drooping in a chair.

The doctor came and went without saying much. Sometimes Gopalan cried out in his sleep; he called his mother or his wife. Indu would not leave his room and often ended up sleeping at the bottom of his bed, with her feet sticking out.

Sometimes she would wake up and see her father quietly watching her. 'I'll be all right soon,' he'd mutter weakly and close his eyes. At such times Indu would sit up quickly and start praying to all the Gods she knew, though she was sure her father didn't believe in any of them.

Miraculously Gopalan started getting better after a week. His cough became less tortuous and he starting drinking soup. Indu massaged his feet and sat nearby, ignoring the visitors who came to se him. The doctor gave more injections with confidence.

Months passed and it seemed to Indu that her father was gaining weight, looking more substantial. For a while he kept away from the beach and the swimming. He tried to cut down on the number of Scissors cigarettes smoked in a day, though there was a red-and-white packet next to him wherever he sat.

Shards of Sunlight

The years went by and Gopalan's coughs and fevers became a fact of his existence in the household; Indu learned to cope with them with a mixture of impatience and nagging.

Indu finished her Intermediate exams in 1952, somewhere near the top of her class, but not quite. This was par for the course; she had too many fish to fry. She had become something of an athlete, playing first team at throw ball and ball-badminton. She continued to read books indiscriminately, the good, the bad and the indifferent, working up a colossal reading speed.

In Government Brennen College, she was renowned for her insatiable appetite for books; she borrowed library cards from all and sundry, until the librarian decided to give her extra cards in her own name. At studies, she was always undistinguished, but her language skills were exceptional and she got into the habit of engaging in college debates and sharpening her skills of analysis, synthesis and argument.

By this time Indu was sick and tired of theorems and lemmas and everything Mathematical. However, in Thalassery, the choice was limited: you could take Maths or History or Economics for your degree. There were no laboratories, so not much else was available. The English Literature course was also not offered because not many English lecturers, city-breds who actually spoke the language with panache, affection, and occasionally arrogance, could be attracted to a remote little town like Thalassery.

Indu knew going out of Thalassery to do something other than Mathematics was not an option for her – who would look after Gopalan and his fragile health? So she decided to settle down, unenthusiastically, to another two years of boring

Shards of Sunlight

Maths. The saving grace was the library and she was sure she could spend two more years, at least, before she exhausted that treasure trove. If it crossed her quicksilver mind that she was shutting off future career options she did not dwell on it.

Sometimes Indu wondered at her father's strangely aseptic attitude to life around him. Indu was beginning to look at the boys around her. One or two would follow her around.

Kuttikrishnan, a boy who was in the same year-group as Indu always got on the bus and kept a seat vacant near him. Girls and boys never sat near each other, what was he thinking? She wondered. She often noticed that he would let a bus go by and wait for her to turn up before he got on.

After two months of this Kuttikrishnan's friends starting teasing him. 'We are waiting for the bus,' they would call out. 'What are you waiting for?'

'Even later still, they would chant. 'She is coming, coming, coming…'

He was oblivious. All they got from him was a smile. Soon they gave uo. He was immune.

When the Intermediate results came in May Indu was pleasantly surprised; she had done much better than anyone expected, considering she spent most of her time reading books, which had nothing to do with her studies. Gopalan proudly completed her application forms for a degree course before he got busy with the wedding scheduled for late May. When the harvest was in, and the fields in front of his brother-in-laws house were dry, his farm workers would erect a thatched tent there to feed the wedding guests and Gopalan would have to play a large part in his niece's wedding.

Shards of Sunlight

Gopalan had many nieces in his village and one got married during October; as was the custom with the Nair caste, the *muhurtham,* the auspicious time at which the wedding should take place was set for the night.

The wedding feast for the hundreds of guests went on into the early hours of the morning and Gopalan was out there in the forecourt seeing to the guests and making sure the drinking on the perimeter of the compound did not get out of hand.

Indu was busy inside the house with her friends most of the time, but out of the corner of her eyes, she could see her father rushing about. She had a moment's unease but it was soon forgotten; in any case what was there to be uneasy about. She told herself he was as healthy as the rest of them and a day's running about would not hurt him.

Indu was wrong. When her household returned to their house in Thalassery after the celebrations, Gopalan was already drooping with exhaustion and running a slight fever. Gopalan's fevers came and went and he usually laughed them off as a residual illness from jail, but warning bells had already started to ring in Indu's mind.

Next morning he was up and getting ready for Court when the first wheezing cough returned.

'Maybe a day's rest,' Indu urged.

'I've taken enough time off for that wedding as it is,' he muttered as he got his stiff collar on.

By the evening he was running a fever and coughing continuously.

That night Indu spread a mat on the floor in Gopalan's bedroom and slept there in case he needed her, but he did not call for anyone.

Shards of Sunlight

In the morning Doctor Madhavan came again and did the usual doctor things.

'His lungs are weak from all that coughing and smoking.'

'Are you giving him an injection?' Indu asked.

Madhavan took his syringe out, but he looked uncertain. Indu did not like the look on the doctor's face, so she didn't go to school.

Gopalan looked wasted after each coughing session; the coughs now had no phlegm in them, but he held his chest as though it hurt. This time the men did not come to care for him; he was sick so often they assumed he would recover.

As the coughs became more violent Devi started camping with Indu on her mat in the night and Doctor Madhavan came daily. He gave injections and shook his head when Indu looked pleadingly at him.

'How long since you slept?' he asked Indu after three days of this. She was dishevelled and desperate.'

'Achan –'

'In God's hands,' Madhavan said, and Indu felt he had somehow relinquished the initiative.

She took to sitting at the foot of Gopalan's bed for long hours. Sometimes she dozed.

When he slipped away into unconsciousness, she did not notice until his breathing got strained. He hiccupped and a little red phlegmy trickle came out of the side of his mouth. Indu shook Devi awake and called next door for Vijayan to fetch the doctor.

When Madhavan arrived the next time Gopalan did not wake up. The doctor felt his pulse and took his syringe out. He gave Gopalan two injections; Gopalan's legs jerked slightly. His hand fell out of the edge of the

Shards of Sunlight

bed. Indu picked it up and rubbed it, feeling its cold inertness.

Indu knew everything was wrong when Devi fetched the thulasi water and Madhavan looked at Indu with pity; he shook his head and turned away.

Devi put a drop of thulasi water in Gopalan's slack mouth. Indu had seen this ritual before.

'No,' she shouted. 'No, he can't breathe. Don't give him water when he is choking.'

The doctor put his arms round Indu and turned her away from her father. 'He has stopped breathing,' he said and sat down on the chair with his head in his hands.

Indu looked frantically from Devi to Madhavan. Tears were running down Devi's face and she was praying under her breath. Indu touched her father again.

'Acha,' she called and fell in a heap on top of him. No one moved her for a moment.

She sobbed a high keening sob that made her catch her breath and then subsided into semi-consciousness, while Shinnu held on to her and sobbed with her.

The men from the neighbourhood took over; this was their territory as much as it was a woman's when a woman gave birth or died. They waited only half an hour before they washed him, dressed him in white khadar clothes and laid him out in the puja room. He looked exposed and vulnerable.

The men tied a bandage around his chin and over his head to keep his jaw from dropping. His toes were tied with pieces of white rags to stop them from stiffening and they placed quarter-anna coins on his eyelids to keep them shut. The sacred lamp was lit at

Shards of Sunlight

his head, and at his feet, two half-coconut shells were placed with lighted wicks.

While all this was going on the women were excluded from the room. Indu knew her father was not hers anymore; in some way, again, he had gone to being the Gopalan who belonged to the whole neighbourhood.

They came in twos and threes, wearing mourning white, and stayed a moment before going out to sit on the veranda. Some looked in on her, but did not say anything.

'He wouldn't have liked strangers washing him,' Indu thought and started sobbing again.

Devi looked at Indu and looked away as though she couldn't bear the sight. Shinnu hugged Indu tighter.

'Why do they do all that? Coins on his eyes and rags on his face? He'd never allow any of that if he knew.'

'Shush,' Shinnu said. 'Don't sit here if it upsets you, we can sit in your grandmother's old room. No one will come there.'

'Can't leave him alone,' Indu said.

Through the morning Indu heard the sounds of the men hacking the mango tree down from the compound behind their house for Gopalan's cremation. Soon after mid-day, four men came into the room where Gopalan was laid out. By this time Indu had stopped looking at his face; she could not bear to look at this effigy of her father, who had been always animated in his life.

The men moved the lamps at his feet aside and started lifting him up.

'What,' Indu shouted, springing towards them. She caught hold of the arm of one man, a nephew of her father.

Shards of Sunlight

'Time for the rites,' he said, looking pityingly at Indu. 'For the cremation,' he said. 'He has no sons, so I am to do it. Light his pyre.'

The rest ignored her and walked out, Gopalan's body sagging a little as they carried him.

Indu collapsed again into Shinnu's lap and Shinnu let her be until she came to a few moments later.

'Women are not allowed near the pyre,' Shinnu said, holding on to Indu when she tried to stand up.

The slow murmur of the *Pujaris* who traditionally conducted the last rites could be heard in a soft murmur and occasionally the crackling of the fresh mango logs as the fire caught. Shinnu closed the window before the smell of burning body reached the room.

Shards of Sunlight

18

Later, Indu would always think of 1952 as the nightmare year when life became a battle to stay afloat; she felt she was drowning in grief and hopelessness. She also suffered sharp pangs of guilt: she had troubled her father so much, refusing to learn this or that, criticising his smoking, his friends and his disregard of health.

She said all this to no one but Shinnu. 'I made him feel such a failure about his inability to give up smoking.'

Shinnu comforted her, 'No, failure he never felt; he was too confident. And you know, you are just like him, full of self-belief. You will be alright, in the end. Wait and see.'

'Shinnuedathy, I was forever arguing with him about my reading, about Hindi…'

'That was just a game to him. He was so proud of you, he wanted to give you more and more things to learn. And you *did* learn whatever he gave you.'

Indu waited for that hard lump in her throat to go down, for the tears poised on the edge of her eyelids to dry up, for the big hole in her life to cover up and grow over. Above all, for the colours to return so that she was not living in a world that was forever grey or black, struggling to fathom the scene around her.

One Sunday in June, while the monsoon was lashing at the windows and the yard was three inches deep in water, Indu sat on her father's reading chair on the veranda, thinking of the uncertainty of her life. Now

Shards of Sunlight

that her father was not there to make her feel special, she didn't think she could be anything she wanted to be.

Indu's uncle, Kannan, was supposed to look after her, but *where* was he? He was far away in Ottappalam, and apparently now about to leave for Ceylon, where he had got a job as a tea estate doctor.

'Rubber estate, tea estate, all the same to me. Even here in Ottappalam all I do is look at the nether regions of pregnant women and help the midwife deliver babies. If I were rich I would never put my hands up a cervix again.'

This, during a quick touch-base visit he had made just before he went away in September.

'Colombo is only a couple of hours in the steamer from Dhanushkodi. If you need me just send me a telegram.'

He sounded as though that was an unlikely event. Incidentally, Mani says she wants to come over this Christmas, spend some time in Thalassery.'

To all this Indu was mute. What could possibly need his coming back? Nice though, if Mani came.

Mani arrived at the end of June; this time she was subdued.

'He was more father to me than my own father,' Mani wailed. 'Never made me feel you were closer to him than I.'

Indu remembered how jealous she was of her father being public property.

Vijayan from next door came to greet Mani.

'Big woman now. Look at you. Can't believe I used to take the two of you to the temple festival.'

'I had to come,' she said to Indu. 'I had to see you.'

Shards of Sunlight

Next day she wandered off in the direction of Gopalan's room. Indu followed her, but hung back when she reached the door. Was she ready for this? But, with Mani, she would be more ready than any other way.

The door was locked. Kannan had locked it soon after the fourteen-days ceremony of purification and no one had gone in there since.

'Doesn't anyone go in here? All Elayachan's things are here. His books, 'specs, gown. Come, Indu.' She stretched her hands out to Indu. 'Let's do this together.'

She went downstairs and came back with Gopalan's keys, which he had always carried tucked into his waist, in the mundu.

Milestones, very long and painful ones, for Indu, but she knew this also had to be passed. She was glad Mani was here to help her but even Mani was not ready for the bereft room with Gopalan's things still where he had left them when he died. His lawyer's gown was folded carelessly into the bottom of the book shelf. A file he had been working on was on the side table and his reference books still under the bed, accumulating dust. The room looked as though he would come in any moment from his bath and get ready to go to the Courts.

Indu picked up the gown and an animal noise escaped her, halfway between a sob and a gasp. She folded it again carefully and looked helplessly at Mani.

'Better put this away; otherwise the cockroaches will get at it. Let one of his juniors use it.'

Indu clutched the gown as though there was an invisible line of young lawyers queuing up to seize Gopalan's gown from her. She looked away, shook the

Shards of Sunlight

garment out and folded it carefully the way her father had taught her: the gathered sleeves first in and then down the middle before the rest.

She saw him in her mind walking down the hill in the evening, gown thrown carelessly over his shoulders, the world at his fingertips. The tears welled up and trickled down Indu's face.

Mani put her hand out and took the gown gently from Indu. She put it away in the chest of drawers. She then wiped Indu's tears away.

'Enough for the day,' she said, seeing Indu's despair. 'Tomorrow maybe. Don't lock the door. Let the light and air come in. Remember how he loved the light.'

'I hate this house,' Indu burst out. 'This wretched house.'

Mani put her arm round Indu's shoulders. 'This is the house your father built for you and it is so him. The large windows without curtains, the parapets and ledges to sit and read, the nooks and corners to day dream in the house and in the garden, all those shelves waiting for the books you will read and cherish. Good heavens, his legacy to you is phenomenal; it will carry you through life and, eventually, you will love this house.

Indu looked unconvinced. 'I wish you lived with us,' she said.

19

The monsoon was at its destructive worst when the College reopened and Indu started her degree course. Devi and Shinnu stood at the gates and waved her off towards the bus stand a few minutes away. She kept looking back as though she had forgotten something, someone. She heard her father's voice, which now lived in her head. *No flowers in the hair today?*

Next morning she took some violet Narayani blossoms from the back-fence and threaded them on a string torn off the outer skin of a banana tree. She put the garland on her hair and walked out as though she had done something special. *There*, she said to the presence in her head. *Flowers in my hair, but where are you?*

Once she was in College, Indu was different, more mature. She did not laugh so easily and was often lost in daydreams. She had much to think about. Devi was voluble about money-worries, almost as though finding money was part of her remit now there were no earning men in the house. Kannan sent money regularly and Indu knew her father had set up a special fund for her education.

Around Indu the girls and boys in the college walked from one lecture to another. The girls talked about their saris, the new Malayalam films and the festivals and looked obliquely at the boys. The boys weighed up the girls and decided who they wanted to pursue. Indu frightened them with her grave manner and absent-minded glance. They left her alone.

Shards of Sunlight

Without trying she established a reputation for wisdom, or was it discretion? that she did not possess. If she did not talk about the pairings that happen ed around her, it was only because she found them puerile.

The Astronomy lecturer, himself just out of College tried to get past her detachment.

'Sorry about your father,' he said to Indu. 'It must be hard.'

She did not know what to say. But as she worked at the dips and declensions she knew it was compassion that made him talk to her. She kept her head down knowing compassion would be hard to deal with.

As the months passed, her grief moved from the front of her head to somewhere safe at the back. She took more interest in her appearance and began laughing again.

There was also this new agenda that kept pushing its ugly head forward. It kept cropping up in conversations she overheard in the house when neighbours visited, when relatives came from the village, and mostly when that creep Ramunni, an uncle of unknown provenance, arrived with his limitless store of platitudes. He had rarely come to the house when Gopalan was alive.

He was a marriage broker and made a living out of finding spouses for families in Kodiyeri. A favourite statement of Rammunni's was, 'Educated girls make unsatisfactory wives and men know that; you'll have trouble finding a husband for this one.'

Indu intended that process to be very fraught.

If Indu had not come back from College early that Friday she may not have heard this new project of that horrible old man, whom she had to call Uncle. He was one of those uncles who came under the *every one who is much older than you and remotely related to you is your uncle* rule.

Indu had good reason to hate Ramunni. So when she saw him sitting on the veranda chewing pan and spitting red betel juice all over their front yard, she was disgusted. She went inside without greeting him.

'I remember his nonsense,' Indu said. 'He tried to stop my schooling when I was still in Primary school, and then again when I was about to go to College. When my father was alive, he didn't dare offer advice on the subject of girls' education. Now he spouts off to Devi. Devi, in any case, does not have much time for education of girls and she doesn't have the courage to stand up to the likes of him. She is beginning to wilt.'

Kannan, whenever he came by, which was not often, was robust on Indu's behalf.

'Gopalan left money for her education and that is what it is going to be spent on. In any case she is my ward and I decide.'

'What about her marriage then?' Ramunni asked. 'Will you also pay for her jewellery and wedding expenses? I am the one who will find a husband for her while you travel the world making money.'

This was a valid point. Kannan was hardly ever in India. He was in Colombo and came home infrequently. Ramunni on the other hand was a permanent if doughty presence and had a reputation as a marriage broker.

Kannan did not bother to reply, but as he went inside, you could hear him giving instructions to Devi. 'Girls who can learn should be allowed to learn. She must get her degree and then we will consider what else to do.'

Shards of Sunlight

'No one will marry girls who study too much. It is so unnatural,' Ramunni said this loud enough for Kannan to hear.

This had a smidgen of truth in it: education *was* a serious handicap in Kerala in the marriage market; men were afraid of girls who had ideas.

Indu had a sudden feeling of guilt; every one was arguing about her future. Devi struggled to make ends meet, often eating her *conjee* with salted mangoes because there was no curry left for her when the household had eaten. And Shinnu wore the same tattered old mundus year after year, while Indu got her four saris a year at the beginning of each college year. Who thought of those two women who lived permanently in the back of the house?

I'll get a job when I get my degree, Indu promised herself. I will look after Shinnu and Devi, buy them lots of nice clothes and good food. If the stray thought intruded that no woman in her family had ever earned a living, she quickly thrust it aside. She'd find something.

She took this idea to Kannan when he was sitting on the front veranda one day, shaving. He was all lathered up and drawing the razor neatly down his chin when she spoke to him.

'*Velyacha*, I'll finish my degree next year. You won't be here when I get my results in August.' And neither will my father, she thought with a sudden lump in her throat.

Kannan turned to his niece. 'I'm sure you'll pass. Pass well, I dare say, from what your teachers say. And we'll celebrate when I come back next year.'

'I want to work after that.'

Shards of Sunlight

Kannan rested his razor on the top of his mug of hot water.

'Come here,' he said. He smelled of shaving soap and she could see bits of his chin, which the razor had missed. 'You *are* full of surprises. What brought this on?'

'Achan always said women should be independent. How can I be free if I have to depend on someone else for money all the time?'

'Do what most women do, marry a rich man. 'Joke,' he said quickly, as he saw Indu frown. 'Mani is working in a firm in Bombay. Maybe you should come and live with us in Colombo for a little while, check the place out, get some tips from Mani also when she is around.'

'That would be wonderful, Velyacha,' she said joyously.

Indu finished College in May and waited impatiently for August when she would know how well she had done in her exams. She spent her holidays helping Shinnu in the kitchen and daydreaming.

'When I start working, we'll go to a lot of Malayalam pictures,' Indu said to Shinnu, who had a passion for four-hour-long Malayalam epics and a crush on Thikurishi, one of the lead actors. Indu often felt that Shinnu was one of those women who had fallen through the sieve when fate handed out luck. No one ever thought of what Shinnu wanted; yet it was Shinnu who had looked after both the girls in the house, plaited their hair for school, combed lice out at weekends and made sure there was something hot for them to eat when they came home from school, ravenous and tired.

Shards of Sunlight

'Working,' Shinnu said thoughtfully. 'Will they allow you?' That amorphous *they* who made decisions on all and sundry, the keepers of the laws and protectors of maledom. 'What if they arrange a marriage for you?' That ubiquitous word again.

'Wait and see,' Indu retaliated with spirit, but she knew Shinnu had a point.

Shinnu was proved right soon enough. Ramunni came to the house one afternoon in July; he did not come empty handed. He called Devi out on to the veranda and spoke to her at length, in whispers, showing her what he was holding: a faded yellowing piece of paper, almost tearing at the folds.

Shinnu and Indu could not hear any of the conversation but, as he left later, Ramunni called out from the walkway. 'It is not easy to get such a good connection. Especially for a fatherless child.'

When Devi eventually came inside she looked shamefaced. 'What can I say?' she said, avoiding Indu's eyes.

'No, to start with,' Indu said.

Devi moved over to the kitchen parapet and collapsed on it. 'Wealthy,' he says. 'A once-in-a-lifetime chance. Perhaps you should think about it.'

Indu felt her stomach clench. She looked at Devi, willing her to look back, but Devi's face was averted.

'Always bothering the child, you lot,' Shinnu said angrily. 'Ask that old fart to go somewhere else for his lunch when he comes into town. That's all he comes here for, and then he leaves a bad taste in our mouths when he leaves.'

Shards of Sunlight

Shinnu went up to Indu and patted her. 'You don't have to do anything you don't want.'

'But *we* do,' Devi interrupted. 'You and I always do.'

'That's because you have no means of earning a living,' Indu said. 'Depending on this brother or that.' She realised what she had said and her hand came up to her mouth. 'Sorry Ammamma. I shouldn't have said that.'

'It's true though,' Devi said heavily. 'And what are you going to do that is different?'

'Work is what I'm going to do, Ammamma. Look after you and Shinnu. Make enough to tell all these old hyenas to keep away. Stop sniffing around for the next carcass. I am *not* getting married to anyone. Yet. Things to do.'

Indu flounced out, her voice trembling, betraying her agitation. She knew she was talking to herself.

Indu had forgotten about the whole issue when Ramunni next turned up. He held a small folded cloth packet in his hand and looked pleased with himself. He called Devi out for another whispering session.

When Devi went inside, she looked defeated. 'I can't talk to him; he just talks over me. He's brought the horoscope of that boy and wants it checked with Indu's for compatibility.'

'And?' Shinnu asked with contempt.

'Looking at the horoscopes doesn't mean anything is decided. I'll give him her horoscope; that'll keep him out of our hair for a little while.'

Indu realized she was not winning this round, so she decided to get help; she disappeared into her room

Shards of Sunlight

and searched for the last letter she had received from Kannan. He wrote so rarely, she must have thrown it away long ago. As she rooted among her papers she found an old birthday card, which had his address. She copied it down imagining he would come to her rescue if she really needed him.

Actually, she had more faith in his wife than her uncle; he never asked her about the things that mattered to her. His conversation was limited to, 'How old are you now?' – as though he didn't know – and a sweeping 'How is college?' She generally ignored the first question and said 'fine' to the next. What was the point?

His wife, Kamala, on the other hand, took her out when they came and bought her clothes. She took her to the cinema and the temple festival and asked her about what she was reading and what she wanted to do when she finished college.

'You know what? You are not like all the other girls here,' she would say, smiling that infinitely warming smile of hers. 'You can do anything you want – Gopalan made sure of that. What a father! But there are no Masters Courses here, what can you do in this little town? Come to Colombo with me and you can at least gain time, think about things.'

'I want to work, Velyamma,' Indu said once.

'The thing is, there are few jobs here in Thalassery except teaching and that is merely dogsbody work. You are too clever for that. Will they let you go to Madras to find work? I doubt it. A single girl going that far to a city alone? No, it is not going to happen.'

'The money is so little it is not worth teaching here.'

Shards of Sunlight

'As I said, come to Colombo. You will get a decent wage there.'

It was a long way away, but Indu was excited. However she had to finish her degree first, and now it seemed, she had to keep Ramunni's marriage plans at bay.

Weeks passed and Ramunni did not visit. Indu decided he must have given up the whole idea of her marriage. Exams were looming and Indu was deep into Partial Fractions and Differential Equations when Ramunni reappeared on a Sunday afternoon. As he walked up the walkway to her house he pursed his lips and spat a red jet of betel juice into the hibiscus bush. Indu disappeared into her room as soon as she saw his grim face.

He summoned Devi and spent a great deal of time whispering to her; when he left, Devi appeared very subdued.

'What's he said now to upset you, Devi Ammamma?' Indu asked that evening, as she ate her conjee and plantain mash.

'He's started that marriage talk again.'

'So let him talk. You don't need to worry, because nothing is going to happen.' Indu spoke with more certainty than she felt.

'He says some people are coming to see you as soon as the exams are over.' The 'see' was a loaded one. As in the bridegroom's people inspecting a prospective bride.

'I don't want to be 'seen' by anyone,' Indu said, as she flounced off to wash her hands.

Shards of Sunlight

In the middle of May, when exams were long over, and the heat had built up to irritation levels, Ramunni announced the day of the 'seeing.'

'They want to fix the wedding for *Chingam*,' Ramunni said to Devi. *Chingam*, between mid-August and mid-September, when the rains had petered out and the harvest was in, was the festive month in the Malayalee calendar, so it was considered an auspicious time for weddings.

'The groom is returning from Dubai especially to get married and we need to move quickly,' Ramunni added.

'She is not interested in getting married; I think we should wait till her uncle comes back from Colombo.' Devi's voice was tentative.

'Good proposals don't grow on trees. Waiting for Kannan! What's he done so far? When you wanted to fix that roof in the kitchen, water coming down on the hearth and the fire hissing out, it was to me you came.' Indu listened from the corridor, seething.

Devi was too scared to mention the 'seeing' ceremony to Indu.. Until the day before the event.

'Moley, tomorrow these people are coming. To see you.'

Devi had picked a time when Indu was chopping vegetables for lunch; she could not get up and run away at that time. Indu put her knife down and looked up from the chopping board.

'Which people, and for what?' Indu's voice faltered on the last syllable as she realized how hedged in she was. 'Well, they can't. *See* me. Like looking at a goat you are going to buy. Probably want to feel the udders.'

Shards of Sunlight

Shinnu laughed out loud and looked up from the sardines she was scoring with her sickle, clutched between her toes as she sat on the low wooden stool. She saw Devi's frown and quickly damped down the laughter.

'Do this one thing for me, Moley. You can always turn them down later. I just want to get that old man off my back. 'You can say anything you like later.'

'Why are you so sacred of that man?' Indu asked. 'What does he do for you?'

'He's a nasty old man, but I owe him.'

'Owe?'

'Last year, when we had no money to repair the leak on the roof and we were placing buckets all over the kitchen floor to catch the downpour, I had to ask him. And he helped. But now he thinks he owns me. He shouts at me.'

'Right, we owe him money. Let him wait until I get a job.'

'Just this once…' Devi pleaded. 'Wear a decent sari and be civil to the women who will come tomorrow. You are not agreeing to anything by just being there.'

Indu's face became red with anger and frustration.

'Yes, we are, Ammammey. We are making that Ramunni think he can tell us, me, what to do with my life. And you should not let them come and look at me as though I'm up for sale, like an animal. I thought you had more pride than that.'

'I won't ask you again, Moley. This time, I've given my word.' Devi looked defeated.

'Just for you, Devi. But I am not marrying anybody to pay your debt.' Indu dumped the knife in her hand with disgust and walked off to the veranda.

20

When Indu thought about it, it wasn't Devi's debt at all. It was hers as well. She knew her college fees and clothes cost more than all the household expenses put together. Devi had never said anything, but Indu suspected the money her father left for her education had gone long ago. Fees had increased so much in the last few years. And Kannan was so far away, what use was he in an emergency?

Results of the degree exams were late that year, something to do with confusion with the moderation in Madras University. Indu knew she'd pass. Getting a good pass? That was another matter. Jump the gun and start looking for a job, she thought.

She went to the lawyer's house down the road to borrow their English newspaper, The Indian Express to check for vacancies. Time was running out. She remembered the days when her father had two daily papers, one Malayalam and one English; now they had no money and had to borrow papers from a kind neighbour.

Indu collected the paper eager to look at the vacancies page. The State Bank of India had advertised for Junior Managers, but Indu knew no woman was ever appointed. There were some vacancies in the District Courts nearby for clerks, but they would pay even less than the teachers got. And what a dead end that would be after her father's dreams for her. If nothing turned up, she'd have to go to her old Convent and ask for a teaching job.

Shards of Sunlight

On Sunday, Devi called Indu out of bed early. 'Get bathed and dressed quickly, they are coming at ten.'

Indu grimaced but decided it was simplest to obey.

The kitchen was bathed in sunshine when she came for breakfast. Shinnu, stood at the stove frying plantain chips at top-speed, and Devi was hanging around, as usual giving instructions to the maids. The kitchen smelled of caramelised sugar and ripe fruit.

'Stop wasting time – go to the front yard and make sure that it is clean. Swab the veranda and dust the chairs. I don't think anyone ever dusts anything around here.'

'It's the dust from the road,' the maid answered listlessly.

Shinnu had spread fresh cow dung in the middle room of the house and in the kitchen the previous night. The dry-straw smell reminded Indu of the times she had 'helped' Shinnu with the cow dung. When she was about twelve years old and Mani had left with her parents, Shinnu often indulged Indu when she was doing the rooms on Fridays. The cowdung mixture was black and green and Shinnu took the undigested grass out of it before giving Indu a smooth liquid in a half-coconut shell. Shinnu allowed her to do a corner, before her evening wash. The cowdung felt a little sticky and gritty at the same time.

It was quite a conspiracy as both Indu's father and her aunt did not approve of such kindnesses. Indu remembered how she dabbed the cowdung on the floor, watching Shinnu to learn how to do it properly, so that it dried without lumps.

Shards of Sunlight

Today, however, Shinnu looked more than usually busy. She left the plantain chips to drain and started slicing bread for savoury egg-toast, fighting with the blunt knife, which was all she had. Bread, Indu thought, a rare delicacy in the house. The ghee on the griddle pan was bubbling as she dipped each slice of bread in the beaten egg, spiced up with the usual suspects mashed together: ginger, onions, green chillies and garlic. She then gently placed them on the pan to toast. The toast sizzled and Indu escaped quickly; she was allergic to the smell of cooked eggs.

Half the bread was kept aside for sweet toast. Shinnu browned these separately and sprinkled sugar on top. In between she chopped up potatoes for a stew to accompany the bread. All to impress the marriage party.

When Shinnu caught Indu's retreating back at the door, she called her back. She put two doshas on a steel plate with some coconut chutney and brought it to her.

'You come first,' she said. 'The rest don't count. You better eat this; no point in waiting for the stew. It will take time and Devi wants you to get dressed and look pretty.'

Shinnu was whispering, so Indu whispered back.

'And I think I always look pretty.' She was whistling in the dark, and Shinnu would know that.

Shinnu put the spatula down for a moment and touched her face lightly.

'All these monkeys. Don't worry. You'll be all right. You wait and see.'

Shards of Sunlight

Indu wondered what in Shinnu's book meant all right. Shinnu, who seemed destined to follow in Devi's footsteps looking after the children of others.

The dosha stuck in Indu's throat as she hurried to get it down.

'What a farce,' Shinnu remarked. And to Devi: 'She can't get her breakfast down, she's so nervous. I don't know why you can't leave the girl alone.'

'Is your hair dry?' Devi asked Shinnu. 'Plait it anyway and have you got some flowers for your hair?'

Shinnu looked up from her dosha mixture as Indu burst into tears.

A memory. Her father at his desk in his study with clients, preparing for the morning's work. Indu walking past, throwing a quick glance at him. Hurrying for that bus because she had been late getting up.

'What? No flowers in the hair today?' he asks, pencil poised over his writing pad, smiling. A quick conspiratorial smile.

'Sometimes we women have to do things we hate doing,' Devi said. She went up to Indu and touched her cheeks. 'Wear that new green sari; you look good in green.' She wiped the tears. 'Powder will get streaky on your face if you cry.'

Indu never wore powder, but Devi didn't know that. Indu felt powder did not improve her light brown complexion and it dimmed the colour in her cheeks. The most she did was dab a bit on her nose after an oil bath to take the shine away.

Indu went to the veranda and let her waist length hair down; it was still damp from her bath. She stood in the sun on the east end and passed her fingers through her hair, taking the knots out and drying it in the heat of the morning sun. This had been a ritual with

Shards of Sunlight

her ever since her hair grew to shoulder length; her father used to watch her in the sun and smile his special smile for her, the smile that seemed to send out beams of love that wrapped her up in safety. She thought about all the changes in her life.

I wonder what Achan would say to a marriage proposal, she thought, and nearly laughed out aloud. He never had time for the likes of Ramunni and treated him with scant courtesy when he came. So much so he rarely came. All this frequent visiting had started after her father died, like a vulture moving in on a weak prey.

When her hair was dry, Indu went upstairs and found her green sari at the bottom of the pile. She searched for the blouse to match, one that Kannan's wife had given her on their last visit.

As she got dressed she wondered what she was supposed to do when the 'seeing' crowd arrived. This was a first for her and she did not know the protocol.

Devi set her right when she came down.

'The women will come in and make small talk; you don't need to be there at that point. When we serve tea and snacks to them, you must carry the snacks in to each of the visitors. After that you can stay in the room or go; they might ask you to stay. If they ask you any questions, answer politely but you don't have to volunteer any information. The less they know about us the better.'

'You sound as though you are ashamed of me,' Indu teased.

Devi was in no mood for repartee. 'It's me I am ashamed of at this moment, putting you through this nonsense.'

Shards of Sunlight

Indu went up to her and put her arms round her. 'Who cares, Ammamma, it will all be over in an hour. This is just going to be a pantomime and then we can all get back to our normal lives. So long as you know this is nonsense.'

'Ye-e-s,' Devi answered, but she sounded a great deal more uncertain than Indu.

Must write to Kannan Velyachan, Indu thought. Does he know what is happening here?

The seeing party arrived late, almost mid-day. They walked slowly up the walkway, looking around them as though to take in the house, surroundings and neighbourhood and assess them. The old man who came with them pointed things out to them: the coconut trees, the nutmeg trees Indu's father had planted and which hosted rat snakes through the year, and the fields on three sides of the house, where the rice paddy grew strong and gold-tipped. When the wind rippled through the paddy fields, a soft murmur could be heard as though of muted prayers.

Indu saw the old man and thought, Ramunni number two.

She didn't want to be in the sitting room, so she hovered in the kitchen. When the kitchen got too hectic she went out on the veranda at the back and looked unseeingly at the paddy fields, where two men were inspecting the sluices.

Devi went to the door to greet the visitors and the women came in, leaving the sole male sitting on the one chair outside. He had no part to play in the next part of the script. The women were dressed in temple best and looked self-important. After all, they owned the big prize – the *Man*

Shards of Sunlight

Shinnu came out to join Indu. 'The curtain rises. Scene 1, Act 1,' she said with not a little contempt.

'Shinnuedathy, did you ever go through this drama?' Indu asked.

'Who will want to come to see me?' Shinnu asked without emotion. 'No father, no money, no brothers. You now, they see this house and they think, "house, money, property." Your degree of course will not go down well and don't even mention jobs. They like a School Leaving Certificate at most and not much brain. Come to think, you might be a worse catch than me. I'd like to see their faces when you open your mouth.'

Indu was beginning to relax. 'Devi said not to say much.'

'Devi is caught between that devil, Ramunni, and the deep Arabian Sea just round the corner; she means well. You know something? She will never allow anything that will hurt even a strand of your hair.'

The summons came a few minutes later.

'Bring the tea,' Devi called out, darting to the kitchen door and back to her guests.

Shinnu poured hot tea into stainless steel tumblers and arranged the toast and other delicacies on plates. 'Save some for us,' she said and put some back.

Shinnu handed the toast to Indu and sent her in. Indu took care not to look at any particular face, but went round serving the toast. All the women were sitting on a long narrow mat and Devi in front of them, on a wooden stool, with her pan-box in front of her. The old woman in the group, possibly the mother, picked up a slice and nibbled it. The two younger women, sisters? refused politely.

Shards of Sunlight

Indu looked at Devi who gestured for her to put the plate down. She put the toast down and waited undecided. Go or stay? Had they seen enough? Nothing at College had prepared her for this scenario.

'*Irikkoo kutty,*' the old woman said with authority. Sit down, child.

Indu drew up another mat rolled up in the corner and sat next to Devi. She wondered if her uncertainty showed.

Shinnu brought plantain crisps and put the bowl in front of the guests; she went back for their tea. Tea came in stainless steel mugs; it would be some time before they would be able to pick up the burning hot mugs.

Conversation died down a little when the guests started picking up the plantain crisps. The smell of hot coconut oil and hot tea, typical of all such occasions spread through the room.

One of the sisters was plump and wore a considerable amount of gold around her neck; she kept fingering a chain and looking furtively at Indu between bites.

'Don't like jewellery?' she asked Indu, attempting a smile.

Devi had reminded Indu to wear her black-bead-and-gold necklace, her *karimanimala*, but Indu had forgotten.

'Oh, no. Just forgot,' she answered.

'Girls these days…' Devi said apologetically.

Indu wondered when she could slip away, but they were all now focused on her.

'When are you expecting your exam results?' the thinner sister asked. 'Must be soon now.'

Indu let that pass.

Shards of Sunlight

The two sisters said something under their breaths and addressed Devi. 'Who does this house belong to?'

'This is the house Indu's father built a few years ago – for her. She owns it.'

Don't go there, Indu thought. Let's not mention my father. He would have made short shrift of you lot. Starting with the man sitting on the veranda, probably chewing pan.

'Can you speak English?' the other sister asked. 'These days people are going to *faren* countries, they need to know English.'

Devi answered for Indu, quickly as though avoiding an outburst from Indu. 'She reads many English books; so I suppose…'

'I do speak English,' Indu said, standing up as she spoke. 'Most girls at the convent do. I'll take these plates back.'

Indu picked up some of the mugs and plates and walked away.

When Indu reached the kitchen she put down the plates on the table and looked into space. Time for action, she thought. She vanished upstairs and pulled out her uncle's address in Colombo from her writing desk and tore off some paper from the back of her Calculus note book.

She thought for a moment, and started writing:
Dear Velyachan

I was going to write to you when my exam results came, but the results are late this year. Something came up and I think you should know.

Ramunni has been pestering us with talk of me getting married. Now he has brought this proposal and insists we have to go along with it. Those people have come to 'see' me and I had to be on show for Devi's sake. She seems really scared of Ramunni, exactly why no one knows.

I have looked for jobs in the papers but there is nothing suitable that I can apply for. I would love to get away from here until all this marriage talk blows over. I don't want to get married at this point and I am sure Achan would not have wanted it either. He always said I should become independent and not be afraid of any man, ever, in my life.

Did you mean it when you said I could come to Colombo for a little while? I must get out of here; otherwise I don't know what will happen.

If I can come to Ceylon, won't I need a passport and visa? Please tell me what I have to do.

Devi and Shinnu are well and we look forward to your next visit. I hope Velyamma is well. When will we see her next?
Affectionately,
Indu.

She folded the letter, put it into an old envelope from her desk and licked it closed. Devi called her later when the guests got up to leave, but Indu pretended she had not heard.

Next morning Indu went to Devi to beg money for a stamp.

'Writing letters – for whom and for what?'

'Kannan Velyachan. I write to him now and then.'

Devi gave her that squinty look which meant she was suspicious. Indu called it her X-ray look, seeing into the speaker's heart. Nothing got past Devi.

'You'll need a lot more than two annas to send a letter to Colombo – if it ever gets there.'

Shards of Sunlight

Devi took the letter from Indu and put it on the lintel of the door. 'I'll get Vijayan to post it for you tomorrow.'

Indu thought of Vijayan next door, not unlike Devi, slowly growing old, looking after his extended family. He had always run errands for Devi since the time Indu's father went to jail. Now he was thought of as almost family after the way he had tended Gopalan through that last bout of pneumonia.

Indu quickly pushed the thought of her father away; it would just make her weepy and ineffectual. She had things to do.

21

Indu had not thought this whole thing out, she knew that. What was she to do about this interfering old man, Ramunni, and what was she hoping would happen after the letter to Kannan?

As she looked out at the road from her desk, she stuck her thumb into the waist-band of her petticoat. At nine in the morning the road was awash with school children. Some wore the blue –and –white uniforms of the Sacred Heart Girls' High School. Others were in maroons and whites. The town buses careened past heedlessly as pedestrians jumped out of the way. The lone bullock cart trundled along, oblivious to the bustle around it, as the bullocks snorted through their nose-rings and tossed their heads. Occasionally the cart-driver wielded a whip and cried, 'ho-ho' but without much intent.

Somewhere in the house someone was tossing onions and mustard seeds in hot oil; the smell was enticing and Indu realised she was hungry. She ran down the stairs to the kitchen, where Shinnu was making the tastiest *uppumavu* in the world. As Indu came through the door, Shinnu threw curry leaves into the oil and poured the semolina in. She gave it a moment and reduced the fire beneath by removing two of the pieces of firewood that were blazing vigorously. She stirred the mixture for a few minutes till it turned a light golden brown and poured cold water to cover. The bubbles burst and plopped as the water hit the semolina and Shinnu continued stirring, slowly now, till all the

Shards of Sunlight

water was taken up. She threw in a handful of scraped coconut and turned to Indu.

'Hot, but it is ready now.' She served some out to Indu. 'Salt enough?' she asked.

'Mmm, Mmm,' Indu answered as she tasted the uppumavu, slowly first and then wading into it, eating quickly as it cooled down.

'I love the onions in this,' Indu said. 'Is it the shallots or the big Bombay onions?'

'Shallots always for taste,' Shinnu said. 'Yes, you better start learning to cook. Then Devi won't have to lie if any more of those proposals come your way.'

'Did she say I can sew and sing as well?'

'Probably,' said Shinnu as they both laughed. 'Count on her to say whatever they wanted to hear.'

As the days went by Indu's hopes about a rescue by Kannan faded. Surely Velyachan would not ignore her letter, she thought now and then, but not for very long. She started rushing downstairs in a hurry whenever she saw the postman walking down the road in his khaki uniform, carrying his red letter-bag.

After a few days she would wait on the veranda when it was time for the post to arrive. So much so the postman would say to her, 'Nothing for you today, again.'

'Like a cat when the fish is being cut, why are you hanging around the veranda?' Shinnu asked when this became conspicuous.

Thereafter Indu pretended to read a book at the window, knowing full well that it fooled no one.

After a month she gave up. No letter and no hope of one. What could she do next?

Shards of Sunlight

Meanwhile Ramunni came back with the verdict on Indu. For once he beamed at her.

'Not particularly fair or anything, but they thought you would suit their 'boy.'

'They liked you, it seems,' Shinnu said to Indu later that day. There was a warning note there. 'It seems he wants to come down and take a look at you himself.'

'That's all I need,' Indu wailed.

'He has to get leave from his job, will take time.'

Indu wandered off in the direction of the upstairs window again, the one overlooking the road. She pressed her face against the vertical iron bars on the window and looked out unseeingly. Events seemed to be steamrolling on with their own momentum and it was *her* life that was being carried along with them.

A woman with a wicker basket of red spinach on her head walked by; she was dragging a reluctant goat on a rope with her, probably for sale at the market. Must feel like me, that goat, Indu said to herself, wryly.

A rickshaw came down the hill fast, so fast, the man struggled to gain control. He went past the house a few yards and stopped. He then turned round and came back to put his shoulder-load down on the ground. A small canvas bag came out first, then a man. He paid the rickshaw man off; Indu looked hard at the man.

Couldn't be, she thought, and then, Velyachan.

She went down the stairs two steps at a time and got to the veranda in time to greet him. 'Velyacha,' she said with great relief.

'Did you think I wouldn't come?' he asked.

Kannan bathed, had lunch and slept till evening. He didn't raise the topic of Indu's 'seeing' until Devi brought him his evening tea.

'Long time since we've seen you,' Devi said as she put down his mug on the parapet of the front veranda.

The implied criticism was well-measured. Not too much to cause anger, but enough to make the point. He appeared thoughtful.

'So - difficult to get away. As it is… I had a letter from Indu.'

'I know. Ramunni…

'Yes, Ramunni… High time that old renegade minded his own business.'

'He has helped us when we needed help. That kitchen roof…'

'I get the picture,' Kannan said angrily. 'And how many days a month does he come here and spend the day here. Expect you to give him lunch, have his siesta here and then get up to lay down the law. Now that Gopalan is gone…'

'True. But the picture, you don't get. I have no one to turn to when there is an urgent need. Are you where you can hear when I call you? That Vijayan next door is more use.'

Devi was much older than Kannan; he let it pass.

Indu provided a diversion. She had washed a voile sari and came out to hang it on the rope to dry. It dripped on her as she walked even though she tried to hold it away from her. Kannan watched her quietly, his face thoughtful and a little uncertain. Finally he called out to her.

'Come here, Moley.'

Shards of Sunlight

Indy blinked and turned. She looked stunned. That was how Gopalan called her, Devi thought, and the two brothers had identical voices.

Indu swayed a little, almost tottered, and took a few steps towards him; she wiped the shock off her face, pretending to clean her face with her sari end as she did so..

'Come closer,' he called out. 'You look like you've been drinking toddy early in the morning,'

Indu rubbed her wet hands on her hitched-up sari and walked across.

'What's this I hear about you kicking up a fuss about this proposal?' He smiled encouragingly, inviting comment. 'Don't you like him?

'Haven't seen him to like or dislike,' she said, shortly, a little wearily.

'D'you want to?'

'No.'

'The 'no' was sharp and certain. No hesitation there.

'Start again,' he said. 'Don't you want to get married?'

'No, Velyacha, not yet. I want to work. Maybe study more.' She came to a hesitant stop.

Kannan looked at Devi; she shook her head slightly as though the world was beyond her understanding and went inside.

'You don't have to do anything you don't want to. Now. Sometimes we have to. But maybe not just yet.'

'There are things I have to do,' she pleaded, thinking of Devi and Shinnu and their meagre lives, but that was not something she wanted to talk to him about.

'Such as?'

Shards of Sunlight

'You know.' The naughty grin surfaced. 'See the world?' She looked at Kannan to see how that went down.

'I knew that was coming. All those books you read, there are lots of worlds there, I suppose. You're something, you know.' He smiled indulgently and changed the subject.

'Let's go out tomorrow and get you some saris and stuff. That one dripping on your feet looks like it's had it.'

'It's okay. Actually, I have enough clothes. But it will be nice to get out.'

The next day, Kannan ordered a jutka and Velyachan and Indu went out to the Big Bazaar where the textile stores were lined up on one side and dry good stores on the other. Kannan got off in front of Warrier's Emporium and Indu followed him. The emporium was a big square hall with a narrow ante-room at the back. On all three sides away from the entrance the glass-fronted shelves were stacked with saris and textiles of all hues and provenance.

'Choose four saris for College,' Kannan said, settling in a chair at the entrance.

Indu took a good look around and made for the almirah in which *Khatau* voiles were displayed. She selected four saris; Kannan paid up and asked, 'What else do we need?'

Indu needed many things, but she did not feel right asking him for everything. Couldn't ask him for cloth for home-made bras and knickers, she decided. Too personal and he might be offended. Her knickers were beginning to wear at the crotch and the tie-up bras, the *rowkas*, had begun to yellow under-arm.

Shards of Sunlight

'Right,' he said. '*I* know what I want to do. Let's go'.

They walked across to the solitary professional photographer in town and climbed up the steep, gritty stairs to his den at the top with the open skylight. The smell of chemicals grew stronger as they went up.

Light flooded in, almost blinding the visitors.

'Passport pictures for this young lady,' Kannan instructed.

Ghani was a foreigner in Thalassery, the way everyone was an alien who had not been born there. It didn't help that his Malayalam was stilted.

'Simply stand here,' he said, gesturing to the wall, on which a white cloth had been hung. He pulled a rope tied to the window sill and closed the skylight partly. Indu was entranced, watching the way he managed the light.

The man put his long-legged tripod up and disappeared behind the dark material hung on the back of the camera. He fiddled with the lens and pronounced the apparatus ready. He positioned Indu next to a vase of paper flowers on a stand.

'No, 'Kannan said. 'What we need is a small face shot without any decorations.'

The man moved the flowers away and came closer. He clicked and turned and clicked again. When he finished, he said the proofs would be ready in three days.

Kannan was busy the next week, filling forms and getting papers attested. Soon the proofs of Indu's passport photographs arrived. If Devi noticed anything she wasn't commenting.

Shards of Sunlight

'When did you get these?' Shinnu asked when she saw them.

'At Ghani's in town. Which one is best? I have to choose, Velyachan says.'

Shinnu took the photos to the window and scrutinised them. 'They all make you look older; no sparkle in them.'

'Shall I ask Ghani to put some sparkle then?'

Shinnu was clearly following another train of thought. 'Will you come back soon, after you go with Kannammaman.'

'Can't stay here with Ramunni at my heels. Why is he picking on *me*? There are so many girls about.' Indu put her arms round Shinnu. 'Shinnuedathy, whichever way this pans out, I am on my way out. Dubai, married to Ramunni's 'boy' or Colombo, take your pick. At least, with Velyachan I know I can do something for us - you and Devi and me. Look at us – dependent on all these men. And what's all my learning for if I get married and spend the first ten years having a baby every year? I need to control my own life; I don't want some strange old man deciding my future.'

'I don't like it; will I see you rush down those stairs with wet hair every day saying, "I am famished?"'

'I promise I will come back soon, soon, soon.'

Shinnu's eyes were filling up. 'Now it will be two old women… I knew you'll have to go some time, but -'

'I'll take you both with me as soon as I can,' Indu promised. 'I'll write every week.'

Devi came in unheard on this scene. She stopped short and looked at the two women. She picked up the proofs and put them down again.

'I hope Kannan knows what he is doing.'

'Don't worry, Ammamma. I am the one who should know which way I turn. And I do.'

Devi looked non-committal. But that was Devi.

22

The day after the passports arrived, Indu began getting ready for her trip to Colombo. She took down Gopalan's old suitcase that had been rusting in the loft. She laid it down carefully on the veranda floor and fetched an old cigarette tin containing kerosene. She applied kerosene carefully to the latches and buckles to clear away the black dots on them. As the smell of kerosene spread, she started sneezing loudly and remembered the last time the suitcase had been polished. It had been Gopalan then because he knew Indu was allergic to the smell of kerosene.

The sneezes brought Kannan to the door.

'What's upset you?' he asked Indu.

'This kerosene-'

He went upstairs and came back with anti-allergy pills.

'What's this?' Indu asked suspiciously. 'I am not sick; I don't need pills.'

'Makes you a little sleepy, but it will stop you sneezing.'

Indu got a glass of water and washed down the pill.

Kannan took the kerosene-soaked rag from her and settled down to polishing the metal on the case. Then he rubbed the tan leather down slowly and lovingly.

'I gave him this case one time when I returned from Penang' he said. 'A long time ago.'

Shards of Sunlight

Indu knew who he was talking about. She brought her face down to the suitcase, risking another sneezing bout and smelled the leather. 'He took it to jail,' she said. 'I am glad I'll be taking that with me.' She passed her hand over the lid lovingly.

'There, all ready for you,' Kannan said after a while. 'Now you have to decide what you need to take with you. They only allow forty-four pounds.'

'There go my books.'

'I didn't bring much,' Kannan consoled her. 'You can put some books in *my* case. Here, don't go wild,' he admonished as Indu's face relaxed. 'Not that Bernard Shaw your father carried around with him. More a doorstop than a book.'

Life in the fast lane: the days went by like an animated cartoon, packing, visiting friends and family to say good-bye, shopping for odds and ends for Kamala. Indu had no time to stop and fret, except when she caught up with Shinnu now and then. In those moments she would ponder Shinnu's diminished life and make fresh resolves as to what she would do for Devi and Shinnu.

She must find work quickly, send money home, and new clothes for Shinnu and Devi. There were moments when she suddenly lost faith in herself. Where were those results and those certificates to come from her studies? She went to the College and asked the office: did they know when to expect the results?

'Not really, but soon now.'

She started borrowing the Indian Express from Damu's house daily to scan the middle pages for the exam results. Sometimes Kannan would go out and get a copy for her.

Shards of Sunlight

Finally a day came when he came hurrying back waving the newspaper. 'Results,' he shouted from the gate.

'Did I pass?' Indu asked anxiously and then. 'But you don't know my number, do you?'

She grabbed the paper from him and sat down on the veranda steps. '5460,' she said. '5460, 5460... My number is not here. Velyacha...' Her face was beginning to crumble. 'I didn't pass.'

'Nonsense. Give it here,' he said. He had a quick look. 'There it is: A second class in Part one, Maths, and second in English and second in Malayalam too.' Indu seized the paper again. 'Where, where is it?' She was jabbering nervously and her hands shook.

Kannan picked up her trembling figures and put it on the number. 'There.'

Indu looked again. 'I didn't look there,' she said. 'Among the students in first or second class. I just looked at the passes. Never thought I'd do better.'

'You are the only one from your college to get second classes right through. A few firsts in Maths and one in Malayalam. But no one's as consistent as you.'

She rushed off to the kitchen. 'Shinnuedathy, Shinnuedathy, I passed, got a second class even. I passed, I passed, I passed.' She danced a little jig.

'Stop it; you'll get the evil eye on you,' Shinnu said.

The evil eye was a constant of life in Thalassery; you had to watch out for it. If something wonderful happened to a person, there was bound to be some other person who was jealous or just plain malicious.

'As if anyone doubted you will pass, you silly baby. As if...' Shinnu was

Shards of Sunlight

grinning from ear to ear. 'The first B.A from our village. Must make milk *payasam* tomorrow to celebrate.' This was Indu's favourite sweet.

The word spread quickly in the neighbourhood, over bamboo fences and across backyard vegetable plots. Damu came by to celebrate. Indu could see the thoughts in all their minds: if only Gopalan had been here, he would have been so proud.

She was not going there. That could come later and in private.

Meanwhile, according to Devi, the evil eye had to be dealt with immediately. She prepared a betel leaf, folded, with *karpooram*, - incense - and whole black pepper seeds inside it. At the pointed end of the leaf, she placed a lighted wick made out of old cloth and tucked it into the leaf. This required considerable dexterity of hand and Indu watched the ritual, amazed at Devi's efficiency with the betel leaf. Her father had always laughed at what he called hocus-pocus; Indu's attitude was that there was no harm in it and if it made Devi happy, it was well worth doing.

Indu was instructed to sit cross-legged on a prayer mat in front of the plaster and poster deities in the puja corner. She had to sit down because she was a clear head and more taller than Devi.

This was the hour of dusk when the day had not quite finished and night waited in the corners of the room to creep in. The devotional lamp was already lit and Indu could smell coconut oil in the well of the lamp and the sacred ash smeared on Devi's forehead. Indu's father had claimed the ash was well-burnt cow dung, so Indu should give it a wide berth.

The five wicks on the lamp had a mesmerising effect as they waxed and waned, so Indu looked away

Shards of Sunlight

as Devi muttered incantations under her breath, while making circular motions with the betel leaf around Indu's head. Then she brought the leaf to Indu's face and motioned Indu to blow out the wick. Devi would not talk till the ritual was completed and evil dispersed. The contraption was swiftly carried into the kitchen and thrown on the embers in the fireplace. They spluttered and caught for a moment and died out.

Devi pushed the leaf forward into the embers and turned to Indu, satisfied. 'Crackled properly. Means I got all the evil into the leaf.'

The days gathered speed as September, with the occasional rain, slipped into the dry, colder days of October. Kannan cursed the bureaucracy that kept him in Thalassery.

It was as well Indu had little time to dwell on her going. She signed more papers and Kannan sent telegrams to Madras for the visa. Late in October of 1954, everything came together and it was time to leave.

Indu had never gone in a plane, had no concept of Colombo beyond a calendar she had once seen with colour spreads of tourist spots: white women reclining on beach- beds in bikinis on Mount Lavinia beach, the big façade of Galle Face Hotel with the evening crowd enjoying the sea breeze, tea estates with mist hanging over them and Nuwara Elia, with its resort bungalows.

When Indu packed away her precious books inside the almirah where her father's law books were stored, she saw the silver fish and the inch-deep trails they made in the old paper. She took all the books out and cleaned the glass and wood with soapy water. When it was dry she dusted all the books down and sprinkled DDT powder inside the shelf. She opened a few books and stayed a moment with the Criminal Procedure Code, which was her father's daily reference book. His sloping signature was sprawled across the top of the first page and the date, 1934, probably when he bought it. The pages were yellowing and the ink fading on the signature. She passed a finger slowly on the signature and sat down with it, lost in thought.

What would her father make of all the changes in her life? Her going away from home? But he would have been so proud of that second class. Of that she was sure. He would have boasted in the Bar Association Library until other lawyers ran away from him.

'We did it, Acha,' she said quietly as she put the law book back. 'All those things we talked about – I'm going to make them happen.'

23

Indu left on a Wednesday morning, which the astrologer had declared auspicious for a long journey.

'Colombo is so near, an-hour-and-a-half from Madras, for heaven's sake,' Kannan burst out. 'And what does that old man with the top knot have to do with the future?'

Indu's thoughts exactly, but Devi insisted on the advice of that man and paid him for it. Can't do any harm, she thought, remembering the times when her father had refused to have anything to do with the astrologer.

The whole neighbourhood turned out to see her off, Vijayan in front with home-made sweets, which Indu liked. Shinnu was biting her lips and Devi looked on impassively.

'Stop that snivelling,' she said to Shinnu. 'Mustn't cry when some one is leaving.'

Indu got into the jutka and sat down as Kannan helped the driver to stow the suitcases under the seats.

'Wait,' Indu pleaded, when the driver picked up the bridle again. The horse tossed its brown mane impatiently.

Indu rushed to Devi and hugged her fiercely. 'Devi Ammammey, please think of me. I need your prayers.'

'Ende Moley,' she said, holding on to Indu. 'My daughter.' There was a sob in her voice. 'Go now, go

Shards of Sunlight

quickly,' she said. 'Shinnu and I, we'll wait for you, we'll be alright.'

Indu was sobbing without restraint when she got back into the jutka, and she didn't see anything else through her tears. The horse trotted off and turned the corner, up the hill near her father's beloved Civil Courts.

The jutka went past the courts and on to the straight stretch leading to the town bus stand, the markets, the shops and the world beyond. Indu's small world was made up of college and beach in the main, but also on occasion the new Hema Theatre, Thalassery's first all –weather theatre, which she had frequented with Shinnu. That's another thing she thought, who will take Shinnu to her never-ending Malayalam films and the falooda at the small wayside shop afterwards? Falooda, they called it, that pink, frothy mixture of milk, sugar and food colouring. Shinnu could finish one in a minute, while Indu lingered over hers; eventually Shinnu would finish it off for her and smile happily with a pink moustache. Indu would lift her sari end and wipe it clean.

She should get married, Indu thought, not I. So much love looking for a place to nest.

At the entrance to the town stood two of her citadels: the Brennan College and the Cosmopolitan Club, where her father had spent many an hour playing billiards or chatting to his friends on the veranda. Indu had been a frequent tag-along, Gopalan's little lamb, until she outgrew the limited reading material on the club news-table, the gloomy rooms where no other child seemed to come.

It was a prime spot in the town. Facing the club was the sprawling Big *Maidanam*, with its quota of

Shards of Sunlight

dogs, goats and cows foraging for food, and the tennis courts where the middle-class men played tennis. The District Magistrate's Court on the corner of the Convent Road was tucked away out of sight, but the mosque across the maidanam was prominent, calling the devout to attention, mornings and evenings.

Towards mid-day now and the town was half asleep. Even the college was quiet, with all the students at lectures till one in the afternoon.

'It used to have a beautiful garden when it was still with the Council,' Kannan remarked as they passed it. 'We got flowers from there when we had to take a bunch to someone for a gift. The gardener used to let us pick the ones we liked. Eight annas for a bouquet.'

The college had no time for flowers, struggling as it was with paucity of resources and a frequent turnover of disgruntled staff.

'It still has a great library,' Indu remarked. 'All of the ground floor of that building. We had to dodge the traffic when we walked from one building to another across a main road. But it was worth it. The language lecturers were exceptional, passionate about their literature.'

'You don't mention Maths,' Kannan said, laughing.

'I could have taken it or left it.'

The journey to the railway station took almost an hour because the level crossing near it was closed and they had to wait there for twenty minutes for a slow shuttle to trundle past.

Kannan fretted about the delay. 'Hope we don't miss the train.'

Indu was of the *if we miss this train there will be another one behind it* disposition, but she kept quiet.

Shards of Sunlight

She was beginning to see how enormously different Kannan was in outlook from her father, though they had identical voices that carried far. *Made for speech-making* Gopalan used to say and *should be a rag-and-tin-man*, Indu would say teasing him. Kannan was not someone she would consider teasing.

She could visualise Gopalan sitting casually in front of that crossing, saying, 'Now do you think we'll have enough time to get coffee from that boutique over there while we wait?' He would light another cigarette and consider the odds. Or start a long, possibly tall story, and leave it half-finished when the jutka started moving again.

Eventually Kannan and Indu managed to board the train to Kannan's conspicuous relief.

'We made it,' he said stowing away the luggage under the seats.

He took a long time settling down, this much travelled man, and Indu could see he had developed rituals and routines. He took their travel documents out of his pouch and checked them for the umpteenth time.

'Remembered your mark list?' he asked, referring to the document, which would be evidence of her qualifications until the convocation a few months away. Indu nodded. He pulled his hand-towel out of the side-pocket of his small case and put it neatly on the seat next to him.

More passengers came in and sat down or stayed at the window talking to family members on the platform. Indu was content to watch the frenetic world on the platform; it looked like a small city out there.

Porters hurried past, red towels twisted under their head-loads, necks bent forward under their weights. The tea and coffee boys with their hot urns mounted on bicycles stopped at the windows, shouting *chaya, chaya* or *kappi, kappi*.

Children screamed and squirmed in the laps of long-suffering mothers waiting possibly for the next train, and men sat on the meagre benches reading newspapers or chewing pan. At the water-fount, waiting passengers gargled and spat, cleansing their mouths after snacks or meals consumed at the station cafes. Indu was content watching this other microcosm; her life for now was in the hands of her Velyachan.

Somewhere round the bend of the track a train hooted and slowly, almost imperceptibly, the station and its occupants receded backwards. Life was moving on.

24

Madras Central Station was a human jungle, with men, women and children sprawled on the cement floors in the vast, high-domed waiting area. As they alighted at six in the morning, weary and dishevelled, the station was in full swing, trains arriving and departing, with tannoy announcements in English and Tamil. Even more porters scurried here than in that small station in Thalassery, bargaining for that extra rupee in the fare.

Outside, the building was an amazing, improbable red-brick structure.

'Where did they think *this* one up? Indu asked Kannan.

'All those books you read and you don't know that? A British man called Hardinge designed this, about eighty years ago. They call it the *Gothic Revival* style, whatever that is. Don't you like it?'

'I'm flabbergasted,' she said. 'You could put the whole of Thalassery's Big Bazaar in this and still have space to park buses.'

Kannan and Indu took a taxi to the airport; they had very little time to spare before their flight to Jaffna and then on to Colombo.

Meenambakkam Airport was another blur. Indu watched astounded as passengers were weighed in addition to their luggage. Did she have to be under a certain regulation weight?

Shards of Sunlight

The third person in front of Kannan in the queue, a man huge in all directions, was dragging a canvas case, sometimes pushing it along with his foot, and breathing hard with each effort. When he stood on the pedestal of the weighing machine, he pulled his belt up over his pendulous stomach and stood straight, but the needle still swung madly to the right and hovered in the two-hundreds. When he was given his boarding pass Indu breathed a huge internal sigh of relief; she knew that she would not have trouble.

All that book reading, Indu thought, and I have seen so little of the world, even this country. She was glad she was making a beginning. This is what my father was preparing me for – this caravanserai, which is called living. A journey, many journeys in fact, in front of me, starting with the beginnings, with my far-seeing father at home. Miles to go, she said to herself, and I am ready.

After the check-in there was the Customs to negotiate. The customs officers made Indu open her suitcase and delved inside. They pulled out several books, flipped through a few and looked strangely at her.

'Is this all you are taking to Ceylon? Books? No gold jewellery?' Indu did not answer. They threw everything back untidily and pushed the case to the side, leaving it to Indu to cram the clothes and books in again and close the lid.

Kannan seemed relieved when they reached the aircraft and squeezed into their seats. 'Those customs people,' he said. 'No courtesy at all.'

The Fokker Friendship aircraft seemed barely adequate to carry the weight of sixty passengers, their luggage and crew. Approaching Jaffna, they flew into a

Shards of Sunlight

thunderstorm, which rocked the plane. Several passengers started throwing up and infants screamed. The air hostesses carrying trays dropped on to any vacant seat near them, trays in their laps, and passengers caught in the aisles were thrown from side to side.

The aircraft dipped and rose. Indu felt exhilarated and watched the black clouds speeding past her widow. Achan would have loved all this, she thought. He was so 'up' for any new experience.

When she arrived at Ratmalana airport in Colombo, she was forced to let go of that state of suspended living, which is travel, and begin to become part of the throng again. She was ready to go.

One moment Indu was quietly waiting in front of the luggage carousel, waiting for Kannan to collect their bags, the next, there was a blunt summons and she was being taken away from the crowd and body-searched by an Amazonian woman officer, who had never learned to smile.

'*Yende,*' she said to Indu, come.

Indu had just started pushing her trolley along, wide-eyed, taking in the bustle and the cacophony in a language she didn't understand, when she was stopped

'What for?' Kannan asked. 'They want you to go with them,' he said in an aside to Indu in Malayalam. He sounded bemused.

'For search,' the woman said, not looking at Kannan. She put out her arm and took hold of Indu. She then spoke quickly in Sinhalese to an assistant.

'Please come,' she said again, with more authority.

A tiny worm wriggled in Indu's entrails and threatened to become a full-blown fluttering butterfly.

Shards of Sunlight

She looked at Kannan. He seemed worried, flummoxed; Indu was propelled along to go with the woman.

They went to a wooden cubicle on the side of the customs area and the two women got in with her – the cubicle was tiny and they were pushed up against each other. The walls closed in on her.

'You take off clothes,' the officer said, 'Hang there.' She pointed to a hook at head height on the side of the cubicle.

Indu removed her sari and hung it there, in an untidy coil. She stood in her under-skirt and blouse, feeling vulnerable and scared. The women in that cubicle seemed to have absolute power over her. Where was Kannan?

The assistant pointed to the blouse and skirt. 'Take off.'

Indu hesitated. 'What are you looking for?' she asked, smiling at the assistant. Smiles had always worked for her. 'I am a student visiting my uncle. He is a doctor at Degalle Estates.'

Indu knew the D word was often given God-like veneration. A little sob was trying to escape, but Indu swallowed it.

The two women waited mulishly, there was no response to Indu's overtures, so she removed her blouse, slowly, hook by hook, looking down on the floor.

The assistant patted her back down, hooked a finger under her *rowkah*, and checked for anything in the hem.

'Skirt,' she said, pointing at Indu's midriff.

There was no eye-contact. This is getting mad, Indu thought.

Shards of Sunlight

Someone knocked on the cubicle door at that moment and spoke quickly in Singhalese. A man's voice, gruff, but urgent. The women sighed, looked at each other and didn't look pleased.

What next? Indu thought. She could not guess what they were saying.

The officer pulled the blouse and sari from the hook unceremoniously, crushed them together in her hand, and thrust them at Indu.

'Put on now. Finish.'

Indu got her clothes on, relieved but wondering what was going on. The women unbolted the door and walked out, leaving Indu to find her way back to the concourse from which she had been summoned.

When she came out to Kannan in the Customs Hall, he was red in the face, apoplectic. He was shouting at a gentleman in khaki shorts and shirt.

'Nice way you've got of welcoming a person new to Colombo. A young girl at that. Useless busybodies.'

The man looked subdued, almost scared. 'Mistake,' he said, again and again. 'We are sorry.'

Kannan starting pushing their luggage trolley out without further comment. He didn't say anything till he reached the taxi rank and loaded the cases in.

'They had intelligence apparently that someone was coming from Madras with plenty of gold coins and Indian currency, so they were instructed to search anyone who looked a likely suspect, boarding at Madras. They pick on you. Where are you supposed to be hiding these coins anyway?'

Kannan was in a foul mood by the time he got home.

Shards of Sunlight

Home for him – and now Indu - was a little two-and-a-half bedroom bungalow in Colpetty, in one of the quiet, residential areas of Colombo. A lush pink Oleander was in full bloom in front of the house, on the verge; forever afterwards, when Indu thought back on those Colombo days she would see the image of that glorious tree.

The house couldn't possibly accommodate the kind of existence Indu was used to in Thalassery, with family often dropping in and staying overnight as a matter of right.

The half-room was a box room with a little bathroom, the size of a large wardrobe. So Indu's bag went into the second bedroom, where she shared a bathroom with Kannan and Kamala.

Her room was immaculate. On the neatly made bed there was a bed-spread of thick cotton in splashes of pastel colours. Curtains of the same material hung on the windows and the dressing table had a runner of it too, with an edge of broderie anglaise. Indu put her handbag down in front of the mirror and had a quick peak at herself.

'That was unpleasant, Acha,' she said to the constant presence in her mind. 'But I'm here now.'

Indu knew Kamala had a thing about clean bathrooms and kitchens; she was forever trying to improve the soot-ridden kitchen in Thalassery. That passion for order and cleanliness was evident all round Indu.

She went into the bathroom and washed her face at the sink; she wanted to wash away the horror of those big women frisking her, their palms like spades moving across her defenceless midriff. She wiped her face and neck and shuddered.

Shards of Sunlight

One thing worried Indu: could she really perform sitting down on that toilet seat after using an outside latrine all her life? She pushed that thought away and concentrated on putting away her meagre possessions in the wardrobe. The books went into the floor of the wardrobe as there didn't seem to be any special place for them.

Indu walked through to the living room when she had finished her ablutions. She sat passively, with a deep tiredness inside her, which was more mental than physical. Kamala and Kannan talked to each other in a comfortable murmur; Indu for the moment was content to let the world go by.

For the first time in her life Indu saw at first hand the workings of a marriage. Kamala found a set of clothes for Kannan to change out of and hung it in the bathroom. While he bathed she helped the cook, a middle-aged Singhalese *cokie*, to make string hoppers and coconut chutney for their breakfast.

Kamala called Indu to the dining table and served her and Kannan. She asked him about Devi and Shinnu and made a great fuss over Indu's success in her B.A. Indu, having grown up in a house run by spinsters and a widower, was fascinated to see how Kannan relaxed and the woes of the journey fell away from him.

Soon he was describing the day's events to his wife.

'I mentioned that I was a doctor and worked at Degalle. That seemed to floor them a bit. Then – and this is what I am surmising – I think they found the real culprits. A man and woman. I saw them being taken away by two officers. They looked like newlyweds. Anyway they let us go in the end.'

Shards of Sunlight

'Indu must have been petrified.'

'I didn't know what they were going to do next. Especially when they took me away from Velyachan,' Indu said. 'I couldn't understand a word of what those women were saying. And they were quite brusque.'

'What a way to start life in Ceylon,' Kamala exclaimed. 'You poor thing.'

My father had none of this companionship, Indu pondered, watching the way Kamala calmed Kannan after the unpleasantness at the airport. And he was only thirty when my mother died. He should haver married again, had a proper family. I was all he had, really.

Indu had heard that Kamala and Janu, her own mother, had been friends. Perhaps she could ask Kamala about her mother, but not yet. She wondered whether Mani would come visiting her parents. How long before this house and this country felt familiar?

25

Indu took a week to settle down and shake the sorrows off from leaving her family. Kamala took her out to the market when she went to buy groceries, and to the beach in the evenings when Kannan was about. Kannan lived a peripatetic life, monitoring several groups of labourers in three tea estates. He was often on the road, sometimes for days, turning up unexpectedly at odd times from his journeys.

When a week passed and no one mentioned Mani, Indu enquired; she was eager to see her again. 'Velyammey, when will Mani come?' Kamala did not answer for a moment. She appeared to be thinking.

'She doesn't come that much,' Kamala said finally. 'I don't think Mani likes it here.' Indu heard the sadness in Kamala's voice and didn't probe further.

The next time Kannan turned up he appeared dispirited. He moped around the house and didn't talk. 'Snake bites,' he burst out finally. 'A little boy, only eleven. He died of snakebite today; I couldn't do anything for him. I can't get the workers to stop going to the native snake doctors and coming to me only when it is too late. We lose two or three a year. We have the anti-venom if they come soon enough, but generally, they are in a coma by the time the poor worker or child gets to me. Snakebites and pregnancies and deliveries. The job here is no different from that of Sungei Patani or Penang or even Singapore, in spite of their urban sophistication.' He came to a stop and stared out of the window disconsolately. 'Anyway, I am here

Shards of Sunlight

now for a day or two. Good time to start talking about what you plan to do now that you are here,' he said, turning to Indu.

'What about work permits?' Kamala asked. 'They are fed up here of Indians coming to work and sending money out to India. There are restrictions on who can come or what you can send. I hear they are clamping down on all those unskilled workers from Tamilnadu who come as cooks and gardeners.'

'You unskilled, Indu?' Kannan was teasing her.

'Yes, Velyacha. At most things. What do I know?'

'What you know is the English language; there must be a use for someone who can write as well as you. Anyway, have a look in the Times *Vacancies* and we'll discuss what's on offer.'

Indu enjoyed reading the Times. She found the prose fluid and the content interesting. Sir Kotelawala was Prime Minister, but elections were looming and the feedback from the country was not favourable to a conservative government like Kotelawala's. He was old school, hide-bound, they said, with all those letters after his name, courtesy of the British queen. Bandaranaike was waiting in the wings and the Buddhist monks were becoming more powerful by the day.

Cokey, who seemed to have no other name, would often call Indu into the kitchen to break the eggs for omelettes. She would make the most delicious omelettes with fillings of tomato and cheese and coriander leaves, once the sin of killing the egg was committed by a non-Buddhist.

'She eats omelettes, the hypocrite,' Indu said to Kamala one day.

Shards of Sunlight

Kamala laughed. 'You know, some orthodox Jains walk about with a net across their mouths, so they don't hurt a fly by mistake. Now, *they* are totally vegetarian. Buddhists are not.'

'I don't know any Jains,' Indu said. 'But this cokey here eats fish and meat and chicken.'

'I expect you wouldn't have known any Buddhists till you came to Ceylon.'

'When we went to Kelaniya the other day, I was enchanted with the monastery. All those statues of the Buddha and the monks with saffron robes engaged in prayer. It is really tranquil. So many people worshipping.'

'The women wear white,' Kamala said. 'They bring fruit and flowers for the orphanage that the monks run. Tamils say the fruit is weighed and sold before the end of the day. Still, those monks have to live, don't they?'

'We must go again on *Poya* day. Buddhists celebrate the full moon with prayers and offerings. And of course, Cokey will take the day off.' Kamala smiled.

As Kamala talked she turned the pages of the *Times of Ceylon*.

'Have a look at this, Indu,' she said.

Kamala's spectacles were perched somewhere between her brows and the tip of her nose, but definitely not framing the eyes. Her wispy shoulder length hair was beginning to show grey; as Indu looked at her she felt a sudden surge of affection.

Indu knew no way to express this affection without embarrassing both of them.

'Velyammey, are you trying to get rid of me – so's I am out of your way during the day?'

Shards of Sunlight

'Mmm. I don't know whether this involves leaving the house, but it is worth a try.'

She read it out. 'Wanted: In-house copy editors and content writers for *The Times*. Salary subject to negotiation. May work at home.'

'Doesn't sound like a real job unless you wear a sari, comb your hair and go for the day. Still -'

Indu had taken to wearing the ubiquitous housecoat which women in Colombo seemed to wear late into the day. She knew Kamala did not quite approve. The housecoat, however, brought out the holiday feeling in Indu. The belief that she was here in Colombo only temporarily, she would be going back to Thalassery – and Shinnu and Devi – quite soon.

Kamala looked at Indu indulgently. 'That housecoat won't have to come off. That's why I thought you might like this job.' She was teasing.

'All right, all right. I will change right now. But before that-'

She peered over Kamala's shoulders at the advertisement. 'No harm in trying, I suppose.'

'Go ring them up,' Kamala said.

Indu rang them and someone who said his name was Rajaratne spoke to her.

'They said to go for an interview. He says he is a sub editor in the political section.'

Kamala accompanied her to the offices of the *Times* in the *Fort*. 'Can't park here.' Kamala appeared more agitated than Indu. 'I'll go to *Pettah* and come back in an hour. Might even find that bit of casement I need for the kitchen. Look out for me. Good luck,' she added as an afterthought.

Shards of Sunlight

Indu felt a bit adrift, but she drew her sari-fall across her shoulders and walked in. The receptionist was expecting her. Her and twenty-two others, it turned out, as she was shown to the waiting room. She sat down in one of the plastic chairs without meeting anyone's gaze.

If this crowd were all looking for one vacancy, Indu did not fancy her chances. She didn't have anyone to recommend her either.

A gentleman walked into the room purposefully a few minutes later. He distributed some printed sheets and red pencils to each of the candidates. Indu had a good look at him as he was going from chair to chair.

He was tall and self-assured. Dark brown cotton trousers with a white shirt tucked in and long sleeves. The tie was indigo blue and brown with swirls of cream on it. That print would look nice on a sari, she thought.

'I want you to proof-read this for me. It should come out perfect to go straight into the press. Don't try to improve the manuscript, change words or phrases. That's for the editors to do. I am going to time you all,' he added. 'So, the moment you finish, bring your pages to me. And one other thing – speed is no good if you have to do it all over again because of the errors you have failed to spot.'

He looked at his watch and waited a few minutes until it reached a good place, it seemed.

'All right. 4.15 now,' he said. 'Start. I am in that room right across. My name is on it. Kantha Mahasinghe.'

This is a funny kind of race, Indu thought. She tried to shut the rest of the room out as she concentrated on the words on the page. It was a news item about an overseas trip being made by a cabinet minister. Indu

Shards of Sunlight

tried to forget the content and focus on the words. But the purist in her kept seeing the phrases that were not appropriate, the clichés and the weak words. Not your business, she told herself, trying to focus on the syntax and the spelling only.

The errors were many; someone had gone to town on this to make the document as rough as possible. Indu corrected errors of spelling, of punctuation and grammar. After what seemed like a good half-hour, she looked up: every head in the room was bent over the manuscript. Was she rushing through this?

Indu knew she read fast; she had done so much of it from early childhood. But she didn't want to mess this up, speed-reading. She thought for a moment, then got up and walked through the door to the room opposite, where the board said: Sub Editor, Political.

Indu hesitated; should she have gone over it again? No. Three pages should not take so long. What were the others doing? Did they know something she didn't?

She decided she had been quite careful, knocked and went in.

Mahasinghe looked at his watch. 'Thirteen minutes,' he said. 'That was quick. Hope that doesn't mean-'

Indu did not say anything.

'You may go and join the others now,' he instructed, so Indu went back to the roomful of readers still hard at scrutinising the three pages they had in front of them.

Slowly the others finished and when all were done, Mahasinghe appeared again.

Shards of Sunlight

'We are going to check this and see who we can use. Good luck to all of you. We'll call you when we are ready.'

A bit of an anti-climax, Indu decided, after all the excitement. She was waiting at the entrance to the office when Kamala's taxi drew up.

'How was it?' Kamala asked.

'Don't know, Velyammey. They'll let us know soon, they said.'

'Surely you must have an instinct - '

Indu explained the test to Kamala. 'I finished first, but that does not mean I got all the mistakes. I hope - '

'Now we go home and forget all about this,' Kamala said, brushing aside Indu's concerns.

The next afternoon, Kamala was taking a quick siesta and Indu was writing to Shinnu
when the phone rang.

'May I speak to Indu Gopalan? It's the Times.'
Indu's heart started beating madly. 'That's me,' she said.

'Could you come in tomorrow morning? Our Chief Editor, Samaraweere, wants to see you. Eleven all right for you?'

'I'll be there.

The man did not commit himself, but surely, they called her because they wanted to employ her. Why else would they? Except of course to reject her, but why bother then?

Indu rushed into Kamala's room. 'The Times just called me and-'

'Yes?'

Shards of Sunlight

'They asked me to go back tomorrow morning to meet the Chief Editor.'

Indu barely slept that night; a coiled spring waited to spring in her chest. She turned and twisted trying to subdue that coil, but eventually gave in and climbed out of bed at the unholy hour of four in the morning.

She went through her wardrobe to the sounds of cokie stirring and washing pans in the kitchen. She dumped the contents of her handbag on the bed and checked for unknown things, jittery and unable to settle down to anything.

She was dressed and ready by ten, long before she needed to be for the fifteen minute ride into town. She kept going to the bathroom and looking in the mirror.

'How long are you going to keep this up?' Kamala asked. 'Your nose hasn't changed shape since the last time you looked, has it?'

Eventually the taxi was at the door and it was time to go. Kamala tugged Indu's blouse down from the back and fixed a stray hair. She gave her a hug.

'I can't see anyone not wanting to employ you,' she said.

When Indu was dropped off at the Times, she walked in with a great deal more confidence than the previous day. She was going to meet the Chief Editor.

The receptionist did not keep her waiting for long. This time she was taken to the second floor to be met by the Personal Assistant to the Editor. The PA was a young, immaculate looking Burgher girl of indeterminate age, anything between thirty and forty,

Shards of Sunlight

Indu surmised. She spoke to someone on the inter-com and Indu was buzzed in immediately.

Indu had expected to meet another improved version of Mahasinghe, but this one was a surprise. He was casually dressed in off-white trousers, which hung on a belt under his generous belly. The shirt was all over the place and looked as though he had slept in it. He did not wear a tie and the footwear was Indian sandals, which he got rid off when seated. He stood up when Indu entered, pulled up his trousers, searched for his sandals with his feet, and asked Indu to sit down in the chair opposite. He smiled widely, showing perfect teeth. 'Samaraweere,' he said, putting out a firm hand, given the casual appearance. 'They call me Sam. Mahasinghe says you did the proof in record time: thirteen minutes is quite awesome. Between you, me and the door post, I don't think any of my subs can do it without leaving errors on the product. The question is-' Samaraweere steepled his fingertips and considered Indu carefully over them. 'Tell me a little about yourself.' He suddenly turned tack. 'Education, career ambitions...'

'I am from Kerala,' Indu said. 'My uncle is a doctor for the Degalle Estates. He is my guardian, that's why I am here.'

'Yes, yes – and?'

'I have just passed my B.A, Mathematics Major, with subsidiary English and Malayalam. The English was my favourite bit.' Indu thought for a moment. 'I think I would like to work in an area which utilises my language skills – you could say I have been an eclectic reader. Some might say indiscriminate.'

Shards of Sunlight

She smiled tentatively. 'On the something-to-read-is better-than-nothing principle. That explains the speed,' she added and came to a full stop.

'I'd like to see how you write, Miss Gopalan.'

'Indu,' she prompted.

'Right, Indu.' Samaraweere became businesslike.

'I need to see some of your writing. Please read this book .' He picked up a new-looking paperback from the table and handed it to Indu.

The Order of Things by Gamini Gunaratne.

'I'd like you to do a review. About five hundred words, no more.' He pondered a moment. 'Try to capture the style, the language, the theme. The probable reader experience. Friday all right? Or is it too soon?'

Indu fingered the book – riffled the pages. Comparatively small book, about two hundred pages.

'Friday is fine,' she said.

Samaraweere didn't mention anything about the vacancy Indu had applied for. Was this part of the same selection?

He was standing up, dismissing her, picking up his phone to talk to someone. Indu walked to the door, opened it and hesitated. The editor held up his hand in farewell; the opportunity was lost.

The PA was at her desk. Perfectly groomed, to compensate for the editor? She was carefully adjusting her silk scarf when she looked up and saw Indu. The telephone rang at that moment and the PA signalled for Indu to wait. After a quick conversation, she put the receiver down.

'I am to make an appointment for you to see Mr Sam on Friday. Around now all right? And- oh, my

Shards of Sunlight

name is Janice. Janice Shockman.' She measured out a smile,

'Yes. Friday.' Indu looked at her watch. '12.30 now, so I'll come in at 12.30?'

'With your material, he says. The bit that he's asked you to write. Also your degree certificate.'

'Will bring,' Indu answered, as she walked out.

No sign of the immaculate Mahasinghe, she thought.

The afternoon sun hit Indu's face as she stepped out of the heavy wooden door at the exit. She squinted into the light, all the time wondering what that morning's events meant. The roar of the traffic on the road in front of her formed a suitable background to her clamorous thoughts. Clearly Sam was testing her writing skills – but for what? Would they give her a job as a reporter? Writer? What an achievement that would be.

Kamala drew up in her taxi while Indu was waiting.

'C'mon, hop in. Can't stop here.' She shifted some parcels lying on the seat towards herself to make room for Indu.

Indu put her right leg in and collapsed on to the low-slung seat.

'So?' Kamala asked. Did you get the job?'

'I wish I knew, Velyamma. Today I met the big man. Chief Editor, they said. Guy called Samaraweere, call-me-Sam. He wants me to review a book.'

'Mmm. Maybe he wants you to do copy. Write stuff. But that's not the job they advertised, is it?'

'I'm supposed to do five hundred words, that's about three pages in my exercise book, I think. And see him on Friday morning.'

Shards of Sunlight

'They've gone to a lot of trouble, calling you back. They *must* have something in mind for you. Anyway, I decided you need some new clothes for the office, so I bought you two saris.'

'Office? Velyamma. I don't have a job yet.' Indu laughed.

'You will, very soon. I'm sure.'

As soon as she got home, Indu opened the parcels. 'Saris; I don't think I've ever seen anything this pretty in Thalassery. Thank you, Velyamma.'

The silk was soft and light as she unfurled the one on top. It was peacock blue with a paisley mango design. *The pallau* was made up of huge mangoes in rust and red.

Indu gasped. 'This is beautiful. Much too good for office. I think you were looking for an excuse to buy me clothes,' she added with a smile.

'Well, Mani hardly ever wears saris these days; it's all skirts and dresses. I'm glad you are still wearing a sari.'

'She looked really smart, the last time we saw her in Thalassery.' Indu remembered the last time she had seen Mani. 'I miss her, Velyamma, sometimes.'

'I miss her – all the time. But she wants to work in Bombay. And when she comes here, she is in a hurry to go back. She hardly talks to me.'

In Kamala's face, Indu saw a sadness she lived with. If only Mani would come for a holiday; Kamala did not deserve this unhappiness.

26

Indu tried to keep her restlessness at bay and picked up an old favourite, *The Oxford Book of Sonnets*, but couldn't immerse herself in the verses. She fetched old editions of the Ceylon Times from Kamala's waste bin, where they awaited the monthly cull for the paper-and-old-bottles-man. She spread them out on the floor, generating a damp-paper smell in the dining room.

Indu read the old book reviews and waited for her book-instinct to kick in, noting the gaps in the review or the bias in the narrative. When she felt her critical faculties up and running, she picked up her book, a pencil and paper, and started making notes. Soon she was in full working mode, all those years of intellectual cut and thrustwith her father providing the processes.

'Velyammey, how do I know my work is good enough?' she fretted, as she turned the pages.

Kamala did not need to be told what work this was – the conversation these last few days were about the article to be written. 'When you've done the best you can. And, the main thing is, don't get distracted. Read through once without stop, I'd say and go back and read, looking for all the things you would expect in a review.'

She stood up. 'Stop acting like a baby, Indu. You've got a life-time of books inside you. Nobody needs to tell you anything.'

Shards of Sunlight

'Ye-e-s,' Indu said, not very confidently. Indu had a reputation for getting lost in books, coming out at the other end without remembering very much.

Kamala relented. She went across to Indu and touched her cheek lightly. 'That Sam person. He'll be lucky to have you.'

In the event, Sam took exactly ten minutes to read Indu's review and make a decision.

'I see what Mahasinghe meant,' he said when he finished. 'I have already discussed this with the board. We think you are too skilled to be wasted in the proof room. What we thought was – if you agree – we could start you with Mahasinghe on the write-ups for the political section, and take it from there. We call him Kantha, by the way. That's his first name. Mind you,' he added. 'It will be a lot of donkey work, with a bit of writing thrown in, you'll find out. Janice, my P A will get you an identity card. Could you start a week from now? There's a lot going on now and Kantha needs a helping hand. Welcome to the clan. We'll send you a contract showing pay and so on – it will be better than the proof's. So I guess you will be happy.'

When Indu staggered out, dazed with the speed at which it had all happened, the PA was talking on the phone. She put the phone down and smiled at Indu, all frostiness gone. 'You'll be all right here – Kantha will work you to death and back, but he is a loyal man. He'll take care of you.'

The Times got to work early and stayed late. When a political fracas was on, late merged into early the next day and Kamala got used to having Indu turn up ragged at breakfast time. Kannan, when he was around,

Shards of Sunlight

grumbled, saying respectable Indian girls should not be working late with men; what's the world coming to?

Indu laughed his concerns off. 'I'm not the only girl, Velyacha, and everybody is too busy to notice whether you are male or female.'

As the months passed Indu became familiar with the local scene, learned a smattering of Singhalese and became part of the office. She had a long way to go but she had friends, liked what she did every day and knew that if she stayed with this work, she could become very good at it.

As she honed her writing skills, Indu was given short assignments to report on events in Colombo. She attended some of the meetings organised by the Tamil federalists. She learned Speedwriting of a very personal kind, inventing symbols for oft-used sounds as she went along, and taught herself to listen and remember events and statements.

Three years passed in accelerated motion. Indu wrote to Mani every month, but never got more than a postcard in return. They came from all over the world, but she seemed to live in Bombay. She came to Ceylon rarely and did not stay longer than a week when she did.

On one such lightning visit, Indu accosted her.

'Velyamma waits for you to come and when you do, nothing is quite enough, but you never stay long, do you?'

'I guess I don't,' Mani said.

Mani was standing in front of the mirror on the door of the wardrobe in Indu's room, pulling up a very tight pair of jeans. She went close and looked at a blackhead on her chin and scratched at it.

Shards of Sunlight

Mani had become a tall girl, fair and elegant. She didn't wear any make-up, but washed her hair daily and took great pains to keep it shining. It was shoulder-length now and she wore it loose except on the very rare occasions that she wore a sari. Indu also knew that she had a packet of *Charminar* cigarettes and a lighter in her handbag and smoked behind the house when Kamala was not about.

Indu persisted with her line of enquiry. 'Is it that you don't get leave or something?'

'No-o.' She turned and sat down on Indu's bed.

'Well?' Indu said.

'The "little one" has grown big and is asking *big* questions now.' She pulled Indu down to the bed, to sit next to her. 'My mother and my father – they were really not there when I was growing up, remember? They came and went, and during the war, I didn't see them for six years. I don't think I have to pretend now.'

'Pretend what?'

'That I love them. I don't mind them; they are okay I expect, but I don't know them well. And listen, Indu. When I left Thalassery I went from one boarding school to another for seven years. What kind of parenting was that?'

'Kamala is sad, Mani. Don't be so harsh towards her.'

'Indu, she could have stayed behind sometimes when my father went chasing the next rainbow. I pleaded with her. But she went after my father, leaving me here and there like lost luggage. They didn't seem to want me to be with them. You know what? The only parents I ever had were your Achan and Devi and Shinnu. They are my real family. I see them regularly and I send them money. That's enough.'

Shards of Sunlight

There was no answer to any of this.

Kannan was an intermittent presence in Indu's life as he came and went from the tea estates. Indu and Kamala were company for each other and a strong bond of affection and respect grew between the two women. Life held few surprises, but Indu was happy with that.

Every year Indu went back to Thalassery for the *Onam* festival, with clothes and money for Shinnu and Devi. The first time was in the September of 1956.

'You've brought light back to our lives,' Devi said. 'Once again there is laughter and singing in this house.'

'You mean *you've* stopped singing all those devotional slogans,' Indu teased. 'I'm relying on you to keep the deities happy for me.'

Shinnu went into a cooking frenzy. She made *vadas* and *bondas* and the *undas* that Indu loved so much.

'You're spending all your time in the kitchen, Shinnuedathy. Come and talk to me. Tell me about the neighbours and all the gossip here.'

Shinnu went on cooking. She fried dry rice in a wok till it turned golden and pounded it in the mortar. She sifted it and added scraped coconut, jaggery and two pods of cardamom. Then she mixed everything into a soft dough using the mortar and pestle. After that Shinnu put some coconut oil on her palms and rolled the mixture into ping-pong sized balls for Indu's tea.

'Your *unda* is food-heaven, Shinnu,' Indu said.

'What does Kamala make?' Shinnu asked.

'She does a lot of fancy cooking too, but not these country delicacies that I like.'

Shards of Sunlight

Indu had brought georgette saris for Shinnu from Colombo. She draped them on Shinnu and pestered her till she sat down so that Indu could plait her hair and put it up. She fetched Narayani blossoms from the fence and made it into garlands for Shinnu's hair. 'You look pretty like a bride,' Indu said.

'That's one thing I have to think about, Indu,' Devi said. 'Must get this girl married before I die. I'll have to get hold of middle-men from Kodiyeri to find a husband for her.'

Shinnu grimaced but kept quiet.

'So long as you don't ask that Ramunni,' Indu said.

Indu stayed for a month and returned to Colombo with renewed self-belief. She knew she was some way towards taking charge of her life. She also realised that that little town, Thalassery, was the one place on earth where she was at home however far she strayed.

'Something going on in Kelaniya, people gathering.' Kantha phoned Indu early one morning in the middle of a cold but glorious February day in 1958. 'Please be ready to go there around three in the afternoon.'

'What was that?' Kamala asked as Indu came off the phone.

'An assignment in Kelaniya.'

Kelaniya was only a half hour away by car, so Kamala did not dwell on it.

By the time Indu got to the office, the urgency levels had risen to emergency. The team for Kelaniya got into the Times field vehicle, a clapped-out Austin 35 and sped off. Kantha sat in front with the driver, Girithelis, and the cameraman and Indu were in the

Shards of Sunlight

back. Every one was anxious as they drove in silence. Disturbance was a euphemism for what happened in Colombo when the Singhalese mob decided to go on a rampage. And the Buddhist monks had been getting a bad name for inciting violence against the Tamils. They were becoming politically powerful. Kelaniya's famous Buddhist monastery made no excuses for dabbling in politics.

The rumours had been of a meeting that had become unruly, a brawl, a riot and everything in between. The team was not prepared for the scene that met their eyes when they reached it.

'Trouble,' Kantha said under his breath.

'Oh my God!' Indu gasped as she took in the woman sprawled untidily in the middle of the road; two men bent over her trying to gather her and her screaming three-year-old, out of the way of oncoming traffic.

A group of young men wielding sticks were running away from the scene and several other men and women of all ages were disappearing into the side-roads, dragging children with them. Men called to each other in Tamil, Sinhalese and English and women wailed.

Indu jumped out of the car a moment before it came to a standstill. All she could think of was that child.

'No,' shouted the cameraman. 'No. Stay inside the car.'

Kantha tumbled out too and chased after Indu. He caught her arm, trying to restrain her. 'You don't look Singhalese with that *pottu* on your forehead. Take that pottu off.'

Shards of Sunlight

A small group of young men, in colourful lungis folded half-way to their knees, were chasing after some people who had been selling vegetables on the side of the road. Torn up cabbages and cucumbers were rolling across the road and the debris was splashed red with trampled down tomatoes. There was a pervasive stink of mud mixed with raw and rotting fruit. A fishmonger put his stinking basket down on the ground and joined the shouting men.

Indu didn't understand what anyone was saying. But there was no time to think.

'That's a Singhalese crowd,' Kantha said, holding on to Indu's arm. 'They are looking for Tamils to attack.'

Indu shook him off, but she wiped the magenta pottu on her forehead off with her sari end. 'I'm not Tamil,' she said.

'Don't say anything,' Kantha whispered urgently. 'And slow down. They often think all South Indians are Tamils.'

The ambulance arrived then and a man and a woman jumped out of the van and gathered round the mother. They pushed through the men around the prone woman and started attending to her. The child was now outside this circle of nurses and wailed louder.

Indu heard nothing but that keening child; it had stopped screaming now and was sobbing in, despair. As she got closer, she could see it was a little girl with a large black pottu on her forehead. It had smeared over her eyelid as she cried and rubbed her face with wet hands.

Indu touched her arm and picked her up gently. She talked softly to the little one in Malayalam.

Shards of Sunlight

'Hush,' Kantha said, seizing her arm again. 'You sound like a Tamil.'

. Kantha started talking to Indu loudly in Singhalese, as though he was describing the scene to her. Indu heard nothing. She carried the child slowly, with infinite care, and put her in the waiting ambulance, where her mother had already been placed. The child started sucking her thumb and fingering her mother's hair; she seemed less traumatised.

Kantha accompanied her, spoke rapidly in Singhalese to the driver, and the van moved off.

When the ambulance disappeared round the next bend in the road, Indu woke up to her surroundings. Kantha was still holding her arm; Indu looked at him and slowly and disengaged her arm. She looked down at her sari and noticed the mud and grime and the damp patch on her shoulders from the crying infant.

'Malayalam is a lot like Tamil,' she said inconsequentially. She began to go cold and started trembling; a moment later she tilted and fell slowly backwards; Kantha caught her just in time and staggered to the waiting car almost dragging her with him.

The unruly mob was looking for more excitement. A section of the crowd surrounded a small black, driverless car; the owner had abandoned the car and escaped. The men rocked the vehicle so violently it was in danger of overturning. Eventually one young man ran away and came back with a beer bottle full of petrol and threw it at the car. The men engaged in rocking the car stopped for a moment and gave instructions to the boy.

'Pour it. All over. What are you waiting for?'

Shards of Sunlight

'Here. Give it to me. An older man snatched the petrol and sprayed it from bonnet to boot, holding his finger on the opening to produce a jet. 'That's it,' he said.

He moved away and took a matchbox out of his shirt pocket. 'Keep away.'

The crowd moved away and burst into *jathas*, the Singhalese hymns, as the man tossed a lighted match on to the bonnet. There was a loud explosion and a series of crackles and splutters. Then a steady flame enveloped the top.

Now the acrid smell of burning petrol and hot metal joined incongruously with that of mud, fish and bananas and every one moved to a safe distance on the side of the road. They watched for a few minutes and wandered off in various directions.

The cameraman was clicking away until the crowd dispersed. 'All in the name of Buddha, the man who preached *Ahimsa*,' he said in disgust as he finished shooting and got back in the car. Indu had recovered enough to open her eyes and register the chaos. She was shivering with shock and shuddered in Kantha's arms.

'Must get her home quickly,' Kantha said, as the driver started the car and turned it around.

'I'm better,' Indu said to no one in particular.

'Next time you come on an assignment you listen to me, all of you. And you,' He turned to Indu, 'Leave the compassion to someone else. You are there to get the news, not play Mother Theresa.'

Indu was too weak with shock to answer. Her eyes welled up and a little sob, like a hiccup escaped her. Kantha was in the back with her. He put her head back on his shoulder when she tried to struggle up. His hand on her face was gentle as though she was a child,

Shards of Sunlight

the pressure just enough to keep her there. He smelled of fabric starch and lemony cologne.

'You gave me a bloody fright – wading into those butchers.' Kantha's trousers, immaculately creased in the morning, were now crumpled and dirty from carrying Indu; his shirt was hanging out at the back. He uncuffed his sleeves, rolled them up and dusted his knees. Then he turned to Indu and settled her snugly against his shoulder again. His careful touch belied the anger in his tone.

'Rest now,' he said, to Indu. 'We'll get you home. You need some hot, sweet tea and your mother.'

Indu didn't bother to tell him it was her aunt at home. And it felt comfortable where she was. She closed her eyes again.

When Indu turned up for work the next day, she swept the papers on her desk away and started on her story about the riots. The words flowed without effort and she had written a page of it when Kantha walked into her cubicle, clipboard in hand. 'How are you feeling today?' he asked.

'All right.'

He went round the desk and had a look at what she was writing. 'That story has been done,' he said. 'I wasn't sure you'd be in today.'

'What? Who wrote my story? What d'you think *I* am meant to do?'

'I didn't think you'd come in today; you looked ill. I had to write it myself; it couldn't wait.'

Indu knew she saw little of the events the previous day focussed as she had been on the infant. She wondered whether he had come to tell her off about that. She kept her face bland.

Shards of Sunlight

He stood in front of her, turning his attention to the clip board. Was he going to sack her?

'Sorry about yesterday,' she said finally. 'I didn't focus on the job. You've said so many times-'

'Van langenburg got a great picture – of you carrying that infant to the ambulance. It's on our front page today.'

He hurried off and came back with a copy of the paper.

'There,' he pointed.

Her face was bent over the child and the little girl nestled in her left arm, wide eyed, apprehensive.

Indu looked at the picture carefully. The caption said *Times journalist rescuing a little girl at the riot scene in Kelaniya*. She considered herself quite unphotogenic but she looked almost pretty in the snapshot.

'He's touched it up to make me look nice,' Indu said.

'You don't need touching up,' Kantha said.

Indu burst out laughing and Kantha's face flushed a deep mahogany.

27

Indu did not see Kantha for about for two days. He was covering a story in Batticoloa somewhere in a tea estate. On Friday morning he walked into Indu's office, beaming.

'That was a great trip. It's heaven up there in those estates. We Colombo lot don't know how lovely it is in the hills. Miles and miles of green tea bushes and gardens nearer the owners' houses, laid out with Hibiscus and Canna and Bougainvillea…' He was glowing with joie de 'vivre.

'I've never been up country, but my uncle is always talking about how lovely it is.'

'Next time a team goes out there you should come with us.'

'So what was happening there?'

'Labour dispute. The problem is the labourers are mainly Tamils, though not all, and the owners are Singhalese. So there is an element of race to make matters dire. These guys are second or third generation – hardly migrants.'

Kantha walked to the map of Ceylon blu-tacked to the wooden partition of the cubicle and pointed to the Batticoloa area with his finger.

'Here,' he said. 'Way things are here, Indu, it's all going to blow up in our faces one of these days.'

Kantha fiddled with his clipboard, as though he was looking for inspiration in it.

Shards of Sunlight

'Never mind,' he said and turned. Took a few steps. Stopped again. H seemed to have some unfinished business in the room.

'Never mind what?' Indu persisted. She was so relieved he hadn't sacked her, she had become forward.

'I was wondering,' he said. 'I have got my father's family visiting at home. Lots of squabbling children and ayahs and confusion. So I thought I'd go see a picture today. Care to come along?' Kantha made it sound very take-it-or-leave-it.

A warm glow of happiness spread inside her and she smiled. 'What's showing?' she asked.

'*Roman Holiday*. Meant to be good. But not much fun on my own.'

'I'll tell my aunt I'll be late,' Indu said. 'My uncle's home; she won't mind an evening without me hovering about.'

When the working day was over in the evening, Indu went to the ladies' room and looked at herself in the mirror. Inside one of the cubicles, Soma, a colleague, started talking to her.

'You walking to the bus stop with me? I need to get some lentils for my mother.'

'Can't. I am off to a film today.'

Soma came out to where Indu was washing her face and wiping it with her sari end.

'Here,' Soma took a tissue out of her hand bag and passed it to Indu. 'If you are going out, don't ruin your sari.'

'It's only Kantha. He wants company, he says. For the show.'

'I bet!' Soma said, grinning at Indu's face in the mirror. 'We've been taking bets as to when he'll get round to asking you. He's got a crush on you and you

Shards of Sunlight

don't notice. Serves him right for all the girls he has ignored in the office.'

'You lot have nothing to talk about,' Indu parried. 'So you pair people off. I don't think Kantha fancies anybody.'

'We'll see,' said Soma with assurance.

In the event, the film proved quite engrossing.

Kantha bought devilled peanuts in paper cones and they munched their way through the entire holiday in which Audrey Hepburn went AWOL with Gregory Peck.

'Loved that film. Didn't like the ending, though,' Indu said firmly, with an image in her mind of the press line-up. 'Greeting her as though she was just another princess, not a woman he had spent a glorious weekend with.'

They were walking down the plush red-carpeted stairway of Elphinstone Theatre, Indu trailing her hand on the smooth banisters.

'You're incurable romantics, you girls.'

Progress down the stairs was painfully slow with the people in front trying to get down to the milling crowd in the foyer, getting their bearings in the harsh lights, and mustering children.

'And I suppose you guys are so immune. Wait till it hits you and you go chasing after that special girl.' Indu looked up at Kantha, taunting.

'How do you know I don't have a special girl now?'

He was teasing, an infuriating secret smile on his face.

'Well – you wouldn't go to a film with me for one thing. She'd strangle you.'

Shards of Sunlight
Kantha's answer was to pick up her hand. 'Don't want you getting lost in the crowd,' he said.

Colombo was still buzzing at 9.30 when Indu and Kantha came out of the theatre, blinking in the neon lights of the lobby.

'Could grab a quick bite,' he suggested.

'Postponing going home, are you?'

Kantha smiled sheepishly and they walked in the direction of Maradana. The *Buhari Hotel* was in full swing, crowds of diners walking in and out through the narrow doors, ordering take-aways at the counter, seeking tables or private dining rooms upstairs. The smell of Biriyani and hot ghee wafted into the reception area as Kantha ordered two *kiribaths* at the counter to take away. The rice when it came was wrapped in banana leaves and newspaper and hot to the touch.

Indu had never seen this part of Colombo and its unbelievable vibrancy at this time of the night. People and taxis rushed past to Fort and Pettah stations nearby and buses sailed majestically on the road surrounding the bus stand.

'The transport hub of Colombo,' Kantha said. 'Isn't it amazing? But now I want to show you something special.'

They walked back to the car and Kantha started up the engine as she climbed into the passenger seat. He drove slowly out of Maradana and on to the Galle Face, and parked on the roadside. They collected their *kiribath* and walked to the edge of the ocean. There they sat on a cement seat and opened their food parcels.

The yellow rice was rich with coconut milk and spices, and the sharp tang of cloves hit the back of Indu's palate, followed by the soothing cream of the

Shards of Sunlight

coconut. She had never eaten this rice before and fell to it with enthusiasm.

'Try the *lunumiris*' Kantha suggested, pointing in the direction of a dark, chilli- coloured pickle on the side.

Indu tasted it gingerly. 'Hot,' she said, and wished there was water to ease its path.

Kantha seemed immune to the stuff. 'Should have got some lemonade,' he said, laughing. 'You look as though your mouth is on fire.'

Indu opened her mouth and panted trying to get some cool sea breeze into her mouth. 'Do you eat this a lot?' she asked between gasps.

'Not really. It's special occasions food. Though the *miris* often comes with the *string hoppers* for breakfast. The kiribath is too rich for every day. You'll get used to it.'

'We do something similar in Thalassery – to go with *idiappam*. Kamala makes it often with stew.'

'Is that where you come from? Thalassery? Is it near Madras?

'It's a little town on the Arabian sea coast, nowhere near Madras. We're on the west coast and Madras is the other side. Thalassery is tiny, quiet, not much really, but everyone knows everyone else on the street.' Indu explained with patience. 'We speak Malayalam and listen to film music on Radio Ceylon- it's called, *Binaca Geethmala*- in the evenings.' She turned to Kantha and laughed.

'We have one college – where I went - and a few secondary schools. Not much, you would think, but most every one can read and write.'

'I have heard of the Kerala passion for learning.'

230

Shards of Sunlight

'But the streets are not clean like here. The public places in Kerala can be filthy.'

'D'you miss it then?'

'I miss my family, my cousin Shinnu and my aunt Devi.' And I keep my father in my heart all the time, she added in her mind.

'Don't you have brothers and sisters then? I have two – a brother and a sister. All married and gone.'

'No one. I did have Mani, uncle's daughter. As near to a sister as can be. But she went away too.'

'Is that why you read a lot? Being alone?'

That's my father, he was –' Indu stopped.

'I'm sorry, I know.'

Indu looked far away into the distance, where all she could see were the lights of the Galle Face Hotel, shimmering at the far end. She heard the intermittent, background sounds of the waves as they rolled in and out and smelled the familiar salty smell of the sea, a mixture of wet sea weed, rotting debris and broken-up shells, but all she was seeing was another sea, a beach without lights in a little town on the edge of the ocean. Where the night sky was jet blue and the stars were strung out like *Deepavali diyas*.

Indu was silent for a while and she was glad Kantha let her be.

Eventually she shook herself awake from her reverie. 'Sometimes I don't know why my circumstances seem so different from every one else's.'

'That's not so bad, is it?' Kantha asked gently. 'I think we all have things in our lives, which seem out of the ordinary. Those things make us unique. Time to get you home, or your aunt will be worrying.'

Shards of Sunlight

Kantha picked up the paper and banana leaves as he spoke and carried them to the car. He put them on the back seat and started up.

He drove to Colpetty, humming under his breath. 'Good night,' he said as he dropped her off at her front door. 'That was fun. Must do it again.'

Indu walked to the front door and turned back briefly as she reached it. She saw Kantha waiting; she waved and went inside.

Indu was now in her fourth year at the office and she did more assignments in the field, covering local meetings and events. Kantha was occasionally part of the team, but mostly it was the camera crew with her.

She loved walking into the office of a morning, when staff in the outer office were removing covers from the sleeping typewriters and the place still smelled of phenol and Vim from the cleaning crew. The floors shone with Cardinal polish and wax, the women in saris lifted their hems up when they walked in. She had a sense of ownership of her own little domain – the wooden cubicle with the swing door, the old, chipped cup with the pens and pencils, her ruled notepad and the little fern she was nurturing on the window sill. Kantha walked in frequently in as she was starting to write and her heart would lift, a slow smile lighting up her face.

He brought his list of assignments and his mug of tea in his hand. He gave her her tasks and then went to the window and looked out for a minute or two before wandering off. Indu knew that once again there was one person in the world, all hers, like her father had been, though nothing had been said between them.

Some mornings, he brought her a cup of tea, sat down, and discussed work: length of features, write-ups

Shards of Sunlight

of events and where what might go. He brought snap shots in and pored over them with her, asking her opinion of which was most striking or appropriate. She liked that, their heads close together, the smell of his cologne.

Indu felt accepted in the office, as the girls came in to chat while she worked, or some one asked her to go out to the Victoria Café to grab a quick sandwich at lunch time. Kantha did not join the crowd.

'You going out with the gang?' he would ask her. 'That Victoria Café. The sandwiches are like rubber. Let's go some place else.'

The girls made sly remarks. However, they conceded that, in some odd way, Kantha was 'taken.'

'Wants you all to himself, does he?'

Indu learned to grin and let the small talk float past her. But, in some subtle way she knew she was claiming Kantha. What was the nature of that claiming? she wondered, but didn't delve in her mind for details, content in the camaraderie.

In May that year the Times decided to run a feature on indigenous birds and the team went to Nuwara Elia as there was a bird sanctuary near by. Indu's work was to sift the material and do short write-ups on the hoof, to be ready for final editing when they got back on Thursday. She was apprehensive as she knew little about the locality or the Ceylon birds. They lived in the local guest house up on the hills. It was bitterly cold and the men had brought a crate of beer with them. To 'warm us up' they said. In addition to Indu, two women accompanied the group: Madhuri, an authority on birds, and Kanchana, who was born in Nuwara Elia and knew the habitat well.

Shards of Sunlight

Gautham, a young Singhalese boy, took it upon himself to organise the evening's merriment. He opened up the century old piano in the chintzy sitting room and fiddled with the chords. He poked inside the belly of the monster, trying to tune some of the errant notes and was soon producing recognisable music.

Catch a falling star and put it in your pocket and ...' he sang in a surprisingly pleasing tenor. He also set up the drinks.

If Gautham had not had that one Becks too many to drink, if Kantha had not started doing the *Byela*, if Madhuri had not dragged Kantha off to the middle of that long wrap-around veranda... Indu sat in the shadows looking out on the terraced hills as her colleagues sang and danced; life seemed complete, fulfilled, totally tranquil. Until Gautham coaxed her on to the floor a little unsteadily and started a very personal byela of his own. Drunk, he was if anything more graceful than ever, abandoning himself to the music, trying to get Indu to move to his rhythm. Suddenly, there was Kantha at her shoulder.

Indu had never danced any kind of dance, leave alone that very Singhalese expression of the joy of living.

'My turn now,' he said, moving in between them.

'Didn't know you could dance,' Gautham taunted. Kantha ignored him.

'*I* can't dance, anyway,' Indu said, irritated that she was in the middle of some private quarrel.

She walked back to her chair and plonked herself down. Life had been good until the men started acting up.

Shards of Sunlight

A little later, the music and laughter in full flow, Indu slipped away to find her room, which she was to share with Madhuri. She went in the general direction of the bedrooms, but in the long, dark corridor she was lost. Her room had a white sticker with a big three on it, but she saw 1 and 4, but not 3. It was there Kantha found her after a few minutes, frustrated and edgy.

'There you are,' he said. 'You were gone, suddenly. 'I'm sorry about me and Gautham, it's nothing to do with you. He can be a little rough with a girl sometimes.'

'I would have found out soon enough,' Indu said wearily. 'Can't find my room – number 3.'

Kantha walked up and down the corridors and found the room tucked away on the other side of the bathroom. He walked her there and stood, undecided.

'What's the matter?' he asked. 'Something's upset you. Did I – or Gautham – say something? We're all a bit drunk.'

'Not you. It's me. Wonder why, but I feel alien today,' she said, a little bewildered. 'All you guys entertaining yourself in your way – I find myself totally out of it. The music, the dancing, the small-talk – they are all so new to me.'

'You're just tired. You keep us, me, sane.'

He opened the door and let her in, touched the top of her head in benediction. 'We need you. *I* need you.'

'Thanks,' she called out as he walked away but he didn't respond.

The next morning the gang assembled for a breakfast of *aapams* and potato stew, with pineapple and *papaya* to start off. The men were hung-over to various

Shards of Sunlight

degrees, swallowing pills and looking glum. Kantha did not turn up for breakfast.

'Where's the boss?' someone muttered.

No one bothered to answer. They were like children who had misbehaved, waiting for a parent to come in and tell them off.

Indu relished the *appams*, biting into the lacy, crisp surround before breaking into the soft, semi-sweet interior, which smelled of yeast and toddy.

She had had the full Malayalee bath early in the morning, oiling her hair and face before she soaped it off. This was her remedy for when she felt low. Now her damp waist-length hair hung loose behind her. Her face gleamed in the half-light of the hill-country morning, and the bones and planes were thrown into high relief. The wet wisps of black-brown hair had dried on the sides of her face, not pulled back as usual on a work day.

'You disappeared early,' Ashoka said.

Gautham was keeping a low profile, looking down on his plate and pushing his *aapam* about.

Kantha came in then, wiping his hands on a greasy rag. 'The car needed oil and water. And I think there is a problem with the exhaust.' He wandered off in the general direction of the bathrooms.

'Sleep well?' he asked Indu as he passed her.

'Mmm,' she answered, looking up from her plate and catching his eye.

She saw weariness there and uncertainty, as though he did not quite know what to say or do next. She put out her hand as though to comfort him and then withdrew it. He went a few steps, then turned, came back and took her hand.

Shards of Sunlight

His red T-shirt showed grime from the car and his hair was dishevelled, like a little boy out of sleep.

He looked at his hands and hers and smiled.

'Clean up,' he said, as he walked away. 'Come back and have coffee with you.'

By the time Kantha came out, bathed and dressed, the team had wandered off, some on to the veranda for a quick cigarette, others to get their equipment together. He was back to his usual self, cow-licked and elegant.

The long-sleeved grey Van Heusen was well tucked into his jeans, the sleeves rolled up, a minor concession to this world of field work where other norms applied. Madhuri had shed her sari to don trousers and the other men were in shorts.

Kantha sat down opposite Indu and poured himself some coffee. Indu picked up the coffee pot and cupped her palm round it. 'Cold,' she said. She went off briskly to the kitchen and asked the cook to make another pot. When she got back to the table Kantha had not started on his breakfast.

'What's the matter?' she asked.

He appeared pensive. 'Just tired.' He made as if to pick up the cold coffee.

'Hot coffee is coming,' Indu said. 'Don't drink that tepid water.' She got a plate and put an *aapam* and stew on it and placed it in front of Kantha. 'We've all eaten,' she said.

Kantha looked at Indu's face and smiled. 'You looking after me? I'm a little fragile today. That long drive. And the night went on and on. Couldn't get to sleep either.'

Coffee came then and Indu poured. She brushed back the damp wisps of hair on her face.

'A Degas portrait,' Kantha said. '*Girl pouring coffee*. You look absolutely ravishing.'

He concentrated on his breakfast as though he had said too much.

'Thanks,' Indu said quietly. 'Sometimes I need someone to say that.'

'You know I love you,' he said quickly. The words seemed to have escaped unwittingly.

Indu smiled. Words seemed unnecessary.

She went out to the veranda where the team had assembled. The terraced hills glistened as the sun melted the morning mists, and far away, Indu could see traffic on the winding roads coming up the hill.

'Magical place,' she said turning to Madhuri, standing next to the parapet. 'Magical and lonely.'

Kantha came out to the veranda a minute later, looking at his watch. 'Must get started.'

He came up to Indu and brushed a strand of hair back from her face. And Indu wondered why it felt so right to her, a small-town Malayalee girl who never allowed any man to touch her.

28

'D'you like these field trips?' Kamala asked, almost too casually one day as she was laying the table for lunch. 'Lots of people go with you?' Clearly some cautionary bells had started ringing in Kamala's acute brain.

Indu registered the probe. 'Usually it's the whole team. Cameraman; steno, she transcribes the day's reports; driver; boss though not always; one or two others who are in training some times.' Indu came to a full stop. Was she saying too much?

Kamala continued to set the table walking round it as she did so. 'Is it fun?'

'Can be. But there's a lot to do generally. We get tired by the end of the day. We don't get to go out for a meal or anything unless we are staying over the weekend.

Indu got up and walked to the window. Outside, the children were returning from school, swinging satchels and talking to their mothers or ayahs. She listened to the words tumbling out breathlessly, one on top of the other.

'Sarala Miss said you have to make a pointmen.' A little boy of five or six was chattering to his mother. He skipped along to keep pace with his mother.

She stopped and turned to him. 'Pointmen?'

'To see her. You got to come to school.' He put his hand out for his mother.

Shards of Sunlight

'Oh! Appointment.' The mother held his hand and then him, laughing out loud. 'I'll make the *pointmen* tomorrow,' she said.

The woman wore a Kandyan sari with the pallau in a long neat fold over her left shoulder. It slipped sideways when she leaned forward and she pushed it back. Light green material with a blue-and-white border.

Indu looked at the fan-like half-circle on her waist at the back, green, blue and white to match her sari. She wondered whether it took a long time to get it looking so neat and the front so flat and functional. Must try one of those, she thought. They look so elegant.

'You have to have a great figure,' Indu said, turning away from the window towards Kamala.

'For?'

'For the Kandyan sari. They look so good. Actually even the fat ones look good in them.'

'Here, do something useful,' Kamala said. 'You could bring the rice and stew, and oh, get the serving spoons too.' Indu went through to the kitchen, humming an old Malayalam tune.

Kamala turned back to the table with a half-smile and straightened one of the table mats.

The next week Colombo erupted. In Wellawatta, Singhalese mobs carrying sticks and cricket bats burst into two Tamil homes. They pushed the women into the kitchens and locked them in, instructing them to remove all their jewellery and hand it over. After that the rioters systematically looted the houses, removing anything of value: watches, cameras, cash. They beat up the men of the house and drove the Singhalese ayahs

Shards of Sunlight

into the road, shouting at them for working for the enemy.

The incidents were reported in the press, but any suggestion of it being a communal attack was sanitized out of the account. In the papers it was another break-in: rogues out for a quick haul from the rich homes on the seaside.

Kantha walked into Indu's office cubicle early the next morning, before she had put away her handbag and pulled out her chair. He looked agitated.

He drew up a chair and bent forward, whispering. 'It has begun – what all of us feared. The mobs are out to subdue the Tamils. The police insist they were common burglaries. Then why beat up the men? Why throw the ayahs out? No, this is the beginning, but our editors won't let us mention the Tamil - Singhalese factor.'

Indu had heard about the *Mopla* rebellions in Kerala in the 1920s from the old women at home. How the moplas had gone on the rampage, looting, raping, forcibly converting the Hindus into their Muslim faith. The Hindus had been equally brutal in their retaliation and they had the advantage of being the majority. Hundreds had been killed on both sides and the police had been powerless to stop them. The stories had given her nightmares.

Indu stared wide-eyed at Kantha.

'This will get a great deal worse,' he said, 'and I don't think the Government is going to do anything much,' he said.

'You have to be careful, Indu. You are not Singhalese; it is easy to see. These monsters will think you are Tamil. Better you say at home for a week or two until all this blows over.'

Shards of Sunlight

'No-o. I'm sure I'll be alright. There are so many girls working here.'

'Yes – but no Tamils. They are Burgher or Singhalese. There are some older Tamil women, but wait and see. They won't come in tomorrow.'

Kantha was right. The Tamil women did not turn up the next week. In town matters got worse and the papers started reporting them graphically. The looting and beatings increased each day and in some areas the Tamils started forming vigilante groups. In many parts of Colombo, Tamils fled their homes. Makeshift camps arose overnight on the Golf course and in the Royal College grounds. During the day Tamils kept their front doors shuttered and they cowered inside in silence. Indu stopped going to work.

After a week she ventured out one afternoon and walked on the periphery of the golf course. The women toiled at the doors of the tents, washing infants, handing out food to the family. Clothes were hung out to dry on top of the tents, and Indu smelled the all pervasive smell of fear and hopelessness.

Many rich Tamils started the exodus to the United Kingdom and The United States – these were professionals who took with them skills, which would get them good jobs overseas.

'What are we doing here?' Kamala burst out one day at the breakfast table.

Kannan had been home for two weeks because the estates where he worked had become trouble spots. Most of the estate labour was Tamil and they did not know which way to turn.

'We could go back home,' Kamala said.

Shards of Sunlight

'Could,' said Kannan. 'But, maybe we should wait a little. No one has threatened us so far.'

The household lived in a state of suspended animation. Nothing was as it should be though all the rituals of meal times and baths were maintained. Going out to the market was risky, so Kamala had to improvise. She made gravy with potato, onions and chopped tomato cans. They ate many different kinds of lentils and rice dishes. Sometimes Cokie went out to the fish market and came back with sardines and mackerel, which Kamala cooked with tamarind and chilli. She claimed that living for the war years under a Japanese regime had taught her to make-do.

Kannan walked up and down the living room like a caged tiger. Sometimes he took phone calls from his employers in the tea estate, but they made him even more jittery. Eventually they asked him to go back to the estate.

'Does that mean it's safe there now?' Kamala asked.

'I doubt it.'

'Maybe you shouldn't go then.'

'I need to know what the future is, make some decisions. And I can't do that without seeing them.'

He packed his overnight case and left the next day.

For Indu, going back to India was not an option. How could she leave Kantha?

'Are you planning to go back to India?' Indu finally asked Kamala one day. 'Is that why Velyachan looks so worried?'

Kamala took a moment to answer. 'I was going to tell you: he's lost his job. His boss said they didn't

Shards of Sunlight

want a non-Singhalese in such a trusted position. He's very upset and livid with rage.'

'Velyammey, I have to stay here.'

'I knew you'd say that. What am I to say to your Velyachan? He can't leave you out here alone.'

'I can find lodgings.'

'Indu, you're not Singhalese – they will see you as an enemy. What if you get attacked?'

'There is Kantha.'

'Who is Kantha, Indu? You have to see you have no lien on his loyalties.'

'That's not fair. He would do anything for me.'

'And you think Velyachan is going to leave you here on the strength of that?'

'Velyammey – am I to follow you around from country to country? Or go back to India? I have to have a life of my own. I am twenty-three now.'

'Would you stay here if not for Kantha?'

'What am I going to do in Thalassery anyway? Nothing for me there now. Shinnu and Devi are quietly getting old. I love them both but I can't dump myself like a sack of rice on them.'

'That's the other thing. I think your Velyachan wants to return to Malaya – he's been applying for jobs over there. You can come with us.'

'Velyammey. Time for me to stand on my own feet. I have a job here that I like.'

'Moley, I don't think your Velyachan will let you stay behind when we leave.'

Kannan's temper had not improved with the trip to Degalle.

'The sheer arrogance of it. All the prosperity there is due to the Tamils who toil on their estates. They

Shards of Sunlight

are treated like slaves; they have no rights at all. They have to buy Indian rupees at black market rates to send home to their families. And they cannot afford to go more than once in three or four years. Some have no papers and can't go at all. The older men will put up with it, but the young, who are born here, they are not going to stand for all this.'

Indu waited for Kannan to calm down. But all he did was go quiet for a few hours and then start fuming again.

Early next week, Indu approached him; decisions *had* to be made, and soon. She was twisting the free end of her sari on her finger, not knowing where to start.

'I-'

Kannan looked up, his face was impassive. When Indu saw the face, she turned as if to take flight.

'Sit down, Indu. You've got this far.'

Indu perched on the edge of the chair in front of him and shook her head as though banishing unpleasant thoughts.

Kannan offered no help.

'Velyacha. Velyamma says you might be leaving Ceylon.'

'Not much choice, is there? There is madness here at the moment. I have no job – and I don't want one here now.'

Indu looked down at her toes. 'If you go, I want to stay here.'

'It's that man in the office, isn't it? That Singhalese fellow.'

Indu flinched as though slapped at the distilled contempt in Kannan's tone.

Shards of Sunlight

'No, Indu. You can't stay here when I go. Are you mad? This country is breaking up like rotten wood and I'm supposed to leave you and disappear? Not on, Indu.'

'If it gets dangerous, I'll leave then. Not now.'

'No. You go with me. You have a choice. You can come with me to where I go – it looks like Singapore now – or you can go back to Thalassery. And rot.'

'I need time, to make up my mind about my job – and other things.'

'You go with me, Indu. I brought you here and I take you back.'

Indu turned and left the room. In the corridor she found Kamala.

'Velyammey, Velyachan is so angry with me.' She went to Kamala and fell on her sobbing. 'What am I to do?' Indu felt abandoned.

Kamala hugged her.

'Velyachan always starts like this. Be patient. And remember he loves you. He'll come round.' But she did not sound hopeful.

The next few days were unreal, in that the three people who lived in the same house forgot how to communicate with each other. Indu felt the thoughts in her head clamouring for escape, for answers, but the words encountered an obstinate lump in her throat.

This lump also prevented Indu from eating. She sat at the table and fiddled with her food, attracting questioning looks from Kamala. She dwindled and started spending large tracts of time in her bedroom. She stopped reading and that, to Indu, was the clearest indication of her malaise. After a week of this hibernation, she emerged and sought Kamala out.

'Velyammey, I was thinking-'

'Is that what you were doing hiding in the room?' Kamala asked, but she went to Indu and gave her a crushing hug. 'I miss you when you lurk in your room like a hurt animal. And, what was this thinking about?'

'I need to go to Thalassery – see how Devi and Shinnu are managing. I'll feel better when I have seen them. Haven't seen them for a while.'

'But you get letters, don't you?'

'Post cards and short letters from Shinnu. Saying not much. Can't forget them. And I need to take some money and things. Check my house.'

'Have you said anything to Veyachan?'

'I'm a little scared. Maybe-' She grimaced.

'Oh-oh. *I* have to talk to him. Right,' Kamala said after a moment. 'Maybe a trip to India will help.'

Next morning, as the family ate breakfast, Indu realised Kamala had made Kannan's favourite food– pittu with chick peas.

'Great food,' Kannan said. 'You serve food like this, I might decide never to go to work again.'

Kamala gave Kannan a second helping of the kadala curry 'Indu needs to go home for a little while,' she said, sounding casual.

Indu's head descended another inch towards her food.

'Didn't say anything. To me. Indu?' Kannan stopped eating and waited for Indu to respond.

'I thought, maybe, I could see Devi and Shinnu and make sure everything is… Only a week or two.'

Shards of Sunlight

'Glad you got your voice back.' Kannan sounded fed up.

'Can I go?' Indu asked. '

'What about your work? Aren't you supposed to be back next week?'

'Yes. But I am owed some leave.'

'Go if that's what you want. This is not a good time here for anyone.'

Indu got up and walked to her bedroom.

The next Monday Indu went back to work; it had been eight days since she had seen Kantha.

He wandered in with two cups of coffee halfway through the morning. 'I was scared to phone you,' he said. 'Didn't want to create trouble.'

Indu took the coffee from Kantha. 'This is good. Being looked after. Thanks. But there are too many people doing this right now and I am a big girl. I'm getting confused. What I need is a break. Would you mind very much if I took a few days off? Go to India and see my family.'

'I'm your boss. What if I say you can't take leave?' He was smiling.

'I'll bribe you,' Indu said. She went round the table and hugged him. 'Must sort things out – and then I am all yours.'

'Right then. You need a Resident's Permit to get back – if you haven't one. And a letter of authority from us. I'll get those organised. So don't fix a date yet. You *will* come back, wont you?'

'What do you think?' She felt sure of herself, the old Indu, focused and certain. 'I'll miss you all the while I am there.'

248

Shards of Sunlight

It took Kantha a week to get a Residents' Permit from Immigration and a stamp on her passport saying she did not owe any taxes to the Government.

Kannan talked to Indu before she left.

'When you are there – think about what you want. Your job, this boy…' His voice, which sounded just like her father's had lost its harsh edge. Hearing him, she longed for her father.

'I need to see Shinnu and Devi too. No letters for a long time.'

'Yes. Here's something for Devi.' He handed Indu a buff envelope.'

'*I'll* give them some too. The office has promised to get some Indian rupees for me.'

'Gopalan,' Kannan started hesitantly, and came to a full stop.

He started again. 'Gopalan didn't care about caste or community. But I worry. It's hard to live with a man of a different culture.'

Kamala walked into the room then. 'And if it is the same culture? Such a lottery anyway.'

'Her father-' Kannan started as though a thought needed to be completed.

'Her father would want her to make up her own mind, don't you think?

29

Indu travelled back to India on a bright November morning. She had sent a telegram to Shinnu. A bit like letters in bottles dropped into the sea; you never knew where they ended up.

As she boarded the small Fokker Friendship aircraft that took her to Jaffna and then on to Madras, she felt isolated from the rest of the world, even her family, like a leaf lifted up in a wind with no control over what was happening. Taking this break was a way of trying to get the initiative back, shaking off the barrage of instructions and advice she got from all around her, finding a quiet space in which to think.

In the plane Kantha was a warm presence in her mind, one that she knew would always be on her side. Is that what love was?

Jaffna was a hurried transit, showing passports and getting on the next sector. Madras was only an hour away and she heard a few Indian voices on board. The Indian Airlines plane had a stewardess from Kerala and Indu began to get intimations of home. When the plane touched down at Meenambakkam, tears welled up in Indu's eyes. The hot tarmac with steam rising, the familiar humidity with sweat breaking out all over her body, the smell of drying cowpats and too many people – no place else would ever be home.

The morning sun was fierce on her back as she walked towards the airport buildings. Nothing could faze her, not the customs minions making her open her suitcase and scattering clothes all over the worn

Shards of Sunlight

wooden surfaces, not the surly porter who asked too much for carrying her case to the taxi.

She drove straight to the Central Station to catch the evening train to Thalassery. In spite of the pushing and shoving at the ticket counter she considered herself lucky to get a berth in the third class ladies' compartment.

Indu spent the long hours before her train journey catching some much-needed sleep in the station waiting room. An early morning flight and a long wait before that at the airport had left her tired and wilting. The pleats on her yellow voile sari – clearly not the garment to be travelling in – were crushed to a shapeless mess. Kamala had told her she would need nylon to travel in, but Indu thought it would make her more hot and sweaty.

She figured the chances of sleeping in a noisy, crowded compartment full of weary women and fractious children would be minimal, so she resisted all attempts by others in the waiting room to draw her into conversation. As she dozed off, the familiar languages, Tamil and the occasional Malayalam, interspersed with sounds she interpreted as North Indian, were strangely comforting, like the noises of a home as it closed down for the day.

In the train, there was pandemonium. Women, with children, bundles, bedrolls and tiffin carriers, struggled to find room under the seats for all their paraphernalia of. Indu drew her legs up to allow others to arrange things and helped older women to settle into their seats without tripping over babies or suitcases. Men hovered near the windows as the train puffed steam and hooted before beginning the journey.

Shards of Sunlight

As the passengers saw the concrete pillars of the station receding, the uxorious husbands and urn-toting tea boys with them, they relaxed into their hard wooden seats and looked around at their shelter for the night.

Indu delved in her tote bag and pulled out her book for the day, *Two Leaves and a Bud* by Kamala Markhandaya, placing it on the tiny stand in front of her. She had started on it during the time she immured herself in her room, trying to make sense out of mixed feelings, her heart and head sending out confusing messages. Apt reading, she had thought: a story about tea estate labourers, trampled down by unfeeling employers.

Looking back, her feelings about Kantha were unequivocal: he was her best friend, the brother she never had, the one person in the world to whom she totally belonged. She could trust him with her life. And there was Kannan, her guardian, who came to rescue her from a nightmare proposal and gave her a loving home. She owed him; how could she cause him grief? This eighteen-hour journey to the West Coast would be a time for thinking.

The train gathered speed and industrial Madras gave way to the suburbs. Behind the warehouses the sun was a final splash of pink and orange in the distance. As the steam engine went round a slow bend it blew soot into the eyes and noses of the passengers and Indu had to bring the glass shutters down.

She settled back in her seat, looking out into the growing darkness as trees became taller and industrial buildings gave way to the thatch-huts of the outskirts. At a level crossing, the cyclists waited, one foot on the ground, one on a pedal, while cars idled and pedestrians

Shards of Sunlight

gathered around, waving at the faces looking out of the windows of the train.

Somewhere, leeward, someone spat betel juice out of a compartment and it flew towards the back of the train, a red scattered stream, slowly falling away. Soon the darkness took over and the trees became a black-green mass, a giant shadow on the other side of the tracks.

In the cocoon of the train the children fell asleep on the laps of mothers, themselves half asleep. Apart from the wails of a baby now and then and the snores of adults, the compartment gradually fell quiet. Indu slept fitfully and didn't know what was real and what dream.

Indu was suffocating. Yards of cotton cloth were wrapped round her face and nose; she tried to fight her way out.

She woke up, aware of where she was. The end of her yellow sari had fallen on her face as she slept; earlier she had wound it round her ears to stop the soot from getting in. She took the material down from her head and arranged it on her shoulders.

An old woman from the upper berth was looking at Indu .

'Can't sleep?' Indu asked.

'I never get to sleep.'

The woman turned ponderously over in the narrow berth and was snoring in seconds.

After the dream, Indu was unable to get back to sleep. Her mind felt like a box into which people had thrown bits of paper, some of them essential. She couldn't find the pieces she needed. They whirled inside her mind and settled in unlikely places.

Shards of Sunlight

It would be good to see Shinnu and Devi again, she thought; this was one of the few certainties in her life. Shinnu would cook her favourite things and wrap her up in unconditional love. Indu needed that.

As dawn broke outside the window, most of the people in the compartment were fast asleep. Indu watched the darkness retreat into the far hills. The morning mist hung over the flatlands that they passed, with trees still out of focus. Men came out into the empty rail-side land with bottles of water, to defecate, unconcerned about the strangers in the passing train. No women to be seen.

When the train stopped at stations the tea and coffee vendors clambered into the train with smoky glass tumblers and steaming urns. Sleeping women stirred and felt for their purses tucked into their waists. They pulled their shawls and blankets tight around their shoulders as the morning chill came into the compartment with the *chai* boys.

Indu bought a glass of hot coffee for two *annas*, and held it in both her hands to feel the warmth. The coffee was scalding hot and sweet and it spread warmth in her as it went down. South Indian coffee, nothing anywhere to beat it at this time of the morning. The thought of home was warm and sweet in her.

The morning benediction was long gone by the time Indu's train, The Madras Mail, approached Thalassery. It was delayed twice for a half-hour each at Farook and at Calicut. By the time it clattered into the little station of Thalassery at two in the afternoon, the passengers were hot and perspiring, clothes dishevelled and unsalvageable. Sweat had left wet patches on the backs of blouses and underarms, showing darker than the colour of the garments. Indu's waist felt tight and scratchy and she wanted to change out of the sari, but that had not been possible in the crowded compartment. The morning procession to and from the toilets had left wet patches in corridors and the whole place smelt stale and stifling. Soot blew in, but it brought the cold air with it and this was better than the fug inside the compartment.

The porters with their khaki shirts and red cloth turbans ran alongside the train as it slowed down at the station. They were in and picking up cases even before the train stopped. The train would halt only for five minutes in this small station, so Indu tugged her case out from under the seat and handed it to a porter. She clambered out quickly and walked fast to keep up with the hurrying porter. At the rickshaw stand she didn't bother to haggle, finding a rickshaw and handing over the rupee - much too much – the porter demanded.

It was siesta time and women would be resting after closing down the kitchens until the evening. So Indu was not surprised when she reached her home to find the front door closed and the house quiet. She knocked joyously, sure of her welcome, eager to find her family, the women who had looked after her till she left for Ceylon. When she didn't hear any noises inside, she was perplexed. She went round the back of the house; there was an air of desuetude there. The coconut fronds were rotting outside the kitchen door. The grinding stone was dry and abandoned on the floor of the back veranda, and there were cobwebs on the kitchen door.

Indu went to the front again. She beat on the front door with her palm helplessly. What was she to do now?

Someone was calling her name. Was she imagining it?

'*Indoo. Kutty.*' It was the woman who lived in the house across, Rema whose daughter had been a school mate and friend.

Indu crossed the road and walked across.

'No one there,' the woman said. 'They all left. Some months ago.'

She looked kindly at Indu's face, disappointed and lost. 'Come, Indu,' she said, picking up her hand. 'Come and have something to drink.'

Indu went meekly with her and sat down on the front veranda as Rema made a glass of lime juice and brought it out. 'They went to their village. It was hard for them here with no one to help. Devi was getting old. Couldn't manage.'

Indu felt as though the ground had been swept awy from under her feet. She gulped the juice down quickly.

'Can I leave my case here with you?' she asked. 'Just take a few things with me.'

She started pulling out a few items of clothing and her toiletries out of her suitcase and stuffing them willy-nilly into a plastic bag.

'We'll keep your things. Sure. But why don't you rest for a bit before you go off to Kodiyeri? You look weary.'

Indu tried unsuccessfully to smile. 'I'll be less tired when I see them.'

'Right then,' Rema said. 'When you get to the end of the bus route get someone there to show you the way.'

'I have no change for the bus.' She started crying; suddenly it was all too much.

Rema hugged her. 'Shh,' she said. 'It's not that far. You'll see them; they'll be so happy.'

Rema went into the house and came back with two five-rupee notes and a handful of change.

Indu wiped her tears away, hauled her suitcase into the inner corridor of the house and left, thanking Rema for the drink and the money. 'I'll be back soon. Bring them back with me,' she said as she walked away.

Rema looked doubtful, but said nothing.

The city bus was just turning around near the Courts when Indu reached the corner breathlessly. She rushed and got in as it was starting off. The conductor recognised her.

'*You've* not been around for a long time.'

'Yes, I went to live with my uncle. In Colombo.'

The bus was slow as it went past the Bar Association Library, which faced the sea. She could see the black gowns fluttering about and a wave of nostalgia enveloped her for the simple days when her father went to the Courts in the morning and came back in the evening and life was predictable.

The bus gathered speed along the narrow road parallel to the Arabian Sea and Indu looked out on a seascape, which had dominated her childhood. The water glinted grey and silver where it caught the sun and the froth that laced the waves was barely

Shards of Sunlight

discernible. The bus went into the centre of town and out, stopping frequently to collect passengers. Some spoke to her, but she did not offer any small talk. When, finally, she reached the end of the bus route, she got off and walked to her father's ancestral home.

It was a long walk, but she covered the distance quickly, carried on an urgency inside her to find Shinnu and Devi. She would not be home until she reached them.

When Indu reached the little thatched house where her father's extended family had lived at various times, she was weary from lack of sleep and exhausted with worry and uncertainty. As soon as Shinnu opened the door, Indu collapsed in her arms.

'No one was there,' she wailed. 'No one was in our house.'

Devi came out then, hearing the commotion. She looked at the girls and rubbed her eyes as though she was seeing a spectre.

'We wondered when, if ever, you would come again. It seemed such a long, long time,' Devi said.

Shinnu clasped Indu close and took her in. She walked her to the dark kitchen and sat her down on a wooden stool. She boiled water at the three-stone fire and very soon tea was ready and Shinnu poured it back and forth from brass tumbler to lotta till she had worked up a sizeable froth. Seeing that froth, Indu knew she was back where she belonged.

Shinnu touched Indu's hair lightly. 'You've become very fair. No sports in Colombo, eh?'

Indu smelled Shinnu's ingrained shallot smell and felt the love in the fingers in her hair.

Shinnu warmed up some old rice and lentils in the earthenware pots and sat down next to Indu as she

Shards of Sunlight

ate, as though she couldn't have enough of the sight of her.

'So much to tell you,' she said. 'But it can wait. You rest first.'

She spread a mat on the floor of the puja room and put a pillow on it, then sat next to Indu while Indu stretched out.

Indu closed her eyes knowing she was with her people now.

As she slipped slowly into sleep she could hear the comforting sound of the familiar voice of Shinnu, the voice that had sung her to sleep as a baby.

Indu floated in and out of sleep as the household lit the devotional lamp at dusk and Shinnu carried it to the veranda, chanting, "*Deepam, deepam*," so that any unclean person, such as a woman in the middle of her periods, could move out of the way.

'I missed all this,' Indu said to herself and was not sure what was in the *all*. She felt cocooned, nothing could harm her here.

30

The rest of the day of Indu's arrival in India went in a tired fug where all that registered was the presence of her family. In the house there were only two lamps: a small bulb-shaped bottle full of kerosene with a wick, which was carried from room to room as needed, and a lantern, which sat in the middle room all night and was doused low when the house slept.

When Indu woke up refreshed the next morning she could see the new home of Shinnu's and Devi's new home in the relentless sunlight streaming in on the east of the veranda. The floor was uneven and the cow dung paste had flaked in places, showing the lighter layers underneath. At the edge of the floor, a thin border of rough hewn red bricks held the mud in place. Plaster was peeling from the wall in places and the same coarse bricks showed through.

My father grew up here, playing on this veranda, going to the one-room Primary School near by, Indu thought. This was his domain until he left to study law. She found it difficult to imagine him in this bare household, with only the essentials to get by.

The furniture on the veranda consisted of one rickety bench and two low wooden stools. It was primitive and thread bare. Life seemed to be pared down to the bone here.

Devi was sitting on the bench with her *pan* box on her lap, preparing the betel leaf, as Indu came to the veranda. Devi seemed to have aged beyond her years. She had not put on her dentures after getting up in the

Shards of Sunlight

morning; her collapsed cheek dragged her face down and made her look woeful.

'Shinnu is making coffee,' Devi said.

She had already lit the sacred lamp in the middle room and lamps flickered in the little houses in the middle distance. Indu could hear the clatter of brass vessels and the slosh of water as Shinnu went about her quotidian chores.

Indu went up to Devi and sat close to her on the bench. 'Shinnuedathy is forever cooking and washing. She has spent her life doing this.'

'That is what women do. Never mind- What is it like in Colombo? Do you like it there?' Devi put the pan in her mouth and chewed slowly with her naked gums.

Indu smelled the green smell of pan and an acidic whiff of *chunamb.* 'It's OK. Kamala looks after me well.'

'And your job?'

'I love it, Ammamma. But you two? - This house is so bare. It can't be comfortable.'

'It'll do. The money you send us is more than enough. And this house has been here a long while. We have coconuts and jack fruit and mango in the compound. Plentiful bananas too. I gather the palm leaves that fall and dry them for firewood. We don't need to buy much.'

'True. But why leave that house in Thalassery?'

'Two women alone. It became a sad and lonely place. And it was expensive. Keeping a servant to fetch things from the market, maid to clean, everything cost more and more. Here we are surrounded by family. Our cousins live in many of these houses around us. They are within earshot. The youngsters help in the garden

Shards of Sunlight

and fetch for us. And Meenakshi, my youngest sister, is near; she sends one of her sons down whenever we need a hand.'

'I suppose.' Indu sounded uncertain.

'And Shinnu will never find a husband in the town, so far from our community. I want to get her settled before-'

'And?'

'Shinnu is going to be married soon. To a man whose wife died last year.'

Shinnu walked to the veranda with the coffee just then.

'Shinnuedathy, are you happy to marry this man?'

'Happy? What's happy got to do with anything?' She smiled. 'Getting old, Moley. Look at me. Must take my chance to have a husband and a family. He has two children who need a mother and maybe I'll have my own too later. And I get a home of my own.'

'He's a farmer in a village near here and every one says he is a kind man. Doesn't drink toddy or beat his wife,' Devi added.

'What about gold and such like?'

'That's the next thing. Money for two gold chains and four bangles. That should be enough. Second marriage for him after all. Meenakshi, my sister will do the wedding feast.'

'I have some gold, Ammammey. From my mother, remember. I never wear the jewellery; Shinnu can have those.'

'But they are your mother's.'

Shards of Sunlight

'Nobody has been more mother to me than Shinnu,' Indu said firmly. 'But what about you, Ammammey? You'll be alone.'

'No. I shall live with Meenakshi. Now she is a widow, she says she would like for us to live together.'

As Indu drank her coffee, warming her hands round the brass mug, she knew she needed to ask some questions.

'I went to our house, Ammammey,' she said carefully. 'The coconuts are drying up on the trees and falling down. Beggars pick them up. And the house needs people in it. I am wondering what to do.'

'Rent it. It will be a nest egg for you when you are older.'

'Don't you want to live there, Ammammey? This seems so-'

'Primitive?' Devi laughed. 'We are used to it now,'

It was a thoughtful Indu who went back to town the next day. She visited Damu, her father's friend, and entrusted her house to him.

'Will you find a tenant for me, Uncle?'

'Easy,' he said. 'You'll get two hundred rupees for that house. Lawyers will come flocking because it is so near the Courts, but they'll be hard to get rid of later. I'll try a bank official. They are not allowed more than three years in any town, so they can't become sitting tenants. 'I can collect the rent for you. But can't send money out of here – exchange control restrictions. So what do I do with the rent?'

'Could you send it to Devi in Kodiyeri?'

Shards of Sunlight

'Yes, surely. It's my village too. I'll make sure she gets it. But- don't you want any of the money? For clothes and all that?'

'No, uncle. I work and my salary is enough for me.'

'Work, yes. But time you got married,' he muttered under his breath.

Indu pretended she hadn't heard that.

While she was there, Indu collected her suitcase from her neighbours and returned to Kodiyeri in the evening.

It was the time when the boys of the village stopped playing in the fields and women called their goats and hens in. In the little houses placed far apart from each other, the evening lamps started flickering between coconut palms and mango trees. Dusk crept slowly into the verandas and hovered, ready to take over in the rooms. At the wells the makeshift buckets made of arecanut fronds hit the water repeatedly as households fetched water and cleaned up for the night to come.

The days went by with visits to family living nearby and Indu quietly enjoyed the undemanding existence in the village. But she wondered how Devi and Shinnu managed this lifestyle after living in the town so long; she had a sudden pang of guilt as she thought of her life in Colombo: Kamala's well-run establishment with window curtains, and rugs on the gleaming floor, polished with Cardinal Red and wax polish. Running water and gas on tap, which even the maids took for granted.

Indu had a sense of being at a crossroads in her life – decisions to make, to convey tactfully to her

Shards of Sunlight

family. As always when hard choices faced her, Indu wondered what her father would have said. *'Never forget your beginnings,'* probably. On the other hand, *'Take control of your life; don't let anyone else manipulate you. Once you let that happen, you are lost.'* Could you do both?

She stared into the distance and tried to get order into her mind. Devi walked on to the veranda. Somewhere from inside the house the strong scent of incense wafted out.

'Almost time to douse the lamp,' Devi said. The sacred lamp would be extinguished and carried back to its normal resting place in the padinjitta before the lantern was lit for the night.

'*Ramaramarama...*' she murmured as she blew and drew the flickering wicks one by one through the oil. 'Coconut oil is getting expensive,' she said.

'Ammammey, I saw Damu vakil today.'

'How is he? Loved your father, would do anything for you. He's been bringing proposals for you, his junior lawyers mainly.'

'Mostly lawyers without briefs – they will live off their lands and never have briefs, ever.' Indu laughed. 'I'll have to work to keep us in food.'

'There *are* some good ones.'

'I don't plan to spend the rest of my life as a lawyer's wife in this town, Ammammey. There is a world out there.'

'Right. Right. Just thought I'd mention it.'

For an uncertain second Indu wondered whether this was the moment to tell Devi about Kantha. She postponed it.

'I asked Damu Uncle to rent out my house – and send the rent to you.'

Shards of Sunlight

'What for? It's your money, your inheritance.'

'Just for now, Ammammey. For Shinnu's marriage.'

'Right, but after that I'll keep it for you.'

'Ammammey, I don't need that money. What about your medicines and clothes when you live with Meenakshi Velyamma? And when you come to see me in Ceylon.'

'There's only one place I'm going now, Moley.' Devi looked up wryly. 'Must settle Shinnu first. Too old to travel. But – your money - I'll put it in the bank and use it only if I need it. I'll know it's there; that's good. You, like your father, think of others, but who will think of you?'

Indu opened her mouth to say something, then shut it again. 'There's someone, Ammammey; I am scared you'll get annoyed with me,' she managed eventually.

Devi looked impassively at Indu but did not look surprised.

'Those letters you write and go personally into town to post – I knew there is somebody in your mind.'

'Kannan Velyachan is not happy.'

'He made his choice when he married in Penang, so how can he disagree? His parents didn't even know until after the event. Still…'

'Still what, Ammammey?'

'I think, what would Gopalan say?'

Indu smiled. 'I think I know. Probably, *let her decide, it's her life*.'

'Yes, but I can see him checking this boy out – in person. Who is going to do that if Kannan withdraws in anger?'

Shards of Sunlight

'He's Ceylonese – a Buddhist Singhalese. Not that that matters to me. He works with me and is a kind and good man. And he wants us to be married.'

'And you? Do you want to spend your life there, with him?'

'Yes.'

'No doubts?'

'None.'

'Moley, I don't know where you will go, what you will do, from here on. But your life will be special, that much I know.'

Shinnu walked in, her face just above a load of dry washing she was carrying. 'Special? What's special?'

Indu and Devi looked at each other and smiled.

'What's going on?' Shinnu ignored the handloom bed sheet trailing on the floor.

'Indu is telling me about the man she wants to marry.'

Shinnu dumped the washing unceremoniously on the low wooden stool next to the front door. Some of it tilted on to the floor.

'Marry? Who? From where?'

'Hold on,' Indu said. 'You get married first, remember.'

Shinnu brushed that aside. 'Me? Yes. Forget about that. It's you we are talking about.'

Indu looked down at her palm and thought for a moment. 'His name is Kantha. He -well, I'll have to bring him here to meet you both. Then you can see how I have chosen.'

The women stayed up late into the night talking about the marriages to come and the families of their prospective grooms.

Shards of Sunlight

Shinnu's final conclusion was: 'Does he read a lot of books like you? If not, he's going to lag well behind.'

Indu travelled back to Colombo the next week, eager to get back to her work, her man and her life of now. Kamala was delighted to see her back.

'I thought you were never going to come back. Can't even phone you in that god-forsaken village.'

'I'm back now, aren't I?' Indu said beaming. 'And I missed you all.'

'I know who you missed,' Kamala retorted, grinning.

Kannan walked into the room hearing the happy noises. 'Nice to see you back,' he said. 'How is my sister? And is it true my niece is getting married?'

'Devi is quite content, though she lives a very simple life. No electricity, running water, no nothing. But she's alright.'

'And Shinnu?'

'Definitely getting married. She is happy to have a home of her own, she says. So little to ask. She has very little expectation, Velyacha.'

Kamala went to the kitchen to make tea and Indu followed her.

'Is Velyachan still angry with me?'

'Indoo. Can you not see how happy he is to see you back? He was forever asking me whether I knew when you were coming back. I think we are used to having you around.'

Indu felt a surge of joy within her. Here also, with her aunt and uncle, she had sanctuary.

31

Indu was not due at work till the next Monday. She was impatient to get back and see Kantha, but she decided she would phone him in the evening.

She was staring impatiently out of the window, waiting for her uncle to retire for the night so that she could talk to Kantha without being overheard, when Kantha's car drew up. She watched as he jumped out, slammed the door and strode to the front door, looking behind him, as he did so.

Indu ran to the door and opened it. Kantha came in and quickly shut the door behind him. 'It's not safe here,' he said. 'There is a rumour; they are coming this way tonight.'

Kantha walked through to the sitting room, where Kannan was reading a newspaper and listening to the radio.

'My boss – Kantha,' Indu said.

'Sit, please,' Kamala urged.

Kantha sat down on the edge of the settee and jumped up almost immediately. 'You have to get out of here, *now*. No time for sitting. Those scoundrels don't know Indian from Tamil.'

'Get out, where?'

'Come with me. Stay in my house for a day or two, until all this dies down.'

'Can't just come and stay in your house,' Kannan said. 'What about your family, parents?'

Shards of Sunlight

'They don't attack us. Anyway, our area is pretty safe. We've had Tamil friends staying with us for some days now. We manage. Please get a change of clothes together and come with me.' He sounded frantic.

Kannan was inclined to refuse but Kamala got some clothes together for them and Indu gathered tooth brushes, towels and combs. There was a strong whiff of desperation in the car when finally they drove off towards Kantha's home.

'After the Japanese in Singapore, I never expected to hide like this again.' Kannan sounded angry and terminally weary.

Kantha's home was a revelation – what had Indu expected? Certainly not the elegant bungalow that greeted the refugees. Cinnamon Gardens was a corner of Colombo, where the houses were large and sprawling and open to the tree-lined streets. Here the rich lived, Tamil and Singhalese, as well foreigners from embassies and owners of estates up country. Here the only distinction anyone knew was that of wealth. These households had lived here, many of them, for generations. You could not imagine this corner being threatened by unruly mobs.

The garden had a neat Duranda hedge, only two feet high, shining gold in places where it caught the sunlight. In the left corner a Frangipani spread its benign branches into this garden and the next, with a carpet of white and yellow blooms scattered at its foot. Underneath the tree a stone image of the Buddha in meditation sat, the flowers sprinkled on its head and shoulders wilting. Someone had placed an offering of red Hibiscus flowers and jasmine at the foot of the

Shards of Sunlight

statue. Hindu Gods also had pride of place, with a covered shrine for Shiva in his cosmic dance. This was decorated with garlands of jasmine, turning brown at the edges. It was an orderly garden, the flower beds and Oleander trees showing loving care.

Inside the house, however, chaos reigned. People walked about from room to room like the dispossessed they were, looking for familiar things to which to anchor their shattered egos. The men gathered on the porch and at the windows, smoking and talking in whispers, as though looking for an exit. The women rushed to and fro from the kitchen, cooking for the adults, making baby food for the little ones crawling under every one's feet, washing clothes in the porcelain sink in the kitchen or in tin buckets outside. Children of school-going age clustered in the garden, making up games to pass time. Time, which hung heavily on them now that there were no markers for the day: no school, no homework, no familiar places.

Indu could see the disgruntled world of bitter men in the living room was not for her, so she went through to the kitchen. She did not know what was expected of her. How could she make herself useful? Clearly there was a great deal to be done, feeding the hordes if nothing else. A middle-aged woman at the kitchen surface was cutting onions doggedly, looking neither left nor right.

Kantha walked in. Indu looked up with question marks in her eyes. 'Should I be helping that lady?' she asked. 'Onions for huge casseroles?'

'That's my mother. This was not how I intended you should meet her.'

He took Indu's hand and walked her to his mother. 'Ammey, Indu.'

Shards of Sunlight

The woman looked at Indu's hand in Kantha's and the look on Kantha's face; a medley of confusion of hope, pride and possession.

'Yes. Of course. Indu. I'm glad you're here. Kantha has said so much about you.'

She seemed distracted; she did not have time for formalities just then.

'I was wondering – why don't I help you cut up the onions – vegetables, whatever you need.'

'There's another knife in that drawer there.' She pointed to the corner behind Indu. 'And I am Sunanda. Call me Sunu. If you could do the *gova*.' She pointed to the two huge cabbages on the kitchen surface. 'I'm making *gova* and fish curry and lots of rice. That'll have to do. The little ones must be getting hungry.'

Indu looked at her watch. It was six in the evening. She fetched a cutting board leaning near the water filter and started on the cabbages, chopping them up into small pieces to go into the curry. She worked steadily for half an hour until all the cabbage was shredded. What next? She looked at Sunu who was peering into the *chatti* in which she was frying onions and decided to get on with it, rather than ask questions. So she searched in the cupboards till she found a colander and washed the cabbage and left it on the draining board.

'Good girl,' Sunanda said, looking at the hillock of cabbage. 'Can you cook it for me? Temperadu first and put the cabbage in with onions and green chillies. You'll need to add...'

'I know. I've seen our cokie do this at home.

Indu heated up some coconut oil and waited for it to start moving in the pan. She dropped two large pinches of mustard seed and four dried red chillies

Shards of Sunlight

broken up into quarters. When the mustard seeds starting popping she threw a handful of chopped onions and a teaspoonful of chopped green chillies. She lowered the heat and stirred for a minute, then added the cabbage a handful at a time, stirring all the while.

She looked around for a coconut for the coconut milk. Sunanda wordlessly pointed to the fridge, where coconut milk had been preserved in two separate mugs, one containing the thick first milk and the other the thin second and third milk.

'I always keep some ready in the fridge,' she explained. 'Never know when you might have to make a little more curry.'

Kamala wandered in at that moment. She came close to Indu and whispered. 'I've put our things in a corner in the hall. All the rooms are full, we'll have to settle in however we can. Your Velyachan is in a state.'

'Not easy for an old person. How about you?'

'I'm all right,' Kamala said. 'Long experience of extended families, mine and your velyachan's. We'll manage. But not for long, I hope.'

'That's Kantha's mother.' Indu gestured with her head in Sunanda's direction.

Kamala went over to Sunanda. A big *chatti* was on the worktop in front of her. Seer fish had been rubbed with turmeric, red pepper and salt, ready for cooking.

'Shall I start on this fish curry?' Kamala asked. 'I'm Indu's aunt,' she added. 'You might want to get away from the kitchen for a bit.'

Sunanda wiped beads of perspiration off her forehead and upper lip with the corner of her sari.

'Yes,' she said, distractedly. 'Must go and see where every one is, get mats out for the children.' She pointed to the little dishes near the cooker. 'Onions, chillies and ginger,' she said.

Everywhere Sunanda went the sharp tang of ginger and garlic went with her.

Kamala added water to the fish and onions, and threw in split green chillies and ginger. As it started boiling she added the thin coconut milk and left it to simmer. Indu meanwhile, had added thick coconut milk and curry leaves to her cabbage and it was done.

'Ready for the crowd,' she said as she came over to Kamala.

Indu put a lid on the cabbage and wandered off, in search of Kantha. She found him in the middle of an anxious discussion with the men in the sitting room.

'This won't last long,' a middle-aged man was saying as though he knew the time table. 'The army will put a stop to all this, no men?' He had hitched up his sarong just short of his knees and his white sleeveless vest stretched tautly over his spherical stomach. As he talked he walked back and forth in the room and appeared to be talking more to himself than anyone else.

'Depends what the army wants to happen. And the government. How come they've not stopped it by now? *Government thamai.*'

'Meanwhile –'

'Meanwhile we hunker down and hope there is safety in numbers.'

Apart from Kantha there weren't any young men about. Most of them were old or on the way there. Kantha's father was one of the oldest and sat quietly in a corner not contributing much to the debate. He looked uneasy and lost.

Shards of Sunlight

Father and son resembled each other: the same strong jaw line and sensuous lips, the thick mane growing back from a high forehead. Kantha was not quite as dark as his father, or as short. The old man was small, sparse and angular. His voice was the most surprising feature of him, on the odd occasion he said something. If Indu closed her eyes, he would be Kantha speaking.

Kantha peeled away from the group when he saw Indu in the doorway. 'I think we are all a little scared and tired – probably of each other too.'

'It's being cooped up in a house not your own. You know how old people want their beds, their bathrooms…'

'Beds! I think it's going to be mats rolled out on the floor for a while.'

In the back garden the children had quietened down somewhat and were trickling in to eat in twos and threes. Their mothers served them at the kitchen table straight from the pans. As soon as they finished eating they were led away to bathrooms to wash and then to the mats spread on the floors of bedrooms. Quiet descended on the house as the children fell asleep and the men nursed their first beers or whiskies of the day.

In the corner of the hallway Indu found her bag of toiletries and went in search of a space to possess. She found it under the stairway. It smelt of old leather and damp socks but she was too exhausted to care. She pushed tennis racquets and shoes back and made a space. All she wanted was a moment of peace, to take stock, to reflect.

Shards of Sunlight

An hour later, she was fast asleep, curled up next to old newspapers and magazines, her head resting on her bag. Later, when she turned over and opened her eyes briefly, she felt disoriented, not knowing where she was. Then she saw Kantha sitting next to her and the events of the day came back. 'I'm cold,' she said, My feet feel frozen.'

Kantha picked up her feet and put them on his lap. He rubbed them with his palm coaxing warmth into it. She sighed deeply and settled back into sleep.

Sunanda found them there, her son reading an old magazine sitting next to Indu while she slept. 'Now you have one more person to look after,' she said.

'Yes,' he said simply. 'I think I need your help.'

When Indu woke up the next morning, she found Kantha had claimed a corner of the bag under her head. He was sleeping at right angles to her and her arm rested on him.

Kamala called them a little later.

'Go and eat breakfast before it's all eaten. It's late. I've saved some food for the two of you.'

Indu looked at her watch without quite seeing the time. She rubbed the sleep from her eyes and looked again. Nine, it said.

She scrambled up quickly and stood. Kantha woke more slowly and when he did, he did not seem to be in any hurry to move.

'Not hungry,' he said.

Indu nudged him. 'Get up,'

She pulled at his arm.

He got up and walked to the kitchen like a zombie. Indu, now wide awake, pushed chairs out and served him and her. Kantha ate slowly, deep in thought.

Shards of Sunlight

All the while, Kamala sat opposite watching the pair thoughtfully.

Kantha pushed his plate away half-eaten and went to the bathroom to wash his hands.

'I think you have a lot to tell me,' Kamala said firmly to Indu. 'Wonder what your Velyachan is going to say.'

'Later, Velyammey. Later. Today is such a mess in my head.' She had to sort that mess out for herself first. Kamala didn't pursue it further.

The next morning Indu decided to bathe and wash her hair early before the rush on the bathrooms started; she felt her hair had become grimy from sleeping under the staircase, with all the shoes and tennis racquets of the house dumped behind her. After her bath she stood in the back garden letting the sun fall upon her and into her hair.

She took a few clumps of wet hair at a time and removed the knots in them carefully with her fingers. She did this slowly, sensuously, unaware that Kantha watched her from the kitchen window holding his breath. The grass green of her sari brought out the streaks of brown in her hair as it caught the sunlight. She looked waif-like standing there, absorbed in her morning ritual. In her face there was repose as though she had claimed the quiet of the dawn and it had come to her.

Indu returned to the kitchen when her hair was dry. The overnight guests started wandering in then and the women got busy making food for the babies: Farex in hot milk and Ribena. Sunanda boiled a big pan of water on the gas hob and threw a handful of tea leaves in. She let it simmer very low for a half-minute and

Shards of Sunlight

strained it into another pan. The women helped themselves to it, mixing hot milk and sugar for their men, children still clinging to their housecoats.

'Shall I put the plates out for breakfast then?' Indu asked Sunanda.

'Just show everyone where everything is. They'll help themselves,' Sunanada said.

Indu opened the cupboards out so the plates and mugs were visible.

Kantha came to her then and whispered. 'We need to talk, Indu.'

'Not here and now, Kantha,' She whispered back. He caught her hand and led her into the garden.

'It can't wait, I need to know, Indu. Will you? Will you be my wife? Stay with me all my life?'

Indu looked at Kantha for a moment. 'I will and I thought you knew that. I don't play games. But nothing is as simple as that. There is my Velyachan for one. And your parents. And God knows who else. It may take time; bear with me.'

'I care only that you are with me. The rest we can deal with.'

'Time to go in, Kantha. We are in a goldfish bowl here.'

'I don't care who knows.'

'Neither do I. But we have to show respect for your family – and mine.'

Kantha put his hand out, almost in supplication, but withdrew it quickly.

32

Two days went by as in a dream. Did Indu think she could control all that was happening around her? She was worried about her aunt and uncle. What was Kannan going to say about her and Kantha? Maybe, if she talked to him again when he was calm and not stressed the way he was right now, he would be more understanding.

In the event the choice was taken out of Indu's hands. Kamala was late coming down to breakfast that day. When Indu went to find her in the corner of the hallway where they had slept the previous night, she was sitting on the mat, talking to Kannan. Kannan was still in his sarong and vest, lying on his back.

The other men and women walked in and out of the hallway, going to various rooms, looking for members of their family, or things they couldn't find. One old man stood in the doorway seeing nothing, scratching his head. If they noticed Kamala and Kannan in conversation on their mat, they stopped a moment and then went on.

Kamala was talking to him quietly and Indu could see she was trying to calm him.

'And you never thought of telling me?' he burst out, sitting up suddenly.

The sarong tucked in at his waist came loose and he pulled the ends together furiously.

'I did not know there was anything to tell. She works with him and they travel together, with his team,

Shards of Sunlight

and that is what the job requires. If you didn't like that, you should not have let her take that job.'

'But I was in the estate – what do I know about what you people get up to?'

'Oh. We throw parties and go out every night...' Kamala hauled herself up and turned. '*Get up to,*' she muttered angrily'

She saw Indu then, at the door, looking aghast, hand to her mouth.

'Velyamma, it is not like that,' Indu said

'What's it like then?' Kannan looked outraged, unable to look at Indu's face. 'Is this what I brought you to Ceylon for? To get involved with a Singhalese boy? What do we know about these people?'

'We know they are kind and caring. Looking after this crowd here. And I know Kantha.' Indu's voice rose. There was an incipient edge of hysteria in it. Kamala came over to her and looked hard at her face.

'He seems a good man, that Kantha. But you can't expect Velyachan not to worry. Let's not talk about this now.'

Indu's face had gone a bright pink and her lips trembled as though there were words trying to get out that she was keeping in.

'Shush,' Kamala said, looking around. 'We are in their house.'

The tears were coming now, trickling down her cheeks and Indu picked up her sari end and dabbed at them

Kamala put her arm out to console her, but Indu walked away swiftly.

'Let her go,' Kannan said when Kamala tried to follow her. 'I'll talk to her later.'

Shards of Sunlight

Indu walked slowly like a sleepwalker. The road outside seemed irresistible. A part of her brain told her it was not safe out there, but she *had* to get away. The confusion inside the house with so many families milling around, she thought, was reflected in the confusion in her own mind.

She slipped through the huge gates and immediately felt diminished in size and vulnerable. But she had thinking to do, she had to find the calm place inside her, which helped her to make the big decisions of her life.

She could walk left or right, she knew. But go right and she would be on the main road, not a place to go just then. She walked left. The street was shaded with many ancient trees on the verge and under the shade of one there was a bus stop and a concrete bench for waiting passengers. She sat down and let her mind drift.

The buses that went by did not stop and the road was near empty. She thought of her father; what would he say? She knew he didn't care about caste or religion, but he would have talked to Kantha, made his own judgements. Kannan would not even talk to Kantha.

Kantha found her a little later on the bench; she realised he had come searching for her, but was not sure she wanted to be found.

When he got near, she looked up and smiled apologetically.

'It is not safe here,' he said. 'Come home, Indu.'

He picked up her hand and caressed it. 'Planning to run away from us, were you?' he asked.

Shards of Sunlight

'No. Only from myself. The house is so crowded, I can't think,' Indu said.

'They are all in the same boat, Indu. Scared and distressed. They all want to go home. Maybe in a day or two when the streets quieten down.'

'Velyachan is furious,' Indu said.

Kantha did not respond.

Indu turned to him. 'When I asked him for help, that time they were planning to marry me off to some stranger, Velyachan came as soon as he could. If he hadn't I might have been married now, against my will, to that man from Dubai. Velyachan brought me here, gave me a home. I can't let him down.'

'What are you saying, Indu?'

'I'm saying... I am saying.'

'Hush. Don't say anything now. Come. Let's go home now.'

Indu went with him meekly.

Two days later, the attacks on the Tamils petered out in the area in which Indu and the other men and women camping in Kantha's house lived. They trickled away slowly, the older men and their women, whose need for their own homes, their own beds, had become compulsive. Nothing could keep them away.

Kannan had also come to the end of his tether. Indu and Kamala could see that he needed to be in his own home. They gathered their scant possessions together. Kamala thanked Sunanda profusely. 'You have been kind – and very, very patient with all of us. I wonder whether I could have shown the same forbearance.'

Sunanda smiled. 'Only for a few days. We all mucked in.'

Shards of Sunlight

'We'll see you soon. So much to talk, think about.'

'Yes.' Sunanda sounded uncertain. 'For now, thank God the attacks have stopped.'

When Indu and her aunt and uncle got to the door, Kantha picked up their bags and took them to his car. 'Better I drop you off,' he said.

'We'll need some milk and bread,' Kamala said.

Kantha drove without saying a word to the nearest grocery shop. He got out and bought bread and milk and waved away the small change Kamala offered.

When they reached Indu's house, Kantha helped them in and left quickly. Indu went to the gate with him.

'I-' she started.

'Yes?' His eyes implored her to say something, but nothing came out.

'I-' she started again.

'Never mind.' He started the car and drove off.

33

Indu waited patiently for three uncertain days, wondering when Kantha would phone or come to see her. This was a time when people did not go on the roads unnecessarily, or so Indu told herself as the days went by and she had not heard from Kantha.

On the fourth day Indu decided this was up to her – maybe something she had done or said made Kantha feel he could not get in touch. Or he could be staying away in deference to her uncle.

She went close to Kamala who was fiddling with spoons in the cutlery drawer, and whispered. 'I need to go to Kantha's house.'

Kamala turned to Indu. 'Just now? Not safe out there.'

'Velyammey...' Kamala looked at Indu's beseeching face. 'Yes, I can see. Go then, I'll tell your Velyachan. But come back soon; I shall worry.'

'Thanks, Velyammey.'

Indu slipped out of the house without her uncle noticing.

A black Morris Minor taxi turned the corner and cruised towards her. She stepped on to the road to stop it. The horn hooted angrily as the car skidded to a stop in front of her.

'Trying to commit suicide, are you, girl?'

She got in and gave directions to Kantha's house. Having found the taxi her uncertainties evaporated.

Shards of Sunlight

The car dropped her off at the gates of the mansion where Kantha lived. Indu tumbled out and walked to the door and rung the doorbell. It was Kantha who opened the door.

Indu put her hand out to him. Kantha took the hand and lifted it to his face. Everything is going to be alright, Indu thought. She smiled and walked in, holding his arm tight as if he might disappear if she did not keep him prisoner.

Sunanda was in the sitting room as the young couple walked in. She moved aside on the sofa to make room for Indu.

It was dark in the room; Indu wondered why the curtains were half-drawn though it was still light. She looked around.

'You don't know, do you?' Sunanda said, sighing heavily. She took a deep breath as though summoning up all her strengths. 'Kantha's father left Colombo; he went back to his village. Couldn't stand it here any longer. Never wants to come back, he said.'

Indu walked to the distraught woman. She sat next to her and hugged her and soon both the women were crying. Kantha looked at them mutely, almost as though he didn't understand what was going on. He shook his head, as though getting rid of a thought, Indu imagined, then walked off in the direction of the kitchen.

'He'll be back,' Indu said firmly.

Sunanda looked at Indu. 'There is something –'

'Hush,' Indu said. 'Hush.'

'No. You *have* to know. About Kantha. Kantha suffered from clinical depression some years ago. Many years ago.' Sunanda held on to Indu's limp hand in her lap. 'His father suffers from it too – it comes now and then. That's why he goes away from us like this. Kantha – he had it just the once, long ago. Six years ago. But since his father went, he is strange. I think it is coming back. I am scared, Indu. And if you also leave him…'

'Me? I'm here. I am not going anywhere, am I?'

'Before my husband went they were planning. Kantha wants to go the UK and study again. And he won't leave me on my own here; he wants me to go with him. But in this state he can't even look after himself, Indu. I am worried about him.'

Indu took a deep breath and thought for half a moment. 'He's upset, of course he is. You are too. Anyone would be depressed. But, I'll be here, won't I? I think we'll all look after each other. I think Kantha and I should get married as soon as possible if that is what he wants.'

Sunanda looked hard at Indu.

'You are a brave girl. And Kantha is lucky. But better you talk to your people first.'

'He's had a shock; you've had a shock. He'll be alright, you wait and see.'

She hugged Sunanda again and walked through to the kitchen. Kantha was there staring out of the window. She went up to him and put her hand in his.

'I know you're sad, but it will go, gradually. Your father will be back; he probably needed a few days to think. The last month – it's been awful for every one. Let's make some tea – and get married.' Indu smiled, looking for answers in his face.

He hugged her. 'Indu, when you are with me, I feel everything will be OK. Even my mother knows that.'

Shards of Sunlight

Indu got mugs and spoons out from cupboards and made tea. Kantha carried the tray into the sitting room.

Sunanda looked at Kantha as she spoke to Indu. 'You make the darkness go away, Indu. I wish you were living with us now.'

'Right,' Indu said. 'I have to get permission from my uncle. I'll come back and we'll be a family, together.'

Indu took the tea-tray into the kitchen and washed up. Kantha followed her and watched, leaning against the door, and for the first time that day, his smile reached his sad eyes.

Indu went to him. 'I have been away for just three days.'

'Three days. Was that it? Too long anyway, felt like forever.' He stroked her hair
and looked into her eyes as though searching for secrets he had mislaid there. 'Too long.'

34

Indu returned to her house. Now she had to seek permission from Kannan to live with Sunanada and Kantha for a few days. She didn't know where to begin.

Kannan sat at the window with an open briefcase in front of him. Papers were strewn all around him and the glasses perched on his nose were way down indicating he was not actually reading anything.

'Hardly talked to you since you returned from Thalassery,' Kannan said when he noticed Indu walking into the room. 'Come here. Let me look at you properly. Hope you've brought a whiff of Kerala back with you.'

'That must be a smell of tapioca and sardines being pounded together for the evening conjee.'

Kamala came out then with a plate of *vadas*. 'You've not eaten much today, the two of you.'

Indu took a vada, bit the end and put it down on her plate. She took her sari end and tucked it into her waist, a little like she was getting ready for some serious physical activity.

'I went to Kantha's house,' she said to Kannan.

He looked up quickly. 'And - ?'

'I think – no, I *know*. I *am* going to live with them for a few days. I *have* to. They are in a bad way.'

'That's all we need now. You deserting us.'

'I am not deserting. You know Kantha's father has gone away to his village? No, you don't. Sunanda is all alone in that huge house. All her family are in

Shards of Sunlight

Kandy and Kantha -' Indu lost a little of her voice there as though she had gulped down a few thoughts and they had choked her. 'Kantha is not very well. They are desperate. Someone needs to be there. Velyacha, I am going to stay with Kantha's mother for a few days.'

'You can't just go and *stay* in someone's house.'

'No different from when we went there – when *we* were desperate. Now *they* need some help. And, in any case – I am going to marry Kantha. Soon, I hope.' She was looking at Kamala now though it was Kannan she was talking to. 'But for now, I must pack a case.' She walked towards her room.

'Wait a minute. You are what?'

Indu stopped and turned back.

Kannan looked at Kamala and Indu in turn beseechingly. 'When did you –she-get these mad ideas? This girl-'

'This girl, nothing,' Kamala said. There was an unusual edge to her voice. 'She is almost twenty three. And she knows what she wants. Anyone who stands in her way will know the stuff she's made of. Like that brother of yours.'

Kamala came towards Kannan and sat on the small coffee table next to him.

'You don't really know where you are going to be next year, do you? What if you move back to Malaya? You have been looking for jobs in Penang. If you go, is she meant to trail after you?'

'No, but-'

'Let her go with your blessings. She'll go with or without.'

She turned to Indu. 'Go and pack an overnight case. And phone us daily.'

Shards of Sunlight

When Indu reappeared a few minutes later carrying her overnight case, she saw a look of resignation on Kannan's face.

'Right. If you must go, I better take you there. Make sure you are alright.'

'I'll be back soon, Velyacha. Please don't be angry with me.'

He looked bewildered, but he walked quickly to his car and started it.

Indu knew she was hurting her uncle, but she was also sure that Kantha and Sunanda needed her and that need could not be ignored.

35

When Indu returned from Kantha's house a week later, Kannan knew he was beaten. He decided to give in with as much grace as he could muster at short notice. His post in Singapore had come through and it was a time for endings and new beginnings.

Indu was determined to keep her wedding simple. All the people who should have been there were in her father's village. Indu decided she would take her husband to meet them as soon as possible. Without Devi, Mani and Shinnu, Indu felt this wedding ceremony was just an obligatory ritual. The real marriage would take place when Kantha went to Kodiyeri with her and received the approval of Devi and Shinnu.

In the house there was much argument with Kamala about what she would wear.
Kamala took Indu shopping. 'Wear it or not, you are getting a trousseau,' she said firmly. 'Your Velyachan insists you have everything a bride would have in Kerala and then some more – so that is what you are getting.'

When Indu started to demur, Kamala looked sad. 'I can't do anything for you girls. Mani won't even come and I don't think I'll know when she gets married.'

She looked at Indu pathetically. 'What did I do wrong?'

Shards of Sunlight

'Oh, Velyamma. You can decide everything about my trousseau; I am lucky to have you with me. What would I do otherwise? It's not as though one gets practice getting married.' Indu laughed her naughty happy laugh and hugged Kamala.

Kamala bought rich Kancheepuram saris in peacock colours and gold borders from the South of India that rustled as they moved. She bought silks from the North, Kashmir and Manipur, with edges embroidered by hand in silk thread. And for the home, cottons from the looms of India at exorbitant Colombo prices. Indu flinched when she looked at the price tags, but she did not say a word, just choosing the colours she loved wearing, which flattered the polished mahogany of her face and shoulders: magenta, emerald, marine blues and creams.

Kamala called her seamstress and gave instructions on the blouses to match and the skirts to go underneath. She went to Cargills and came back with underwear with St Michaels written on them. A frenzy of buying, which made Kamala fulfilled in some strange manner, this woman who never bothered with expensive clothes herself.

Amidst all this frenetic shopping Indu had moments of pure terror. Did I not run away and seek refuge from one marriage? What am I doing getting married in this country now? This is not even my country. I have to go back to India.

She would calm herself down, take a deep breath. I will talk to Kantha about all this; he will heed my fears. Above all she wanted to take Kantha to her village to meet Devi and Shinnu.

Kannan was a passive audience when the women went to Ratnayake's for gold and sapphires. He

Shards of Sunlight

stood at the edge of the shop looking out at the traffic, lost in thought.

Indu went to join him there when she could not stand the dazzle of gold and semi-precious stones anymore. She stood quietly, wondering what he was looking at, but she could see he was lost in not-very-happy thought.

'I miss Gopalan,' he said suddenly and Indu saw his eyes glisten. 'He should be here for this. I don't even know what he would want me to say, or do.'

Indu was too choked to say anything for a moment. She joined him in staring out unseeingly as the cars swung past the corner, competing with each other to produce the most noise on their horns.

'I miss him every day,' Indu said. 'I wake up to him calling out, *"Don't waste precious morning hours."* Only to persuade me to have coffee with him and go for a walk along the railway lines near Kuyyali river. I go to bed wondering what he would have thought about Kantha and then I console myself. *"Is he honest and kind and will he make you laugh?"* I can hear him saying.' The tears waited at the edge of her long eyelashes, held there by force of will.

Kannan turned to look beseechingly at her. 'Please don't cry. Don't cry.'

Indu turned away and wiped the corners of her eyes surreptitiously, with her sari edge. And she smiled brightly, a little too brightly, dragging her uncle back, by hand, to the counters, where Kamala was still considering ear-rings. The gold and gems winked and dazzled and Indu was not so sure she wanted to be any part of all this. But there was no gracious way out.

Shards of Sunlight

Indu wore traditional white to her wedding ceremony, though it took place in a dinghy Magistrate's office. The simple Dacca sari was embroidered at the borders in red, black and white thread, with a heavily worked pallau, tasselled at the edge. Kamala had lovingly plaited her long hair and pinned it up in a kondai at her nape, with a double length of jasmine garland to adorn it. She wore no make-up except a magenta pottu on her forehead and kohl in her eyes.

When she looked in the mirror she saw a grown-up woman with signs of trepidation: her face was flushed and a small tick above her left eye signalled well-hidden disquiet. The butterfly in her stomach had taken wing and would not find a place to settle.

Kantha wore a charcoal grey suit and, much as he tried, seemed out of place in that dusty office. The groom's party were accompanied by a cohort of chattering family. Kantha's father, however, was in deep depression, still in his village, refusing to see anyone. His doctor said he had been traumatised by the communal riots and would need some months to become whole again.

Indu had sent telegrams to Devi and Shinnu to tell them her news but she knew they would not be able to travel, wouldn't know where to begin. She wanted them desperately on her side of that bland table at which the Magistrate sat with holy books in front of him and a huge ledger next to them. If only Mani at least had come.

Kamala tried her best to make up for all the missing family. Indu kept looking at the door as though a special guest was still to come. Until the Registrar cleared his throat and looked up at the group.

Shards of Sunlight

'Sit down,' he said looking into the middle space.

Kamala came forward leading the bride to her place in front of the Registrar's desk. When Kantha's party saw Indu there was a collective gasp: she must have looked like an exotic bird from the other side of paradise. They whispered to each other till the Magistrate shushed them up. As Kantha came up to take his place next to her, the door to the room was pushed open with a bang and a woman hurried in.

'Private ceremony,' the doorman said trying to stop her from coming. Indu turned and –

'Mani!' Indu smiled.

She made as if to get up but Mani signalled with her eyes. They said, sit down. And suddenly, Indu felt the sunlight had slipped in through that briefly opened door.

Mani looked distinctly other in that room, an intruder from alien places. But the smile widened inside Indu's heart. She felt her family had turned up after all.

The ceremony was soon over, the book signed and the guests dispersed to the Galle Face Hotel for a low-key reception.

By the time the wedding party started its journey to the hotel Indu was wilting and Kantha, next to her pulled at his collar and cuffs, unable to sit still for a moment. He took his handkerchief out of his suit-pocket and wiped his face several times. When the hand sought the handkerchief for the fifth time on that short journey, Indu put her hand out and took his restless hand in hers and kept it in her lap. After a moment she could see him relax visibly. He clasped her hand tight.

Shards of Sunlight

Some of Kantha's college friends had been invited to the reception. and he was soon dragged away by a noisy group.

'Why no drinks at all, man?' they demanded.

'Drinks are not served at Kerala weddings,' Kantha explained carefully. 'And my mother is not in a celebratory mood.'

'Kerala? Where's that?'

Kantha led a group to Indu, who was talking to some colleagues from The Times.

'Indu, my college mates,' he said and started telling her their names.

'Jerry here was in my year at Peradeniya. And Vishak is my cousin and my neighbour. He is a doctor…'

Indu knew she would not remember their names – she had reached the point of exhaustion when she might not know her own name. She had slept badly for many weeks and had not slept at all the previous night.

The image of her father accompanied Indu through the day as it had for the last few weeks. She could hear his gruff voice: an accompaniment to her thoughts.

Will be alright, Indu. Wait and see. And look after that family; nice people I think. They are in a bad way.

And, *Good girl. You can dress up and get married to Kantha all over again next year if you want. In fact, you could get married every year in different parts of the world. How about that?*

Later: *You look beautiful, like your mother when I married her. Well, almost. Half your age, she was. A child. I never told you anything about her, did I? I felt*

Shards of Sunlight
guilty about how young and trusting she was. Should've told you – so many things.

For the first time after her father's death, Indu felt that she belonged to someone, and that someone would be on her side for the rest of her life. Her life was in her hands and no one could change that.

Indu made plans.

'When are we going to go to Thalassery?' she asked Kantha the next day. 'You need to meet my family.'

'I thought we were going to Nuwara Eliya for a honeymoon,' Kantha said.

'Ye – es. After that. Early next year?' She wasn't that bothered about honeymoons. Every day is a honeymoon day, she thought.

'If I still have a job after all the leave I take, we can go.' Kantha smiled. 'You are full of plans,' he said. 'What are you going to spring on me next?'

'Well, I thought – lots of children. A dozen,' Indu said. 'Cheaper, by the dozen, they say.'

'Now you'll really make me ill all over again.' Kantha said grinning. 'Twelve? We need an early start then, begin working on that right away,' he teased as he gathered Indu into his arms.

THE END

Shards of Sunlight

Shards of Sunlight
Glossary of relations

Achamma	Paternal Grandmother
Velyamma	Maternal Grandmother or Aunt
Amma	Mother
Achan	Father
Ammamma	Maternal grandmother – also used for older women generally.
Ammaman	Uncle – also used as term of respect for older men
Velyachan	Father's elder brother
Elayachan	father's younger brother
Ettan	Elder brother
Echi or edathy	Elder sister.

Shards of Sunlight

Lightning Source UK Ltd.
Milton Keynes UK
UKOW03f2203300514

232626UK00001B/5/P

9 781784 073442